SHE WAS REACHING FOR THE DOORKNOB WHEN SHE HEARD THE FOOTSTEPS IN THE HALLWAY . . .

Tentative steps coming down the hall toward her, slowly, stopping to look at lettering on doors, moving on. He stopped again, outside her office.

Realizing what she'd forgotten, she pushed the button in the knob which engaged the lock. She swallowed hard, waiting, knowing they were separated only by a door, knowing he must have heard the lock.

He laughed. It was a slow, soft laugh, someone laughing at the helplessness of a child. Finally he stopped: He moved on, back up the hallway. At last, she couldn't hear him anymore.

Ten minutes passed. Fifteen minutes. She gritted her teeth, and opened the door to the hall-way . . .

WOMAN IN THE WINDOW

WOMAN
IN
THE WINDOW

Dana Clarins

BANTAM BOOKS

TORONTO • NEW YORK • LONDON • SYDNEY • AUCKLAND

WOMAN IN THE WINDOW
A Bantam Book / August 1984

ISBN 0-553-24257-1

Published simultaneously in the United States and Canada

*Bantam Books are published by Bantam Books, Inc. Its trademark,
consisting of the words "Bantam Books" and the portrayal of a rooster,
is Registered in U.S. Patent and Trademark Office and in other
countries. Marca Registrada. Bantam Books, Inc., 666 Fifth Avenue,
New York, New York 10103.*

PRINTED IN THE UNITED STATES OF AMERICA

H   0 9 8 7 6 5 4 3 2 1

For George

WOMAN
IN
THE WINDOW

Chapter One

The party was in full swing. Advance copies of *Publishers Weekly* had been messenger delivered to the Danmeier Agency shortly after lunch, and the remainder of the afternoon had been devoted to a celebration. Natalie Rader, the cause of all the revelry, sighed happily. Looking around the office, she couldn't avoid the picture of herself, half a page with an absurdly fulsome cutline calling her "the hottest, newest, prettiest Superagent." But there was no doubt that the long piece detailing the auction she had conducted several weeks before was good both for the agency and for herself. Increasingly, it seemed to her, the style and customs of Hollywood were seeping in and discoloring the publishing industry—but at moments like this her distaste for the phenomenon was kept carefully at bay. Enlightened self-interest, healthy ambition, all that: she wished she didn't enjoy the spotlight quite so much, but then she was only human, and at least she admitted the truth to herself.

1

Her secretary, Lisa, brought her a styrofoam cup of champagne and gave her a proud hug. Donnie, the messenger boy and mailroom attendant, beamed at her and lifted his own cup in a toast. She leaned back on a couch in the reception area and basked.

The article in *PW* was accurate, thank God, and the publishers involved in the auction of this first novel had all told the interviewer the truth. The mega-thriller by the academic in Marblehead, Massachusetts, had indeed brought a $1.5 million advance for the hardback and softcover rights, and Natalie had indeed orchestrated the auction masterfully, assuring the agency a $225,000 commission. She'd been with Danmeier for twelve years, a full-fledged agent for ten, and she knew what was going on. Natalie understood the psychological dynamics of things like auctions. Mastering the elements of the game was almost as important as the property itself. Almost. But she was too smart an agent, and too good an agent, not to know that in the end the book was everything.

From where she sat quietly on the couch, with the secretaries and the two other agents and a couple of lucky strays who happened to be in the office at the right time chatting and sipping and kidding her about the ego trip, she could see through two doorways to her own office, her desk. There in a green florist's vase sat two dozen red roses. The little white card read: *Congrats, Tiger. Tony.*

Jay Danmeier came toward her, smiling, looming over her as he inevitably did. He was a large man, well over six feet and two hundred pounds, incredibly well tailored by a bespoke firm in Savile Row. He had hired Natalie away from Simon & Schuster when she was a beginning editorial assistant only two years out of Northwestern. He'd said later that he'd recognized a born deal maker in her, had said it mainly to tease her because it was the fascination of working with writers that had interested her, not the deal making.

But he'd been right, after all. She was a born angle finder and negotiator, and whether or not she particularly enjoyed it was irrelevant. As the years passed, she did come to enjoy it, as part of the process of handling someone with literary ability. It was that sort of insight and predictive judgment that had made Danmeier himself one of the very best: he could read people; he had understood Natalie better than she had understood herself. Success had fed his reputation over the years until it finally matched his physical size. At fifty, Jay Danmeier let no one doubt that he was just coming into his prime. But Natalie was used to him, used to the tension that sometimes curled out of his ego like the spirals of smoke from his two-dollar cigars.

Looking down at her, he smiled his crocodile smile, sighted down the length of the immensely long cigar, and said, "Well, my darling girl, you've set yourself a hell of a dangerous precedent. What do you do for an encore? In a month this'll be old, old news."

"Sit down, Jay. You don't have to impress me from on high. I'm already impressed."

He shrugged and sat beside her, slipping a heavy arm around her shoulders.

"And you know perfectly well I don't look at this business as a competition," she continued. "The encore doesn't worry me. I'm getting just as big a kick out of the Linehan book—"

"Christ, Nat. Always the idealist!" He made a face and tapped his ash into a tiny Sardi's ashtray. "He's just another drunken Irishman. A psycho mick good for a thousand copies, tops, and not a hope for a reprint sale. Listen to me, it'll be a miracle if you can get him fifteen hundred up front. I know, I know. . . ." He held up his hand and growled like the MGM lion. *"Ars gratia artis."*

"Linehan can write."

"Sure. Just be careful. He's got that look on him that scares me to death." He squeezed her shoulder and smiled. "But, lady, you did a hell of a job on this one."

"This is where I say, 'I owe it all to you, Jay,' and you say, 'That's not altogether untrue, Natalie,' and we chuckle up our sleeves." She watched him reflexively shoot his cuffs, inspect his sleeve for a speck of dust, and she smiled at how transparent he was in spite of all the ego. Or because of it.

"Consider it said, then," he observed judiciously. "But you keep up these big capers and you'll make me jealous—"

"You've gotten all the punch lines for far too long. It's finally my turn."

Jay leaned over and kissed her cheek, got up, and headed back to his office. Impulsively he looked back, saw that she was still watching him. He winked with self-satisfaction and disappeared around the corner. Natalie took a few calls but mainly chatted with the gang, nibbled at snacks from the deli downstairs, and reflected on Danmeier in the corner of her mind.

He hadn't been kidding about feeling jealous. Maybe he thought he was, but she knew there was more than a grain of truth to his remark. He'd always dominated the agents who worked for him. It was part of his plan. But somehow Natalie had cracked the careful mosaic he'd constructed, almost from her arrival in the office. Danmeier's reaction to her had been complex from the start—ambivalent, comprised equally of pride in her growth and accomplishments and concern that she might steal some of his limelight. She had never held it against him: it was just the way he was, and she not only understood him, she could handle him. She had, however, wondered what in the possibility of her success he feared—that was a mystery.

Knowing that he was a man who seldom improvised, a man who thought out his strategies far in advance, she had been surprised recently at some of the risks he'd taken with her, putting himself on the line. Not long ago, he had taken to noticing her again, as he periodically did, citing this time some "appealing, fresh vulnerability" he'd never seen before. She had been amused and he had made a pass at her. No other way to put it.

Caught off guard, she had let him take her determinedly yet gently in his arms and kiss her, had felt his hand on the silk of her blouse, stroking her nipple—it had not been unpleasant, she had not resented it, but she had not been particularly aroused by it either. They had known each other for such a long time: it wasn't an unnatural thing for him to have done. She wasn't challenged, insulted, or driven to perceive it as sexual harassment. It was just Jay and he'd kissed her and touched her. She had let him and thought about it later.

"We work together, Jay," she had said a day later over drinks in the ornate, terribly grand bar at the Palace, "and we work together well. And we're friends. So let's not run the risk of ruining it all with a quick little affair, okay?"

"What if I was hoping for more of a long run?"

"Jay, let's not play games. We're better than that."

He had stared into his perfect Manhattan, gray shaggy head bowed, chiseled features overlaid with the fleshiness of success and the floridness of his age and drinking habits, and had pursed his lips thoughtfully. "You know what Oscar Wilde said, of course."

She'd laughed. 'Maybe you should refresh my memory."

"'There is only one difference between a lifelong passion and an infatuation. The infatuation lasts longer.'" He had sipped the Manhattan. "What do you think of that, dear lady?"

"I think you're wondering if you should agree with my assessment of the situation or not. Do you think you're suddenly infatuated with old everyday Natalie? For one thing, it's a little late in coming, isn't it?"

"Oh, no. I remember quite clearly the day I fell in love with you, Nat." He had looked up at her, for a moment seeming almost shy. "I'm only twelve years late in telling you. . . ."

She had felt the start of tears. "Much as I hate to say it, that's a very lovely thing to hear. And," she had pulled herself together, "it's also not fair. No more lovely remarks. Promise me."

He had put his hand over hers and nodded. "All right. For the moment, anyway. But, goddamn it, Nat, I can't answer now for what might happen later." He had smiled gruffly, removed his hand from hers, and finished his drink.

His promise was still intact, more or less. But occasionally she had caught him staring at her in the office or while they met with a client or publisher over lunch at the Four Seasons, and she'd recognized that look in his eye. Once she had accused him, only half-facetiously, of harboring a lovely thought or two.

"Nat," he had replied, "in the nicest possibly way, may I suggest that you shove it?" They had laughed. But there it lay between them, confined for the moment to his eyes. Sometimes she wondered what he saw when he looked at her that way. It was odd, maybe part of being a woman, or reflecting the times in which she lived: she should have known what signals she was sending, but she didn't—and that was that. They were both stuck with the membrane of tension stretched between them. There was something . . . *something* that kept her from tearing it once and for all. She was at that turning point in her life when the sexual arrogance of youth was gone. You never knew how many more chances there might be, and Jay wasn't easy to ignore or forget. And he cared about her.

* * *

At six o'clock the secretaries left. The suite of offices was empty. Except for Jay. He poked his head through the doorway of her office and harrumphed.

"You're sounding awfully officious in your old age," she said, taking off her reading glasses and looking up from the fine print of a contract. "Positively Dickensian."

"Old age," he repeated. "My God, you have an unfailing ability to inflict a flesh wound in passing when I least expect it. Charming."

"Well, you know what Wodehouse used to say. When he was past ninety?"

"I'm not going to find this terribly amusing—"

"Of course you will. He said, 'As long as you're going to get old . . . you might as well get as old as you can.'"

He couldn't help laughing. "Look, come with me to '21' for dinner. Eight-thirty. I'll fight off all my impulses and not say one lovely thing. We can continue today's celebration. Innocent as the newborn. Come on, Nat." He had a regular nightly table, all part of the Danmeier style.

"Thanks, but no thanks, Jay. I'm utterly bushed. And I feel like I've got a cold coming on—"

"Bullshit. That's what Hemingway used to say."

"Really, I'm sorry, Jay. Another time. The fact is, I got caught out in the rain last night."

"Well, now I'm pissed off. Beware the consequences, my sweet."

"I'll bear up under the pressure."

"Don't I know it." He pulled on his trench coat. "Good night and don't forget to lock up." He went away whistling. She heard the door close in the reception room and breathed a deep sigh of relief. *Jay, you're such a bastard.* And she smiled at the thought. Smiled at his easy persistence. Could he convince her he was serious? And should she give him the chance?

She relished being alone. It had not been that way following the divorce, but she'd worked her way through the worst of it and now solitude was okay. Time to herself, no longer afraid to be alone because then she might start thinking about Tony and louse up everything . . . Solitude was fine if there wasn't too much of it.

Smiling to herself, proud of herself, she poured the last of a bottle of champagne. It was flat and warmish and she didn't mind at all. She had gotten through the psychological firestorm, which was how she thought of the crack-up of her marriage, and now, today, she was back on track, feeling good about herself, calm, whole, able to be alone. Back to being Tiger.

She wandered through the empty rooms. The agency occupied most of one floor in an old, handsomely decorated office building in midtown, six stories with a common street-level lobby and a rickety elevator, self-operated. A design studio, two sets of lawyers, a trade commission from an eastern European satellite—and the Danmeier Agency. It was the kind of building that constituted its own neighborhood, was only a couple of steps from landmark status, and operated on the honor system. Old Tim, the doorman, had once been knocked down nine times in a single round; when he came to, he had a vaguely English accent and longed to be a doorman. He came with the building and there was always the chance that he might actually be on duty. His hours were erratic at best and no one had the nerve to upbraid him. Lobby security never seemed a crucial issue.

Natalie loved the comfortable jumble of rooms, the framed dust jackets, the stacks of manuscripts, the sagging, overburdened bookcases on tatty oriental carpets. Home away from home, that was what the agency meant to her, and that was fine, the way it had to be for her now. Work was your life, life was your work. You worked, you coped, and if there was the time and the opportunity . . . then, maybe, you could love. But work was what you could count on. It made sense. You could—what was the jargon of the day? Validate? Sure, you could validate your life with your work. When you asked people to define themselves, what did they say? They told you what they did for a living. Well, she was an agent, she worked, she coped. Whee.

Turning off lights one by one, she giggled. The champagne was getting to her. A wee bit. She didn't drink much, that was the problem. . . . Giggle.

Back at her desk, the contract lounging in a puddle of soft light, she drained the last bit from the bottle into her cup. The roses were beautiful, still dewy from the florist's spray, darkly red, like blood in Italian vampire movies. So sweet of Tony. But she didn't want to start thinking about Tony. That was where the wild things hid, danced, grinned inanely at her. Tony was a memory, had damn well better stay that way. Memory Lane.

She dictated a brief letter into her machine.

"Dear Mr. Linehan. It gives me a great deal of

pleasure to tell you that the contracts from Hewitt and Sons have arrived and I am reviewing them. You will have them to sign in a few days; a check for twenty-five hundred dollars will follow shortly. . . ."

Tomorrow she'd tell Jay. She'd beaten his estimate on the advance but she hadn't wanted to rub it in today. It would be fun tomorrow, though.

The beautiful part was that it truly did give her more pleasure than the coup that had her spread all over *PW.* You had to keep things in perspective, treasure your integrity. Damn straight. It was what made you an individual, right?

She toasted her integrity. Her individuality.

Which was when she should have packed it in and gone home. Instead, she got up and went to the window.

She never understood what had beckoned her to the window.

Chapter Two

Beyond the tall third-floor windows the New York cityscape had darkened to a December evening, then blossomed into the glitter and sparkle that was the city's trademark. Below her the crowds had begun thinning along Madison Avenue. The light changed at Fifty-third and the headlights began moving again, poking through the thin, slanting winter rain. Across the avenue, the flow of pedestrians leaving work, going to assignations over cocktails in corner bistros, catching a bite to eat before heading across town toward the theater district, straggling home after a wearying day—across the avenue the flow of New Yorkers moved past the endless upward thrust of new, grimly skeletal construction that punctuated each block. Men stopped even in the rain to peer through the peepholes cut into the wooden fencing, staring at the quiet earthmovers, watching the arcs, pink and orange, of the helmeted welders up among the girders.

She had watched the Lossin Chemical building, directly across from her window, rise slowly from the deep square excavation pit, foot by foot, taking its shape—more glass and steel, more boring sameness. As she was glancing vaguely at the construction site, her mind elsewhere—at rest, relaxed—she became aware of a curious movement at the corner of her vision. Erratic. Darting.

Suddenly, unexpectedly, like a cry of fire in a crowded room, there he was. And he was all wrong, didn't fit.

He was running. A belted trench coat. A cloth cap pulled low against the rain. He darted among the shining black umbrellas. A bus bore down, he dashed in front of it, across the street, rain-slick with reflected lights reaching toward him on the wet pavement. A taxi braked, skidded, honked; he was momentarily lost among the umbrellas and the scaffolding arched above the sidewalk. It was New York: he didn't even cause a head to turn.

But from the window where she stood he was caught in a framework. Natalie continued looking, picking him out again, now entirely alone against the wooden fence blocking off the construction site behind him. She was struck by the peculiar feeling that she was the only person in the world watching him: it was just the two of them, the situation almost embarrassing in its intimacy—she was watching him in some private act, but she couldn't look away.

What the hell was he doing?

She gasped, leaned forward: he had taken out a gun.

Quite clearly she saw it, was certain, a gun, a pistol or a revolver or an automatic; she didn't know one kind of handgun from another, but it was a gun. He had pulled it from his trench-coat pocket, stood looking at it as if posed, like Jean-Louis Trintignant in that indelible moment in *The Conformist*, as if he didn't quite recognize it and was undecided. . . . Then in a sweeping motion, his arm held stiffly, he lofted the gun up and over the poster-covered wooden fence.

She squinted into the night. Rain blew across the window.

But, no, it had been a gun. She was sure. . . .

The man stood frozen, looking around as if he expected to be caught in the act, set upon by burly cops and dragged off with nightsticks tattooing his skull. His face was shaded beneath the bill of the cap. The trench coat—she was registering it all—looked like one of the five-hundred-dollar Burberry's with the tan wool button-in lining. Maybe . . . But she couldn't imagine she'd been wrong about the gun. . . . A gun? My God.

It was a New York moment. Strange. Weird.

Utterly objective, yet desperately personal.

Natalie Rader was in her office. A man with a gun was standing below in the street. He had thrown the gun over a fence, into a construction site. An anecdote. Something to tell her friends.

Until the man looked up.

What did he see, she wondered later, a random design of lighted windows in the building across the street? One with a woman silhouetted by the desk lamp behind her . . . a woman staring down at him.

He didn't move. Returned her stare. Their faces in shadow. A man and a woman sharing the unexpected, naked moment. The sinister moment that seemed to stretch out forever.

Crazy. She felt as if there was an unmistakable eye contact. An invisible, taut connection stretched between them, cutting through the wind and rain.

And she was very frightened.

She stumbled back from the window, still watching him, feeling for the desk lamp. Knocking the empty champagne bottle off the desk, she heard its thud on the carpet as she hit the switch on the base of the lamp, plunging the room into blackness. She was out of breath, back at the window, standing to one side peering down.

He watched as if he could see her afterimage in the darkened pane of glass. *He knows, he's seen me and he knows I've seen him. Oh, Christ . . .*

Slowly he pushed his hands into the pockets of his trench coat. He glanced to either side. No one paid him the slightest attention. He looked back at the window. She cringed, as if she were naked before him, even in the dark window.

Then he moved across the street toward her.

She watched him coming, saw him pass from view beneath the overhanging ledge outside her window.

Had he gone off down the street?

Or was he coming into her building?

Natalie backed away from the window. Her hands were shaking and her breath was catching in her chest, coming hard. She felt the fine sweat breaking out, the loss of strength in her legs, the pressure in her chest, the giddiness that meant her brain wasn't getting enough oxygen.

The fear was building in her, she could taste it, like a drain in her belly backing up, sickening her, robbing her of strength and will. Son of a bitch. She hated it, fought it with a string of dirty words, trying to shock herself out of it and bring her back to reality. But the man was real—*sure, sure, Tiger, but you're acting like a nut case. . . .*

But what's so crazy about watching some guy throw a gun away and seeing him watch you, come toward you when you're alone in an empty office and he knows where you are and you're scared? That's crazy?

Just go lock the door. The damn door was always locked during business hours, requiring a buzz and an identification. But not today. Not with the deliveries for the party and the people dropping in to share the moment with her.

If you're so afraid, Nat, just go call Lew . . . call Tony . . . call Jay . . . someone will come and get you—

"I will not call anybody," she said aloud. "I won't do it!"

She began muttering to herself as she went to the closet and took out her own trench coat, wrapped her muffler around her throat, grabbed her briefcase. "Don't forget the Linehan contract," she whispered to herself, "and the first six chapters of the Crawford manuscript . . . and your umbrella."

She dug around in her briefcase for the ancient

Valium bottle, a souvenir from the worst days with Tony. "Irrational terror-stricken woman," she said to herself. There were a couple inches of dead champagne in a cup on the reception desk. She gulped it down, made a face, and then stood still, willing herself to breathe slowly, deeply.

She was reaching for the doorknob when she heard the first footsteps in the hallway.

Tentative steps. Someone had come up the stairs. Past old Tim's deserted post. No swoosh of elevator doors. Someone was waiting at the top of the stairs, probably looking around, trying to get his bearings. The footsteps started again, coming down the hall toward her, slowly, stopping as if to look at lettering on doors, moving on. She bit a knuckle.

He stopped again, outside her office.

Realizing what she'd forgotten, she took three quick steps to the door and pushed the button in the knob, which engaged the lock. It made what she knew was a soft click, though it sounded like a vault slamming shut.

She swallowed hard, waiting, knowing they were separated only by a door, knowing he must have heard the lock.

He laughed.

It was a slow, soft laugh. Derisive. Contemptuous. A rolling chuckle, someone laughing at the helplessness of a child. Finally he stopped. What was he doing now? She sagged back against the wall, steadied herself with a hand on a tabletop. Why didn't he do something?

Finally he did. He moved on, back up the hallway.

At last, she couldn't hear him anymore. Was he waiting? Or had he gone down the stairs as he had come up?

She wished she smoked, wished there were anything she could do while she waited. She practiced swallowing and breathing and telling herself that she was the victim of an overactive imagination. Didn't convince herself of the latter. She hadn't imagined that laugh.

Ten minutes.

Fifteen minutes.

Christ, I'm a captive in my own office. Held at bay by a man who probably isn't there.

She gritted her teeth and opened the door into the hallway.

Empty. Long and brightly lit, polished wooden doors, ancient tiles, beige walls. A few smudged puddles of rain. Footprints.

She pulled the door shut behind her. *If he's waiting in the stairwell for me,* she thought, *I'll never have time to get the door unlocked. Tiger.*

She punched the elevator call button.

When the door slid open a man wearing a trench coat stood inside.

She screamed, rooted to the spot.

"Natalie, for chrissakes, are you all right?"

He was a graphic designer from a studio two floors up.

"Oh, Teddy . . . sure, sure, I'm fine. I was just surprised. Thinking about something else—"

"You sure you're okay? You look like you've seen—"

"No, really, Teddy, I'm perfectly all right. Tired.

Long day. I don't know." She shrugged and smiled, getting in beside him. They descended together.

"Say, I saw your picture in *PW* today." He whistled, his Adam's apple bobbing. His glasses were sliding down his long nose. "Wow. Next stop *Penthouse*, right?" They laughed.

Slippery sidewalks. Teddy walked her to the curb and waited while she waved for a taxi. He asked her again if she was really okay and she looked up out of the cab window. *Sure, Teddy, tiptop.* In fact she was already feeling the slightly numbing effect of the champagne.

Chapter Three

While the cab pushed and shoved its way through traffic slowed even more than usual by the rain and the slick streets, she found that she couldn't just shut off her imagination now that she was safe, heading toward normal. Where had the man gone? Had he waited in the shadows, in the bar with the window on the street across the way, in a crowd of people at the bus stop? Had he watched her leave the building? Had he taken another cab and followed her? God, she really was out of control—

Still, what had she actually seen? He had thrown away a gun. Why? What had he done with the gun? You hold up delis with guns, you mug people with guns, and—well, inevitably, you kill people with guns. So what had this bozo done with the gun? Why throw it into a construction site where someone was bound to find it? Guns could be traced. Or could they?

They were heading up First Avenue, then left in the

Seventies, and she was home. She tipped the driver too much because she wasn't paying attention and let herself in the two front doors. She checked her mail in the common front hallway and heard Sir Laurence coughing and whoofing and scratching at the inside of her own front door. How did he always know it was she? Or did he do the same number every time somebody came in?

She had found Sir Laurence half-starved in a parking lot nine years ago and he'd eaten pretty well ever since. He was presumably some sort of poodle and cocker mixture, with the requisite soulful eyes, thick bushy brows, and a now-gray beard that tended to—admit it—a determined sogginess. His life revolved around Natalie, a collection of six tennis balls, and snacks of something called Bonz.

Opening the door, she saw him backing up, wiggling, and finally depositing a wet, almost hairless orange tennis ball at her feet. She sighed, picked it up gingerly using just two fingers, and dropped it over the balcony into the living room, listening to him crash clumsily down the stairs. She lived on the two bottom floors of a brownstone, with a garden in back, trees and flagstones. Sir Laurence was one lucky dog, indeed, with a yard of his own in the middle of Manhattan.

Some days she couldn't quite imagine what she would do without Sir to come home to. Like most New Yorkers with pets, she talked to him a good deal. Like most New Yorkers' pets, he not only listened but seemed to understand the difficulties of her pressured existence. He, on the other hand, seldom lost his generous willingness to hear her out. A perfect relationship. He even slept with her, a warm bundle who, if he kept his questionable breath pointed in the other direction, was always welcome. He had a tendency to leave sand and grit in the bed, but then, nobody was perfect.

She treated him to a handful of Bonz in the kitchen, replenished his water dish, chatted him up a bit about his day, and he went out his own door to the backyard, where he had a bathroom in the far corner—there were times she couldn't quite face a walk.

She put a Modern Jazz Quartet tape in the deck, set out a piece of Brie and some green grapes, and checked her answering machine. T. Jones over on Third Avenue had called to tell her her new coat was altered and ready; Jay must have just called from "21" to tell her that he really wished she'd change her mind and join him; and Julie Conway, who lived upstairs, said that she'd be stopping down shortly. . . .

Natalie spent ten minutes throwing Sir his tennis balls, then ran a very hot tub, and Julie arrived. She was everything Natalie was not: tall, with long blond hair, once a model who had done a spread for *Playboy* in the late sixties, now a public-relations executive in a major hotel chain. She was a master at what had once been called "staying loose, man," while Natalie was always on the edge of being "uptight, man." Yet—or perhaps because of their differences—they had become good friends. Based on the fact that they lived in close proximity to one another: rare in Manhattan.

Long-legged, broad-shouldered, wearing high swashbuckler's boots and a wildly swirling skirt and vest, Julie looked like an advertisement for a tour of Rumanian gypsy-folklore festivals. She swaggered down the stairs, picked up Sir and rakishly rubbed noses, scaring him half to death in the process, and threw her immense length onto a couch.

"What," she asked, her voice deep and elaborately full of vowels, "do I have to do to get you out for dinner? My spies brought me a *PW*; your picture is so beautiful it made my teeth hurt, according to the story you are also 'hot' and 'rich,' and on the whole it seems like a good idea to be seen on the town with you. So, let's go." She smiled lazily, waiting for the expected reply.

"I may be hot, I'm not rich, and I'm a wreck. I plead for a break. A lonely dinner, a lonely bath, to bed with my dog and a set of contracts—" She was pacing, didn't want to get into offering Julie a drink. Didn't want to get started telling her about the man with the gun. Not right now. For an instant, listening to Julie rattle on, it seemed hardly to have happened at all.

"You must eat. Oysters and tortellini at Maxwell's, a short stroll on a nice rainy night. Nightcap at George Martin, check out the local worthies." Julie's booted foot was tapping the air, already impatient, knowing the argument so well.

Natalie shook her head. Smiled. "Not tonight."

"I worry about you," Julie announced for the seven-hundredth time. "You and Sir are alone too much. He's only a dog—"

"A dog maybe but never *only*—"

"You should be out celebrating tonight, Nat, you know that as well as I do."

Natalie smiled. She might as well have been talking to Jay Danmeier.

"A nice dinner, maybe a new man who is capable— just conceivably, mind you—of conversation," Julie persisted, ". . . and he turns out to be a good lay. Voilà, one celebration, right on the money! Really, be absolutely honest with me, wouldn't you like to just let go and go to bed with somebody tonight? Sort of top off the day?"

"Oh, Jules, what can I say? The answer is no, I really wouldn't want to go to bed with somebody. If there were a man I cared about—well, sure, I'm feeling a little fragile, and making love slowly and for a long time would be the best. But that's a big if, kiddo." She stood looking out into the floodlit garden, watching Sir engage a couple of wet leaves in some sort of contest she would never comprehend. "Look, it's just a difference of outlook, that's all."

"Judge me!" Julie cried. "See if I care—actually, I do care. You always sound like a mature, sensitive, nifty lady and I always sound like a sex-crazed asshole. But," she sighed and stood up, so devastatingly confident, such a soldier of fortune in the sexual wars, "a long time ago I decided if the shoe fit I might as well put it on. I tell myself I merely communicate on an earthier plane than such as you—"

"And more effectively, no doubt." Natalie followed her up the stairs. "Whatever happened to Dave? Or was it Dick?"

"Don. And the Jets are playing in San Diego and Seattle, two straight weeks, so he's out of the picture for the moment. You know, I was amazed—he's a gallery man, hits all the art galleries, they know him, he's a customer, collects drawings, sort of eighteenth century-ish. Unexpected frontiers on the offensive line. I'd rate him a contender. If he doesn't find himself too young for this thirty-six-year-old knockout." She paused at the door. "You'd like him, actually, much more your type than mine. He told me he suspected me of sportfuck-ing—he was really upset. Definitely your type, now that I think about it."

In the hallway she turned back, her face suddenly serious. "Did you see the *Post* today? A nurse was stabbed to death in a nice brownstone three blocks from here last night—doorman building; not a clue. A word to the wise, okay? Put that with all the robberies in the neighborhood—and lock up tight tonight. Promise me."

"Of course." On impulse Natalie crossed the hall-way and hugged her. "And thanks for saying nice things about me and wanting to go out with me tonight. I really am worn out—"

"Listen, I'm the last girl to give up."

"Be careful, Jules." She smelled the Opium per-fume, felt the long, tawny hair against her cheek, suddenly felt herself a short, dark, funny-looking crea-ture beside Julie.

"Never fear. I'm big and tough."

And she was gone into the night. On to George Martin. On through the Upper East Side, leaving bodies floating in her wake. Excelsior!

Natalie lay in the tub, feeling the sweat running down her face, smelling the fragrant bubbles. The telephone sat on the floor, in arm's reach. Sir lay in the doorway, watching her, mauling a yellow tennis ball. She picked up a hand mirror and scowled at the face that always struck her as too much the little-girl's face, too much Natalie-at-twelve. As she had grown into womanhood the face had changed so little: only the addition of laugh lines at the corners of her mouth, a faint spray of lines radiating outward from her eyes. A few gray hairs, which she didn't mind, didn't even consider hiding. The scowl faded, her face fell into repose. She supposed she was pretty, if you liked the type. A smooth, olive complexion, neatly shaped black hair that was presently wetly plastered across her forehead, a slender, pointed nose, dark eyes that could be expressive.

The fact was, she'd always thought of her physical appearance as her arsenal, the weapon she could fall back on when the going got tough and everything else failed and she needed to get her own way. That was her father's fault, she imagined. He had loved to sit and look at her and sometimes she had caught him at it, seeing in his eyes not so much love as a simple fascination at what she looked like, at the fact that she had come at least partly from him. Still, he'd always told her she had a good brain, too. She'd always been the quickest, brightest, hardest-working little thing. . . . She put the mirror down and closed her eyes, pushed her thoughts away from herself.

But she still saw the curious look her father had. She'd seen it in other men, admiring her. She didn't need to share their enthusiasm to use it, to get her way. When she'd mentioned such reflections once, Julie hadn't known what she was talking about. But then Julie didn't reflect much.

Now, Natalie smiled at the Jets' offensive lineman worrying about Julie's sportfucking. It was precisely the same charge that she had leveled at poor Julie a few months before, and as usual Julie had taken it in her stride, faced it, dealt with it, and said the hell with it—I am what I am. Which she was.

But Natalie cared for her and consequently worried about whatever fate might lie in wait for her at George Martin or Elaine's or Maxwell's or Xenon or . . . wherever. The Jets' lineman sounded fine; the prognosis was not therefore terribly promising in Natalie's view. Julie tended to attract her own kind, or at least those who matched the facade she had constructed. Not enough guys like Don the Jet.

She believed that Julie had seriously misread the message of the liberation of women, which was not an uncommon fate to befall women of their generation, caught more or less in the middle. The novels, hopeful and angry and bitter and bemused and frequently very funny, crossed her desk with the regularity of White House claims that the economy was turning around. Novels written by bright, literate women trying to decipher the code of the New Woman—and too often there was an unsettling undercurrent of hatred. . . . Was it too strong a word? Perhaps it was a hatred that the authors might commit to paper but would never act on in the course of life. She certainly hoped so.

A hatred of men. A stifling, destructive, soul-destroying hatred of half the human race, sometimes written out of justifiable personal experience, sometimes academically ingested prejudice, sometimes merely trendy. But the hatred was there and she couldn't bring herself to represent the books. One had gone on to rise as high as seven on the *Times* best-seller list, but she hadn't regretted turning down its representation. There was something so desperately wrong about it. Something so terribly pornographic, in the truest sense of that trashed word. Jay had wanted to handle the book, had sensed its commercial potential, and they had fought the issue to the wall. Natalie, not one to make theatrical gestures, had made one that day: we take on the book and I leave. In the aftermath she felt foolish, ignorant, stupid, not even sure she wouldn't have buckled—but Jay had broken first, and the book had gone elsewhere. Where it had made a mint, he never hesitated to remind her.

Julie . . .

She ran some more hot water into the tub, turning the taps with her big toe, soaking up the steam.

Dammit, it was a dangerous world out there for all the Julies. Rapists, coked-out jerks with too much money, values all backward and running amok . . . herpes, God forbid! Julie was coming off two divorces and looked upon men as something less than people—though she mustn't always have been that way. Now, Natalie was sure, Julie was consumed with a deep, boiling hatred of men, their egos, their toughness, their use of women, and was responding by turning herself into a mirror image of them. . . .

It was so sad.

Chapter Four

She must have drifted off, came awake slowly. She got out of the tub, ignored her reflection in the mirror, weighed herself—112 pounds, soaking wet—and wrapped herself in a huge towel like a winding sheet. She popped out her contacts, creamed her face, wiped it off, and went to bed.

The streetlamps shining, a siren going by, the rain still gently falling, soaking the city as the temperature slowly dropped . . . everything normal. She put on her reading glasses and tried sorting through the stack of books on her bedside table. She couldn't face the work she'd brought home, nor any of the hot new novels: by and large she slogged through the hot and new as part of her job. The worst part. She took instead Wodehouse's *Leave It to Psmith*, which, like *Lucky Jim*, always made her laugh.

But she couldn't forget the man with the gun, the way he had seemed almost to pose as he threw the gun over the fence . . . the slow chuckle on the other side of the office door. She shivered at the thought. She didn't often feel the need to share things: she seemed to end up listening to other people's lives rather than they to hers, but this was different, she wanted to tell someone. But it had to be the right person. Not Julie, who might use it to push her karate lessons; not Jay, who'd think she was dramatizing everything; none of her other friends . . . not even Lew, to whom she'd been running with her problems since college. No, there was only one person she could call. She dialed the Staten Island number and hoped. He answered on the fourth ring.

"Tony," she said, "it's Nat. I wanted to thank you for the roses. Really, they meant a lot to me—"

"And made Jay jealous," he said. She couldn't tell if he was smiling, what mood he might be in. "Two birds with one stone." There was that edge of bitterness: he could never quite get it out of his mind that she was probably sleeping with Danmeier.

"Well, thanks. They were beautiful."

As they talked he softened up, dropping his everlasting guard, stopped assuming the worst of her. He became himself again, at least the self she liked to remember, the self she once had loved. He was writing, working on a novel. She could hear a tape of *Tosca* playing in the background. She pictured him in the study of the old house, a fire going, wearing chinos and a sweatshirt, smoking a cigar, looking like an overage college senior.

She told him about the man with the gun, told him

all the details that she knew he'd enjoy. When she finished he was silent. "Well? Well?" she prompted.

"I'm making notes," he said. "It's a little weird, Nat. There's one big hole—"

"Like what?"

"Like how can you be sure it was a gun?"

"Because it looked like a gun."

"Sure, and it was dark, it was raining, you'd had your share of champagne, and you were three floors up. Across the street."

"It was a gun—"

"Not until somebody finds it."

"So why did the guy come into my building and stand outside the door laughing?" He was making her angry but she was fighting it. He was doing his devil's-advocate thing and she couldn't really blame him.

"You don't know who was outside the door," he said, as if to prove her right. "Could have been a delivery boy, a messenger, a clean-up guy, laughing at the frightened lady locking the door just as he gets there—I mean, it could have been." His patience always seemed so condescending.

"I say it was a gun and I say he came to the door. And I say you're full of it!"

He laughed. "Well, the fact is, you're probably right—"

"You admit you're full of it?"

"No, I admit it probably was a gun and he probably did come to the door. But it's also probably over. You went home and he's hoping to God that's all there is to it." He paused. "It makes sort of a nice beginning for a plot—"

"The author at work! It really happened . . . but yes, I guess it does. It's so New Yorky, isn't it?"

"That's what I mean. It's real, it's full of hints, and you can make up your own story to go with it. I mean, it's my kind of pulpy crap, not like the stuff you handle." He laughed quietly, forcing it. "You know what I mean."

"Don't start on that, Tony. It's a tired story—"

"Well, aren't all my stories tired?"

"Drop it," she said.

"I hear your picture in *PW* is very sexy. I hear it goes on to say that you are hot—"

"Tony, I really don't want to have this part of the discussion."

"Ah."

She closed her eyes, didn't respond. There was nothing to say, it was all too old, too complicated, too insoluble, too ratty and dog-eared.

"Nat, are you there?"

"Barely. Look, I just wanted to thank you for the roses. I have, so now you can go back to work—"

"Hey, wait a minute. Are you all right? You're not upset? I mean, really upset?"

"If you mean am I having an anxiety attack, no, I don't think so. If I do I'll give my keeper a buzz."

"Come on, Nat, don't get snotty. Are you okay?"

She heard the sudden change, the real urgency and concern.

"Just tired all of a sudden. The champagne. Look,

how's the work going out there? All you hoped it would be?"

"Nothing's ever all you hope it'll be, Nat."

There wasn't much more to say, the conversation dwindled away. He was right, of course: nothing ever was quite the way you hoped it would be. Maybe that was the last great secret.

They had married when Tony Rader was thirty-three, a newspaperman, and she was twenty-seven, just beginning to make her way at the Danmeier Agency. Now he was forty-two, a novelist who made his living grinding out paperback originals, action-series stuff and the odd porno here and there. He'd been working on a novel—the quintessential *big novel*—since college days and it remained ever in revision, always unsold. Determined not to live off the earnings of his bright, fast-rising wife, he'd let his own view of what he called his "grotty little failures" grow higher and higher, a wall between them.

Natalie had pressed him endlessly, once they could afford it, to stop writing the pulp novels that he could turn out at the rate of one per month and instead devote all his time to what they called his A-material. But he insisted on paying his own way: if there was time left over, he'd attend to that big novel.

The result, of course, was that he did the junk work at the expense of the good stuff. Nothing ever turned out to be all you'd hoped.

The breaking point had come three years ago, when she went too far, tried to help. Without Tony's knowledge she had taken the most recent revision—the first half of that big novel—along with his carefully worked-out outline of the remainder, and tried to connect it. Perhaps she knew the marriage was doomed on its present course, perhaps she knew there was nothing to lose. Maybe she thought she had a chance with the manuscript. She liked it, she found it a satisfying read, full of strong characterizations, just plain good writing. Maybe she'd been kidding herself. . . . She hadn't been able to sell it. Tony had found out she'd tried.

And that had been the end.

With their lives and ambitions so hopelessly intertwined, there had been no way to smooth it out. Tony went on and on about being robbed of his manhood, his personal worth, his responsibility for his own life. And Natalie hadn't been able to figure out what he was talking about. Two people loved each other, they tried to help each other out: it seemed so simple to her, so wildly complex to him. He was threatened by her success, her power over his life: boring, tedious arguments, human. And she felt that if she wasn't allowed to make a contribution to their life together, what was the point? And he would soar off into flights of self-deprecation, rattling on about his inferiority to her other clients. . . .

The old story. No survivors.

She remembered, as she lay in bed unable to sleep, one of their last evenings together. They had gone to see Harold Pinter's play *Betrayal*. Tony had known the music that underscored the play's most haunting moment: Stan Getz's recording of "Her." Once they were no longer together, she had gone in search of the album and found it at King Karol on Forty-second Street. She had bought the album, *Focus*, and had nearly worn it out in the years since, playing it again and again.

She lay quietly in bed, chewing her thumb, her face wet with tears. She really had no idea what she was crying about.

Nothing ever quite being all it was supposed to be? Maybe.

Sir snuggled up in the curve of her leg, tail wagging slowly.

Finally they slept.

Chapter Five

A couple of days later, the man with the gun already fading in her memory, overtaken by the rush of events at the office, Natalie was slouched behind her desk, her feet cocked up on a lower drawer, shoes off, reading a letter from an angry, disappointed author. It was almost two o'clock, still well within the limits of publishers' lunches and the only stretch of the day when she wasn't on the telephone. In a recent attempt to reclaim time for thought, and to read a bit more, she had ruthlessly curtailed her lunch and cocktail calendar: in the past there had been a business lunch every day, drinks or dinner on business four nights a week. Jay said he didn't believe she could cut it back, said that it would dramatically lessen her effectiveness. She suspected he might be right, but she'd been working too hard, she had to give it a try. And so far, so good. Today she was lunching at her desk. And tonight's dinner with Lotte was only partially business, she hoped.

She was trying to deal with an immensely sticky doughnut and a cup of now-cold coffee, trying to dream up a soothing response for the unhappy writer, when the door to her office opened and Jay loomed, filling the space. She looked up in surprise at his failure to knock and saw that he was waving a folded copy of the *New York Post* at her. As Wodehouse once said, though he may not have looked exactly disgruntled, he was surely far from gruntled. The normal tightness of his expression tended to sag into jowls when he wasn't happy: she recognized the sag of concern.

"You look like you're posing for a statue, Jay," she said lightly. "Would you like to come in? Or do you just want to wave the day's news at me?"

"Very funny," he growled, entering and laying the paper on her desk. He was just back from the Four Seasons and she couldn't bear to tell him there was a little spot of something on his blue-and-white-striped shirt. "Your fame spreads, Nat. But if I may offer an opinion, it sounds a little scary to me. . . ."

"What are you talking about?"

"Look at Teddy Garfein's column, my dear." He stood over her, frowning, staring down at her, making her slightly crazy. There was that fine patina of criticism in his voice and it pissed her off, frankly.

But that was forgotten when she saw Garfein's tidbit.

This week's hot, glamour-girl literary deal-maven, Natalie Rader at the Danmeier Agency, had one of those spooky midtown glimpses of the underbelly of life that makes this truly a Wormy Big Apple. Sometimes, anyway. Working late—as deal-mavens always do—our Natalie witnessed what we can only assume is the postscript to a—dare we say it?— murder. Say, how's that for a title, Nat? Would it play in Peoria? Anyhoo, she saw a gunsel de-gun himself on a Madison Ave. streetcorner, pitch his weaponry over a fence and into a building site! And naturally nobody noticed . . . but eagle-eyed Natalie. So what's the upshot? Is there a pistol-packin' construc- tion foreman now on the loose? Who got blasted in the hours before the gunsel threw his gun away? And can Natalie find someone to turn her glimpse of murder's aftermath into a hot property? Ira Levin, where are you when Nat needs you?

"I don't believe it," she said. "How in the name of God—"

"You mean it didn't happen?"

"No, it happened. It was the night we had the party here."

"And you didn't tell me? Christ, Natalie, sometimes I just can't cope with you—"

"Why in the world should I tell you about some- thing I saw out the window? I don't get it—is everybody crazy? What's this doing in Garfein's stupid column?" She was breathing too rapidly. She waved a hand as if to eradicate Garfein and knocked over the cold coffee, desperately began dabbing at it with Kleenex. It soaked into the *Post*. She felt Jay's eyes boring into her.

"Well, you told somebody, Nat."

"Jay," she said, trying to hold her voice steady, "why

41

do you come in here looking like the wrath of God and start picking on me? Who do you think you are? And what the hell do you think I've done? What's my crime? I didn't throw away the gun and I didn't call the *Post*—"

"Somebody did."

"So what? It's my problem, not yours. So why the dark looks, that see-me-in-the-principal's-office tone? Really . . ."

He looked at her and she saw his eyes soften. Her fists were clenched in her lap and she knew she'd stuck out her lower lip like a little girl about to cry. She sat there looking up at him, aware of his softening, wondering if she was doing it all on purpose. All her life, the pose had worked. But it wasn't a pose: it was just her, just the way she looked. Oh, who could figure it out?

"I'm sorry, Nat," he said quietly, closing the door behind him. "I didn't mean to play the heavy."

"Well, you should watch it. And you've got food on your shirt. Messy eater." She smiled, felt better.

"I don't know, it just worried me, seeing your name in the paper that way." He stood looking out the window. "Over there, is that where you saw it happen?"

She nodded, got up, pointed out the spot.

"The thing is," he said, "whoever threw the gun away—assuming it was a gun, your eyes must be better than mine—may be wondering right now if you saw him, if you could recognize him—and Garfein put your name in the paper. It's not funny. Too many freaks out there, and now this particular freak has your name—"

"So there's not much I can do about it, is there?"

He shrugged his massive shoulders. "If you didn't tell Garfein, who did? Who have you told?"

"Only one person, I'm afraid."

"Oh, no, not Tony!"

She nodded. "I had to tell somebody."

She saw him almost flinch, the question unspoken: Why not me, Nat, why didn't you tell me?

He looked at his watch. "I've got an appointment. Look, we've got to think of something—some means of keeping an eye on you for a few days. I could call a security firm. Or a detective agency. I don't want you just wandering around, a sitting duck." He looked out the window again. "I've had some experience with being scared, really scared. It's not nice."

She took his sleeve. "Don't worry, Jay." If she had told him the rest of the story, the laughter on the other side of the door, he'd have put her in his pocket and not let her go. "Really, I'm not scared. Maybe it wasn't a gun—"

"Don't bullshit me, Nat." He stopped with the door open. "Be careful. I'll think of something." He grimaced, shook his head, and left her alone.

What had he meant? she wondered: *I've had some experience with being scared, really scared.* . . . It was hard to imagine what might scare him. Then she smiled to herself: the fact was, he was a little bit scared of her.

At seven-thirty she met her friend, Lotte Marker, who was a senior editor specializing in mysteries and thrillers at a house with whom Natalie had done a good deal of business over the years. They had been friends since their first meeting and made a point of dining together three or four times a year, which always meant there was a good deal of personal catching up to do. When they settled into one of the corners in the back at Le Petit Robert in the West Village, Natalie was surprised at Lotte's immediate reference to something other than books and business. The Garfein column. No warming up with shoptalk tonight.

"Well, everybody's talking about it, my dear," Lotte said, fixing Natalie with a quizzical gaze over the tops of her half-glasses. She was holding the menu to one side as if this Garfein thing couldn't wait. "Let's face it, it's so bizarre!"

"Come on, things like that happen in New York all the time."

"Debatable, in my view, but it's not just that you saw the man with the gun. What makes it so precious, so priceless, is that it shows up in the *Post!* That, whatever else you may tell yourself, definitely does not happen every day. That sets it well apart from all the other daily scary numbers, don't you agree?" She sipped a kir and smiled knowingly. "It's rather like having several million people look through your purse . . . or your medicine cabinet. Suddenly everybody knows more about you than you know about them, you're so exposed, so vulnerable—"

"Really, you're making way too much of it—"

"Au contraire, I'm voicing a more or less unanimous opinion based on an informal survey—let me repeat, everyone's talking about it. And of course you're listed in the telephone directory, so he's got your address—"

"Oh, stop, Lotte! I don't want to think about it!" She was beginning to feel the onset of real irritation.

"Nonsense stop! You'd better think about it. If you saw him throw a gun, then he must have had that gun for a purpose . . . and he must be afraid you saw his face. Did you, by the way?"

"No, he was in shadow."

"But he doesn't know that, does he?"

"Lotte, for heaven's sake, what are you trying to do to me?"

Lotte inspected the escargot, popped one into her mouth. "I'm not a mystery editor for nothing, my dear. I know how these stories work, trust me. The point is, there is an inherent danger here and I'm afraid you're not going to take it seriously if somebody doesn't come down on you like a ton of bricks. I've elected myself to do same. The question arises, how in the world did Garfein find out?"

She told Lotte it had to have been Tony.

Lotte sniffed. "Wonderful, just wonderful. Tony. An IQ the size of his penis!"

Natalie laughed. She was lured into recounting the details of the night of the gunman over the fish and the chilled white Bordeaux. She told Lotte how the man had stood laughing at her through the locked door.

"Mon Dieu." She sighed. "Worse and worse. Richard Widmark in *A Kiss Before Dying*. That's sadism, my child. Why, he could be following you to work, watching

45

your house, following you to dinner tonight . . . he might even let you see him just to find out if you recognize him. He's playing with you, Natalie."

"You're absolutely getting carried away. You've convinced yourself of all this—"

"With good reason, I might add. I know what it's like to be scared, I've been scared. . . ."

"What do you mean?" Natalie's attention was piqued: two people had just told her the same thing, that they knew what it meant to be scared.

It had happened the previous summer. Lotte had gotten a telephone call, one of the oldest come-ons in the world, but she'd fallen for it. A young man's voice, all earnest sincerity, an intern at Bellevue, rather apologetic, giving his ID number, naming the staff research director in charge of the project, explaining that he was one of a team doing a survey of Manhattan residents. "No personal questions," he'd said, "and you can just hang up if you don't want to participate, I'd certainly understand. But I do wish you'd help me out." He had laughed in a rueful, self-deprecating way, somehow endearing. Lotte had said sure, go ahead.

The first questions had concerned the extent of her insurance coverage, whether it was group or personal, the costs, if she'd had any claims in the past three years, what she knew or believed she knew about rising hospital costs, and her perceptions of the rise or fall in quality of care. The innocence of the questions had lulled her and she had hardly noticed the slight changes, the way they were edging into her own life. Her views on abortion—had she ever been pregnant, did she regularly test her breasts for telltale lumps, had she ever suffered from vaginal infections of any kind, and were they common among her friends? . . . She had finally objected and the voice had apologized, told her he knew these were touchy areas but after all it was absolutely anonymous from her point of view, and he only had a couple more questions. She relented, "like a goddamn hick," she said, and the next question was one too many. Orgasms. Was she more likely to have an orgasm when she had intercourse or when she used her finger to excite herself? She had gasped, called him a perverted creep, and he had laughed eerily, a different voice, and said, "That's all the questions, Miss Marker. Little Miss Marker. I know all I need to know and now I'm going to get you and fuck you and then I'll kill you. . . ." She had been momentarily hypnotized, frozen with horror; had stared at the receiver, then slammed it down, and sat there while it rang again and again until she had unplugged it. . . .

"He called several more times over the next weeks, always when I was out, as if he was watching me and knew when I was gone, so he could leave messages on my answering machine, that laugh and descriptions of what he was going to do to me . . . and then the calls stopped." She sipped her coffee, for the moment refusing to meet Natalie's eyes. "The thing is, I haven't been able to date a man since—I know, I know, it's stupid, but I can't help it. I just can't help it. . . ." Finally she swallowed hard and smiled edgily. "The point is, Natalie, I'm begging you to take this seriously. Please."

47

In the cab going home Natalie wondered what Jay had been referring to when he'd said that he knew what it meant to be afraid. Men, she reflected, seemed so much less vulnerable, but you never knew. She sighed to herself and was glad to hear Sir yapping and scratching behind the door.

The fact was, she was afraid, and she hated admitting it to herself. Lotte hadn't told her the story just to hear herself talk. Take it seriously, she'd said. All right . . . but Natalie wasn't sure what that meant. Not exactly, anyway.

Chapter Six

She woke up hearing Lotte's story replaying in her mind, had coffee with it, put up with it yammering at her in the cab, and got to the office in something less than a great mood.

Jay was already there, turned out in one of his stunning glen plaid suits with an almost subliminal touch of maroon deep in the weave, dashing from office to office, taking his stance at one window after another with a gigantic pair of binoculars. He would crane upward, trying to get the clearest, most angled view he could, muttering under his breath. He turned to Natalie, took one look, and said, "So what's eating you?"

"Bad case of urban angst."

"Oh, that. Old news, Nat, old news." He grinned boyishly. "The peregrine falcons," he said, "I saw one, he was swooping down from the vicinity of the top of the AT & T building—then I lost him, dammit. . . . We're just too low here for any kind of decent bird-watching."

He put the binoculars back up to his eyes and fine-tuned the adjustment. He'd been a bird-watcher since his Boy Scout days, had shown her his guides—some dating back forty years—which he kept in his office: she was sure it was his most innocent vice. Charming, really, in such a sophisticated, urban creature.

"Well, stay at your post," she said, turning to leave.

"Damn right," he murmured, "damn right," already absorbed in the idea of the soaring falcons.

An hour later on her way to the Xerox room she glimpsed him again, at another window, peering up through the eyepiece.

By eleven o'clock her ear was hurting from the telephone receiver digging into her small pearl earring and she needed coffee. She went and got it herself, brought it back to her desk, and the intercom began its dim, insistent buzzing. Lisa's voice was low and amused: "I've got the fuzz out here for you."

"The what?"

"Fuzz. A cop. Sergeant MacPherson, NYPD. Nice blue suit, brown shoes . . ."

"What does he want?"

"To see you."

"Okay. Have him come in." She'd thought of little but Lotte's fears and warnings through the night and morning. Now, the police. *The police?*

Sergeant Danny MacPherson looked about her own age, central casting's idea of a certain kind of cop: a tweed jacket, brown slacks (belying Lisa's idea of humorous observation), a pale, rectangular face, a level gaze, hair longish and combed back from his flat forehead, a wide mouth with a firm set to the jaw: no colorful little quirks like the guys on "Hill Street Blues": he seemed to date from the early age of television, before ugly and real became beautiful. He walked in, showed her his badge or ID card—she didn't really look—and introduced himself. He didn't smile. She bet he was first in his class at the police academy or the John Jay school.

"Ms. Rader," he said, with acute attention to the *Ms*. "I'm running down this gun thing that ran in the *Post*. And the *Times* and the *Daily News*. Did you happen to see the news last night, by the way?" He sat down, crossed his well-creased slacks.

"No," she said. There had been a surprisingly sardonic cast to his voice and she didn't much like it. An Irish brogue, a smelly black cigar, and hairy knuckles would all have been more comforting.

"Well, I did. Your little incident was turned into a cute closer on the gossip portion of the show—it was practically word-for-word from Garfein's column: a photograph of you, the story of what a big-time agent you are, then the scene you're supposed to have witnessed. All that same garbage about how it might make a wonderful plot for a movie." He folded his arms. "I wasn't amused, Ms. Rader. Can you imagine why?"

"Not really," she said, "aside from the fact that it's not a very amusing story. As well as an invasion of my privacy. Which could conceivably put me in even more danger from the man who threw the gun away." She felt Tony's and Jay's and Lotte's concerns tugging at her, infiltrating her subconscious. MacPherson was bringing it all back.

"I wasn't amused because I don't like being left out of funny things involving guns. Frankly, it made me feel like a horse's ass—do I make myself clear? This part of Manhattan is mine, Ms. Rader."

"How very grand. Does that include all the people, too?"

"When guns are involved, it most certainly does. Now before I hear your story, I have a simple question. I can't help wondering why you didn't report what you saw to us right away. Before you called the newspapers and made sure you got as much publicity as you could. I'm just curious, you understand."

"You tell me, Mr. MacPherson, is this your idea of police brutality? A withering crossfire of sarcasm—"

"Good lord, no." MacPherson's face changed fractionally, whether around the eyes or the mouth she wasn't quite sure: perhaps it was what passed for his smile. "This was more in the line of an insult. But then, I'm not very happy about you and your newspaper friends. And I'm still wondering why you didn't give us a call."

"You tell me this is your turf. My God, if everybody who saw something weird went running to the cops . . . well, we'd spend our entire lives at the precinct house, wouldn't we?"

"But why run to the newspapers?"

"I didn't run to the newspapers."

"You don't say. . . . Well, why don't you just tell me the whole story."

"Why don't you try not to be so supercilious."

"It's a deal, Ms. Rader. Maybe it's out of my

system." He took a notebook from his jacket pocket and a fountain pen, which he carefully uncapped. "And maybe not," he said. "We'll see."

"You aren't my idea of a cop," she said.

"I can live with that," he said softly. "Now why don't we just get on with it."

MacPherson let her tell the story without interruption. When she had finished describing how Teddy had seen her into the cab, she took a breath, looked at him questioningly, wondering if there was anything left to tell him about that night.

MacPherson flipped through his notes, face expressionless. "You know," he said quietly, "it would make a thriller, wouldn't it?"

"No, it wouldn't, actually."

He still hadn't looked up from his notes. "That touch about the laughter on the other side of the door? Frankly, my blood ran cold."

She wasn't sure if he meant it or was mocking her. She didn't much like being off balance. "But it's only an incident, not a plot. The plot is what would come later . . . and there isn't any *later*, if you see what I mean. Life tends to be made up of incidents. The plot only shows up much later, if indeed there is a plot."

"Aha. Well, I'm sure you know far more about fiction than I do." He finally looked up. "The point is, so far as I can see, there either was a gun. Or wasn't. Rainy night, a fair distance, a gun is rather small . . . but somebody did do the laughing number outside your door." He gave a barely perceptible shrug. "We really must find that gun—"

"And wouldn't it be a good idea to see if one was used in the immediate hours before he threw it away?"

"Yes, I'll bet that would be a good idea, Ms. Rader." The faint derision had edged back into his voice and she regretted having spoken. "Now, back to all the publicity. If you didn't tell Mr. Garfein, who did?"

She told him about her conversation with Tony.

"Have you asked your former husband if he actually did mention it to his friend Garfein?"

"No. But it's obvious, isn't it?"

He looked skeptical.

"I haven't spoken with him since. The whole thing made me angry. I didn't want to have a fight with him."

MacPherson seemed to think that wasn't worth a reply. He stood up. "Show me the window. Show me where you were standing when you saw this man. Please."

She got up, pointed, and he made a small, unhappy noise. "Do you wear glasses?" he asked.

"Contacts."

"Could you possibly tear yourself away from being a hot superagent for a few moments?"

"It's imaginable," she said.

"Well, imagine it." He put his notebook back in his pocket, capped the pen. "I want to find the gun."

It was cold, crisp, and clear in the street. She followed MacPherson across to the construction site, to the contractor's trailer, where they confronted a foreman

in tan workclothes and a fur-lined parka jacket. He
looked at MacPherson's badge with considerable dis-
trust, an attitude that changed only for the worse as he
listened to MacPherson's retelling of Natalie's story.

"Nobody here found a gun," he said. "Are you
kidding? We'd all know about it—a job in Jersey City
once, we found a stiff in a piling form, same difference.
Gun—I'd know about it." That seemed to end the
discussion, from his point of view. He was pulling on the
last inch of a cigarette. His face was red, chapped from
the life he led.

MacPherson suggested that Natalie point out the
exact spot the man had been in, the motion with which
he'd thrown the gun, and then the three of them—
ignored by the workmen—tramped around in the pit, far
below street level. It was dirty and uneven and she was
having a difficult time negotiating in her Italian shoes,
which weren't designed for treacherous footing. Everywhere she looked she confronted a sea of hardening
cement, huge forms of wood and steel, machinery,
swearing men in hardhats. The hardhat the foreman had
given her made her feel like she was wearing a soup
tureen, Quixote's helmet of Mambrino. Her attention
had wandered, trying to project where the gun might
have landed, when she noticed that the relationship
between MacPherson and the foreman was not improv-
ing.

MacPherson's voice had gotten remarkably steely.
"Just tear it up, soldier," he said. He was pointing at a
bed of moist-looking concrete that, she had to admit,
looked as if it was in the right place to hide the gun.

"Don't argue with me, just tear it up or shovel it out. I've already got a warrant."

"Fuck you, buddy, just fuck you and this nutty broad!" His voice fairly exploded and several of the workmen looked up, surprised, then grinned at the show.

MacPherson actually laughed. "You're wonderful," he said, smiling, moving close to the foreman, slapping him on the huge shoulder in a comradely gesture. Natalie stepped closer because MacPherson was lowering his voice, still smiling. "How would you like the building inspector's men down here? You want that? Do you have any idea how sorry you and your bosses would be if I got Bracken and a couple of his guys down here? For a very close inspection of all your specs? I'm talking Fast Phil Bracken, get it? You'd be lucky to be a helper-third-class-journeyman-asshole by the time Fast Phil and your bosses got through with you, got done paying the fines. No, maybe they'd just dump you in a form and fill it with cement—now start digging, soldier."

The foreman quietly surveyed the situation, weighing the pros and cons, then nodded genially and went off to commandeer some labor.

Natalie couldn't help laughing. "Very impressive. Fast Phil must be a holy terror."

MacPherson looked down at her. "I just made him up. What do I know about building inspectors? It's sort of the idea—cops have to know how to scare people sometimes; don't let anybody tell you differently." His eyes followed the foreman. "Thank you for coming over, Ms. Rader. I always work better with an audience." He took her arm and helped her back up to street level. "I'm going to hang around here, just in case this guy needs any further scaring. I'll let you know what happens."

She watched him head back into the pit. Crossing the street, she looked up at the agency's windows. In the corner window past the reflection Jay Danmeier stood with his binoculars. He wasn't watching peregrine falcons. He was watching Natalie Rader. She shivered in the cold.

In the late afternoon, MacPherson came back to her office. He wore that shadow of a smile and was carrying a brown paper sack and a newspaper. Unfolding the paper on her desk, he dumped the contents of the sack. There was a heavy clunk.

"That's a .38, Ms. Rader. A gun, you might say."

It was disfigured by clinging bits of half-hardened cement. It seemed large and ugly and frightening. She had never seen a gun before, up close.

"It was right where it should have been. They had to move about five tons of wet cement. . . . I'm relieved there was a gun at the bottom of it, frankly."

"But why didn't someone see it before they poured the cement?"

"Those forms are full of leaves, sandwich wrappers, all kinds of debris. Who looks?"

She took a deep breath. She wanted the gun off her desk. MacPherson seemed to sense her response and scooped it up, newspaper and all, and put it back in the sack.

"What do you do now?" she asked.

"Do a work-up on the gun. Check here and there. We'll keep busy." He had his hand on the door, turned back. "Proves one thing, though."

"It does?" She glanced at him, startled.

"Proves your imagination wasn't working overtime. To tell you the truth, I thought maybe it was. Good afternoon, Ms. Rader."

She stayed in the office until seven o'clock and once outside decided to walk home. She was damned if she'd let fear of the faceless gunman restrict her everyday life. It was a brisk night, dry for the first time in a week, and the bite of winter invigorated her. She walked crosstown to First Avenue and turned left, kept glancing back over her shoulder, feeling foolish, trying to ignore the frisson she felt whenever she noticed a man of a certain build in what was becoming a very common kind of trench coat. She wondered at one point if a trench-coated fellow with clicking leather soles might actually be following her: she had heard him behind her as she passed through the dark shadows beneath the Roosevelt Island Tramway at Fifty-ninth. In the Sixties, still hearing his steady tread, she stopped at a florist's window and watched him pass behind her in the reflection. He seemed utterly unaware of her and she gave a sigh of relief, calling herself a fool in the process. You couldn't live your life worrying about an entire population clad largely in trench coats.

She stopped at a new, gleaming white shop, bought a wedge of cheese, some walnuts, and a cold green-and-white pasta salad. Two doors later she nipped in and bought an already chilled bottle of Orvieto. She was walking more quickly than she liked. In the next block it was a fresh box of Bonz for Sir, and by then she was practically racing.

She got home fed up with her own anxiety, fed up with her tendency to let it discolor a perfectly pleasant walk on a beautiful night.

She fumbled with her keys, her arms full of sacks, and finally managed both locks. Something struck her as strange as she stood silently before the door.

No half-barks and no scratching at the inside of the door. Where was he?

She swung open the door. Waited.

"Sir?" she called tentatively. "Where's Sir? Where could Sir be?" That kind of babbling was sure to bring him.

It was so dark in the flat.

She went in, set the sacks on the mail table, and tripped over something as she went toward the light switch.

She fell to her knees.

She had tripped over the limp body of Sir. . . .

Chapter Seven

It was amazing what the mind was capable of, how many functions could be thrown into the struggle at one time.

On one elemental level, reaching down into herself, Natalie confronted her own sudden vulnerability and terror: she exercised her will. Everything there in the dark was wrong, she sensed it, she knew it, though she couldn't see it.

On another level, she dealt with the limp, warm, furry body of Sir. She registered the thump of the heartbeat within his fragile rib cage. Her circuits were humming beneath the surface: Sir was alive, whatever else might be wrong. His head lolled sideways when she picked him up, and she quickly cradled him as she would have held a baby.

She finally found the light switch and went down to the living room. She turned on a table lamp and in the glow she saw what had happened, went rubber-legged, sank onto a couch with Sir in her lap.

The place had been burglarized. Julie had warned her. But, of course, it hadn't done any good. The door to the backyard stood open to the night. The heavy cast-iron bars had been removed and stacked neatly on the flagstones. Sir opened his mouth in a groggy yawn, whimpered. His eyes flickered. She hugged him to her chest, burying her face in his ears, cooing to him, trying to stay calm, fighting off the desire to cry and swear and scream.

The shelf of glass tigers twinkled at her. The cold breeze from the open door had made the room uncomfortable. She felt the warmth of Sir's body, his breathing growing stronger. He began to squirm halfheartedly. He'd obviously been drugged, which was apparently the work of the humane criminal element these days. She fumbled in one of the sacks, ripped open the top of the box, and held a Bonz under his nose. He licked it, pulled it into his mouth on his tongue. She sat with him until holding him was impossible: he had recovered and wanted to get free, though he wobbled a bit once he was on all fours.

Goddamn crooks!

She looked around the living room, finally got up and did a survey. A small television set was gone, a compact stereo system from the bedroom but not the Bang & Olufsen, which was just too involved to cart away easily, a video-cassette recorder, a Magnavox video-disc player with laser, a couple of cameras from an antique chest, some silver. . . . For some reason they'd ignored the Schiaparelli mink coat, a pre–World War II masterpiece she'd bought a few years before.

She locked the door into the backyard again. The bastards! Her temper kept flaring as she walked from room to room double-checking. Why did they have to pick now of all times? It seemed that her life had speeded up in the few days since she'd seen the man with the gun. Faster, faster, like a carnival ride out of control, like the carousel at the end of *Strangers on a Train* . . .

She wanted to slow it down, get everything back in perspective. Stop thinking about the man with the gun, about Jay Danmeier and his moods and his binoculars watching her, about Tony and his big mouth and his doubts, about MacPherson and his smart-ass attitude . . . and stop thinking about the gun on her desk, crusty with damp cement. . . .

She slowly, carefully made a picnic of her cold pasta salad and wine. She brought her plate and goblet into the newly denuded living room, sat down, and called her insurance man. She left a message on the machine belonging to the man who had made the iron bars for the door.

Instinctively, as it seemed she so often did when frustration and irritation got the better of her, she grabbed the telephone and began ringing Lew Goldstein's number. She hesitated halfway through the process, fingertips poised over the buttons, and wondered if she was acting childishly. Running to Lew . . . She'd known him for nearly twenty years, since they were freshmen together at Northwestern. . . . Never lovers, always pals. And now he was an Upper East Side psychiatrist, lived only a few blocks away, and she still took her crises to him, and he still teased her the half-dozen times a year they saw each other, "still crazy after all these years. . . ." But she stopped, put the telephone down, feeling silly, but still . . .

Dammit, it *was* the kind of experience when you wanted to call a man, just to tell about what a frightening mess you'd found behind your front door. What was wrong with that? She drank some wine and wondered why she was bothering to defend herself to herself. And wished there were a man to turn to . . .

Sir came in and flopped down on the carpet in front of her, his chin resting between his paws, his eyes looking up beseechingly, a crescent of bedraggled, wet tennis ball protruding from his mouth. Ever hopeful. She had to laugh.

Natalie had just changed into jeans and a sweater when Julie arrived, out of breath, bubbling with something she wanted to tell. Then she noticed that things were not quite right, and Natalie told her the story of the burglary and the apparently dead body of Sir, and Julie gasped dramatically, threw her long body into a chair, and began working on her own glass of wine. Once Natalie started talking she ran on through the events of the day, including MacPherson and the foreman and the finding of the gun. Julie was an appreciative audience. Finally, when Natalie had come to a full stop, Julie looked at her brightly: "As David Letterman says, you think that's bad—last night my shoes exploded!"

Natalie searched around for something soothing to put on the tape deck and settled for Antonio Carlos Jobim. She poured more wine and they had a laugh at the thought of calling the police about the burglary, a patently hopeless act in New York City. They sat quietly sipping. "Well, you've let me babble on, now it's your turn—you sounded as if you had something to say when you arrived—"

"Oh, my God, I forgot! It's wonderful—well, it's sort of ghastly but it makes a story that you particularly will appreciate, my dear." Julie forked up a mouthful of Natalie's pasta and settled back, one incredibly long leg pulled up under her. "I had a comparatively shitty day myself—there's some kind of creature infesting one of our hotels in Rangoon and the preliminary reports indicate that it may be eating people, but never mind that—and I retired to Scandals for a drink after work. The insufferable Tillie insisted on accompanying me, unlike some friends of mine, but she quickly saw what an unpromising social desert presented itself and departed for home. At which time this sort of hunky guy moved in—looked vaguely familiar, until I realized that he was a clone of half the guys at the bar, the not-quite-right Burt Reynolds–Tom Selleck look, mustache and curly hair— whatever will finally happen to all these doll men, I ask you? Anyway, he sort of bellied up to the bar, said howdy ma'am, and began to bowl me over with his brilliance and wit. Yawn. But . . . here's where the plot thickens. *He was after you, Nat!*"

Natalie had been listening with only one ear, really, just enjoying having Julie there and talking, and she wondered if perhaps she'd missed something. "He was what?" she said meekly.

"After you. Quite a newish opening gambit: come up to a hot lady at the bar and begin asking about her pal—remember, you did stop in at Scandals with me one night a couple weeks ago—then we went on to Pinocchio for dinner—"

"I remember, sure, but I didn't know the name of the bar."

"Naturally. Well, it was the same place—and this guy wasn't thinking of someone else. He described you, got it all down pat—shiny black hair, purple wool suit with black piping, diamond earrings, little bitty five-three or -four, I mean he was talking about you. He said, let's go back to your place and I can meet your roommate, too." Julie sucked her lower lip back behind her front teeth and cocked her head appraisingly, looking at Natalie from the corners of her eyes. "A secret admirer."

"Just what I wanted. A secret, mustachioed, corny, doll-man admirer." She grinned halfheartedly, a sliver of fear, a memory of the faceless man with the gun tickling at her. "You came running home to give me this bulletin? It passeth understanding."

She was absolutely certain there couldn't be a connection. So why did the thought cling? She toyed with the idea of mentioning it to Julie—the connection she made now with any potentially ominous male—then rejected it. The gulf between them when it came to the subject of men was just not bridgeable. She wished it weren't so, but there was nothing to be done about it.

She wished she had the kind of female friend she could tell anything to, ask anything of, but she knew what Julie would say: *Go for it, give the guy a chance,* which meant, *Go ahead, sleep with him, see how you like it. . . .* For Julie that was always the test. Anything else she'd worry about later. Natalie's loneliness was held inside her, nearly denied altogether, like a secret, shameful illness, while Julie said the hell with loneliness and went off adventuring, her vulnerability cloaked in bravado and drowned out by clattering bracelets. Julie could stand the pain: sometimes Natalie thought she actually sought it, like someone proving a theorem.

"No," Julie was saying, "I came running in because this guy browbeat me into letting him drive me home— don't say it, I'm a fool, I admit it—and he was groping while he double-parked out front and I was trying to get the hell away. He was developing what appeared to be an apoplectic red face and it was not a pretty picture. I finally got the door open and he was talking pretty ugly by then about me and you. The I'm-going-to-stick-it-up-your-cunt-of-a-roommate-too speech, a farewell to the troops. A real charmer—and I knew you'd be pleased that your advice about my frequenting low dives was borne out yet again. . . ."

Natalie sat pensively, watching the glass tigers glittering. Julie wearily threw Sir's tennis ball again and again. Natalie was disgusted and worried by Julie's story: it fit so well into the pattern of the past few days. Upsetting. Someone out there, dirty and vicious, had been watching her. You couldn't know, you couldn't defend yourself. *I'm nothing special, nothing like Julie with her swagger and strut and drama. Just me. And I'm being watched. Welcome to Paranoia, just this side of Breakdown.* She couldn't give her feelings away to Julie. Julie wouldn't have minded being watched: she wanted to be watched, admired, reached for, because it proved everything she believed about herself as well as the men who lusted for her. For Julie romantic love was an absurdity; for Natalie it was the only kind of love worth having. No common ground, not when it came to men. Julie had no illusions about them: Natalie was committed to hers. So her disappointment and fear was the greater.

"Look, Nat," Julie said quietly, "I didn't mean to upset you, it was stupid to tell you after the evening you've had—"

"I'm not upset, really I'm not. It's just an icky experience. I'm sorry you had to go through it. I wish to God you wouldn't end up in places where that kind of stuff happens, that's all."

"Funny thing is, you've just about got me convinced. I should probably wait for Don the Jet to get back from the coast and start going to art galleries with him." She stood up and stretched her arms over her head, like someone getting ready for a slam-dunk. An avalanche of bracelets cascaded down one forearm. "I'm just possibly getting too old for all this carrying-on. Time to pack it in and have babies and move to a farm. Look at all the fun Lady Chatterly had. . . ."

Natalie smiled to herself. She had heard the barefoot-and-pregnant speech before.

* * *

Once Julie had gone upstairs to her own apartment, Natalie was too wide awake to go to bed. Sir was back to normal, bounding around, throwing his tennis ball into the air and chasing it with utter abandon. "Poor old Sir," she remarked to him, "hasn't been for a real walk all week. Good idea, Sir?" He threw himself ecstatically against the front door, rattling his leash that hung from the doorknob. Natalie slipped into her old sheepskin jacket, hooked his chain through the loop on his collar, and set off.

Sir's impatience was showing. He tugged hard, pulling Natalie behind him, heading across First, down to York Avenue, then insisting on his favorite walk—across the footbridge over the FDR Drive, with the endless streams of traffic with the headlights and tail-lights looking like solid, molten streams of brightness below, like time-lapse photography. There were some ships in the East River and steam rising like smoke from the water around them. The wind was cold and clean-smelling, like true winter. For the moment, with Sir and the biting cold and the hum of traffic, she wasn't thinking about any of the events of the day. She felt momentarily free of all that, unencumbered, the way she wanted to feel. The walkway along the fence, with the river coursing beyond, was lit by antiseptic lights on poles separated by pools of darkness between. A man walking his Great Dane waited while the dog barked at a motor launch. Looking out over the water, she felt isolated from the city, from the lights just back across the FDR, past the hulks of darkness that were the hospitals and the condos that lined the eastern boundary of the Upper East Side.

She must have been drifting in her own thoughts because she let the leash slip from her grasp, and Sir, sensing a romp, was off like a bullet, bounding along the fence heading uptown like a dog late for a very important date.

She stood helplessly, watching him go. There was no point in chasing after him. He'd just think it was a game and run all the harder, farther, faster. She'd have to wait him out, just saunter along behind, until he noticed he was alone and began to get nervous. Sir wasn't used to being out in the great world all by himself. Instinctive fear would begin to work its way.

Watching Sir, she heard, riding on the wind behind her, someone whistling tunelessly. Suddenly she didn't want to look back. Now she felt the fear in the belly . . . who was whistling? Had someone followed her? She went to the fence, tried to look casually out at the lights of Queens across the river, straining to see who was behind her.

A man in a trench coat, hands deep in his pockets, stood like Natalie, looking out across the water. Far behind her. The equivalent of a block away. Just a man. A shape. In a trench coat. She bit into her lip, proving to herself that she existed, and set off hurriedly toward Sir.

Sir had wandered to a stop, was sniffing the air curiously. He strolled slowly on, looked back at Natalie, but didn't speed up. He was ready to be taken home, wherever the hell that was: doubt showed in his every step.

He stopped again, stared into the shadows at the bottom of another footbridge across the FDR, where the stairway curled down from above.

His leash lay on the walk behind him, like a fuse.

She looked back. The man in the coat, hands still in his pockets, was walking along the fence, a bit closer to her than before. There was something about him that seemed familiar. She shook her head: imagination out of control. *Don't be a jerk, Nat.*

She turned back, only twenty feet from Sir. *Don't run now, you little bastard. It's been a long day. Just wait for me.*

Sir was standing staring into the shadows. She recognized the pose. Sir, asking himself if he could just possibly pee one more time.

Somehow the leash had gotten on the far side of him.

She had to go all the way to him. She knelt beside him, where he stood rooted to the spot.

"What are you doing, you silly fellow?" she murmured, hugging his head.

She blinked.

Directly in front of her, perhaps two feet from her face, were two shoes.

She looked up.

A man stood in the shadows, grinning down at her.

Chapter Eight

She knew she was stretched out on her back. She felt something wet on her face, then her memory began to function again. Sir was sniffing her face, licking her cheek and nose, whining with impatience. His tongue was slippery and she got a whiff of his breath and pushed his head away with a gloved hand, forced herself to open her eyes.

The man in the trench coat was leaning over her.

"Lew . . ."

She closed her eyes again, then opened one hesitantly, thinking maybe she was hallucinating.

"Natalie, for God's sake, are you all right?" His heavy glasses were sliding down his nose and he jammed them back up. She nodded, tried to say something but her mouth was stuck dry.

"Natalie," he said, as if he enjoyed repeating her name. She heard a blast on a boat's airhorn. The low roar of traffic on the FDR was dragging her back to wakefulness. "You fainted." He looked very worried. "Your pulse is okay. But doctors hate it when people faint. . . . Do you have any nausea? Try to talk to me. Please, Natalie. And get that silly grin off your face."

She wet her lips. "I'm all right. . . . There was a man in the shadows." She blinked and saw him in her mind: the grin, the eyeballs like pinpoints of light in the blackness. An impression of rags, a vile smell, stringy hair . . . Quickly she forced her eyes open, hating the images playing in her mind.

"Yes, there was a man, a bum, I guess." He put his arm around her, helped her into a sitting position. He watched her closely as she took a deep breath. Her face was damp and he patted her forehead with his handkerchief. "Tell me if you feel any nausea—"

"I'm okay," she said. The cold air off the river felt good. "I think I cracked my head—no, really, I'm all right. Just had the pants scared off me."

"The guy took off. All raggedy and with a stiff leg. You gave him a helluva scare, too. Just a crazy. Do you feel like standing up? Here, take my arm. . . ."

She leaned heavily on him, felt a moment's dizziness once she was on her feet, sagged back against him. He held her. There was something wrong, something at the back of her mind— Yes, of course, she had just tried to call him. Now here he was. She was starting to hate coincidence.

"What were you doing out here anyway?" It was a sharp-edged question, not very grateful, but she wanted to know: she was sure he was the man she'd seen behind her, whistling. Lew . . .

"Well . . . I was following you."

"Why? I don't understand." She felt the involuntary shudder of fear running along her spine. *Why?* Why was he following her? And why should she fear Lew of all people? Or was fear becoming a constant in her life?

"I saw the piece in the *Post*, called you at the office, missed you, called you tonight, ditto, and thought I'd drop by your place. You were gone, so I remembered Sir's favorite course. Simple." He had Sir's leash and they were walking back along the river, back the way she'd come. She felt normal strength returning to her legs but she clung to his arm. "And there you were, out cold." He shrugged. "Hell, we haven't gotten together since when, Labor Day weekend? It's about time. And to tell you the truth I didn't like that little tidbit in Garfein's column—I mean, it looks to me like your privacy's being invaded. Who told him the story, anyway? Is it true?"

"Tony." She sighed. "They're pals and I don't suppose he thought it would wind up in the column. Yes, it's true, it happened." They had reached the footbridge she'd crossed earlier and she realized she was a little slow going up the stairway. At the top, on the bridge, he said he thought they ought to stop for a few minutes.

Leaning on the railing, watching the traffic, he scrutinized her clinically. "Feeling bushed? Light-headed?" She nodded. "You really shouldn't be out down here this late . . . certainly not now when there's a guy who might be looking for you. Did you see his face?"

"God, don't you start too. Everyone acts like I'm the only living witness to an ax murder. No, I didn't see his face. And I certainly cannot spend the rest of my life hiding from this guy. Who is probably long gone by now." She watched his breath making little balloons of steam before him. He smiled grudgingly, sighed and pulled her away from the rail, set off walking again.

"Oh, Lew—I don't mean to bite your head off. It's only because I know you're right, I should be more careful. Stupid bravado. I hate admitting I'm scared; it makes it worse. Whistling past the graveyard. I'm very lucky you were there. Who knows what that guy would have done if you hadn't come running—"

"Oh, I think he was mainly interested in getting away. Really." But he squeezed her arm through his, as if he really was her hero.

She asked him what he'd been up to and he said he was still doing his act with the couch and the photograph of Freud. At her house he stopped and gave her the leash.

"Listen, you'd better go right to bed. Fainting really does take a lot out of you. It's surprising. Are you sure you feel okay? Well, I guess I'll head for home, Nat—"

She laughed. "Oh, for heaven's sake, Lewis, we're not a couple of strangers. Come on in and have a coffee or a Scotch. Let me tell you the kind of night I've had—before I went out for Sir's walk."

"Are you sure?"

"Well, I'm not going to beg." She opened the door and Dr. Goldstein followed her inside.

An hour later she'd told him about the burglary and the discovery of the gun on the construction site. She rattled on and he listened, nodding, seldom taking his eyes from her face. Finally she said, "You poor guy, you may not be my analyst, but you still seem to have to do all the listening." She bit her lip and frowned. "I seem to be on some kind of ghastly roll. . . . Oh, and Julie—I didn't tell you what happened to Julie at Scandals. . . ."

That story left him shaking his head. "It's sort of strange," he said, pouring himself another cup of coffee, "but I don't think men generally have any idea of the weird experiences women—particularly working women in these big labor-intensive urban areas—have on an amazingly frequent schedule. Most sort of moderate, vaguely normal—I know, what's normal?—vaguely normal men, who don't do a lot of coming on to women they don't know, don't have a clue about this other world that women are prey to. I hear things from patients all day long, and a lot of this social activity I can't even begin to relate to. . . ." His voice trailed away and he looked into his coffee cup.

"Well," Natalie said slowly, "one of the more surprising things that happened to me ever since I saw the man with the gun—" She heard herself stop speaking as a series of images, psychic flashbacks, suddenly imprinted themselves on her mind: the man darting between cabs in the rain, the cement-encrusted gun on her desk, MacPherson capping his fountain pen, the white teeth gleaming like polished bones in the darkness above her. . . .

"Yes? Go on—" He was watching her closely again, as if she might be showing symptoms of something.

"I'm sorry," she said quickly, shaking her head. "I'm

feeling a little scattered, after all." She closed her eyes, blinked them open to confront his. "You're right, Lewis. I am bushed all of a sudden." She felt as if the room, the sound of her own droning voice, Lew's steady gaze—she felt as if they were all closing in on her. She got up from the stool at the tiny kitchen counter and went into the living room, put on a Villa-Lobos tape and sat on the end of the couch. She told him he should sit down and finish his coffee.

"See how cleverly my plan has worked? I came over here to talk to you over coffee, and by God I'm doing it."

"Fairly circuitous route," she said.

He settled back in his chair, looking around. "Look, exactly how scattered are you feeling? You're pale—"

"Really, just tired but . . . I'm not looking forward to your leaving me alone with my thoughts. Ever since all this started, things have been sort of piling up around me . . . oh, hell, Lew! No point in babbling to you—"

"On the contrary," he said. "But for now I want you to get right to bed. And I'm going to call you tomorrow. I want to know just what it is that's been piling up."

"Oh, please don't worry, Lewis!"

"What, me worry?" He grinned, boyish, like the old days.

She got up and followed him up the stairway to the front door.

He stood there looking at her.

She smiled up at him.

He punched her softly on the arm. "I'll call you, Natalie. Tomorrow."

Once he was gone, once she was standing at the sink

brushing her teeth, she thought how lucky she was that he'd remembered where Sir liked to walk. *Way to go, Lew*. She took a sleeping pill to blot out the images that haunted her and went to sleep with the radio playing softly. And Sir curled against her legs. He began to snore just before she went under.

Chapter Nine

At the office in the morning there was a handwritten letter from Rory Linehan, the novelist whose first book she had recently placed. He was delighted with the news of his advance. He and his wife hoped she could join them for dinner at their place the next evening to celebrate. She was hugely pleased, couldn't stop beaming to herself. Her optimism about Linehan's career was really limitless, if only he had the determination and stability to keep learning, working, disciplining his gifts. She called their number and spoke briefly to his wife, accepting the invitation.

She had lunch with Jay, a fortnightly ritual enabling them to speak of business away from the endless telephone discussions that kept them apart within the office. They had a drink in the tiny bar inside the front door at Lutece, then dined more elegantly than her appetite required in the airy, green and white barnlike dining room. Danmeier was in full cry, running the tab to well over a hundred dollars. Natalie just smiled at his discourse on the wine. He was more wrapped up in his toys than any other man she'd ever known. Still, why not? He seemed to have life so much his own way. Which was doubtless why his inability to forge a personal relationship—a *more* personal relationship, in any case—with Natalie seemed to bother him so. Any resistance seemed to throw him off his game, and Natalie wondered if just maybe she was testing him and his professed interest in her.

"By the way," he said, enjoying what she took for a gooseberry tart with his coffee, "Clive Morrison's over from London. We're having dinner tomorrow night and he specifically asked me to have you join us. Good sign, Nat. He's a distinguished publisher, and we're doing an increasing amount of business with him, as you know if you're paying attention to the contracts file, and he's being touted for the queen's next honors' list. Should be 'Sir Clive' the next time he's over here. Why in God's name are you looking at me that way?"

"I can't go, I'm afraid. I already have a dinner engagement, Jay—"

"For God's sake, Natalie, if it's not with Ernest Hemingway, break the date. Perhaps you missed it, but this is Clive Morrison! He asked for you, he knows about you—it's business, my dear. Not just old Jay hanging around waiting to be turned down as usual." The bitterness in his voice frustrated her: the last thing she needed . . .

"It's just one of those things," she said, knowing already that she was wrong and Jay was right, that she

82

could quite easily beg off the Linehans and make another date for their dinner. She knew it but something was flaring inside her. She wasn't going to change her plans. "If it makes you feel any better, my engagement is business, as well."

"With whom, may I ask?" He sounded very cold. As if he were yet again bearing up under a personal insult.

"Linehan and his wife," she said.

"Linehan." He repeated the name with distaste. "I do wish you'd never heard of dear old Linehan. You can tell from his bloody overwrought book that he's the kind of Irishman who enjoys blowing people to smithereens. I mean, have you read the book?"

"Of course."

"One pussy and cock symbol after another—the man's a raving degenerate. Can't say what he means. D. H. Lawrence might just as well never have existed—"

"Jay, people are looking at you—"

"Good. I like to be looked at. Linehan." He sighed with massive disgust. "I don't suppose I can actually order you to come meet Morrison?"

"You can do whatever you like. But I shan't come."

He finished his gooseberry tart. "Natalie, we've got to have a good long talk. About the agency. About your role in it—you aren't by any chance . . ." He shook his head. "No, I guess not."

"What are you trying to say?"

"Are you thinking of leaving? Raiding the client list and going off on your own?" His face was reddening. She realized the effort the question had cost him.

"Oh, Jay," she said. She tentatively brushed the

sleeve of his immaculate blue pinstripe. His vulnerability, coming as it did out of the blue, touched her. "Jay, really . . . of course I'm not thinking of any such thing. I like what I do. I like where I do it. And I certainly don't want the administrative headache of setting up my own shop—even if I could."

He nodded, recovering. "But you know you could. You could take your share of clients. Very loyal to you. Well, I'll give your apologies to Clive."

They lingered briefly, hostilities ended, and she took his arm on the walk back to the office.

The patching-up process was not, however, wholly successful. Natalie was aware of the tension between her and Jay through the afternoon, though they never actually had occasion to speak. The looks—or lack of them—were enough. He was just going to have a pout and there wasn't much she was inclined to do about it.

And then Tony called. "Your ex," Lisa said, sticking her head around the corner, "on two. You here?"

Lisa was very protective, but yes, Natalie was there. Listening to Tony's voice from the wilds of Staten Island, she was reminded of the fact that she'd not spoken to him since he'd blabbed to Garfein. She felt herself flushing at the memory: anger like a tiny explosion somewhere in her brain. He said he was just heading into town and wanted her to meet him at the Bemelmans Bar at the Carlyle. He said it was important. She told him she'd try to be there by six. "I hate it when you sound so mysterious," she said, but he only laughed. His voice was a little on the high-pitched side and she'd never been crazy about his laugh. He was better in person than on the telephone. The Clint Eastwood syndrome, high voice but sort of gaunt and sexy otherwise. God, poor screwed-up Tony, hammering away at his porn novels and his soldier-of-fortune novels and his treasury-agent novels. . . .

She left the office early and took a taxi home. The insurance man was waiting for her on the front steps. He was a shy young man who made a list, checked it twice, told her that she had been very wise to photograph her valuable possessions and file the photos with the insurance company. He told her he'd get back to her. She fed Sir several Bonz and went to pick up the mail.

A note had been dropped through the outside slot and lay atop the pile of bills and circulars.

Tried to deliver flowers at 4:30. Nobody home. Call 866-9851 for delivery.

Who could be sending flowers?

She looked at her watch and punched out the number while slipping out of the day's clothes, flinging them across the bed.

"Dante's Flowers," the man said.

"You've got a delivery for me. Last name Rader, over on—"

"Yeah, yeah. I got it right here. You weren't home." His voice brimmed over with impatience, as if she'd set out to frustrate Dante's Flowers' daily schedule.

"I'm home now," she said, "if you can step on it."

"Wait a minute." He yelled at someone on his end,

"Can you deliver Rader, Harry? Hey, way to go, man. Okay, Miss Rader, how's twenty minutes?"

"Fine," she said, wriggled out of her pantyhose and ducked under a cold shower, clenched her teeth and waited for it to get hot and steamy.

She was half-dressed in something new and turquoise, drying her hair, when the buzzer sounded. She straightened the skirt and looked out the peephole at the man on the stoop. He was holding a box of flowers and smoking a cigar.

She spoke into the intercom: "Who is it?"

"The flowers, lady, the flowers you just called about."

She buzzed him in and opened her door. It was a very cheap cigar that smelled like candy. He looked like a character in a movie, short, muscular, beetle-browed, holding the box of flowers like a bat against his shoulder.

"Hi, toots," he said, without even looking at her. "It's your lucky day. Here, just sign on the back of this sheet." He wheezed on the smoke, blew a stream past her face.

She signed. "Is there a card?"

"Look, I only deliver 'em, y'know? Card should be in the box."

She took the box. There was an ashtray full of change and a few bills on the table by the door. She handed him a dollar. He folded it, tucked it into his shirt pocket. "I'll buy myself a decent smoke. Thanks, ma'am." He touched the shiny black plastic visor of his hat. "Have a nice night, toots." He was gone.

A dozen long-stemmed yellow roses.

She put them in a Lalique vase on the coffee table so she'd see them down in the living room the moment she opened the door. One problem. The card.

Congrats!

No name, no signature. Just a typewritten, single word.

She was running late, there was no time to try to figure it out now.

She was lucky to find a cab outside the front door and she was off to the Carlyle.

Tony was waiting for her. It had always been his favorite rendezvous with the wonderful Ludwig Bemelmans drawings on the wall. Natalie found it rather impersonal, tables too small, and too much open space. But then there had been a lot they didn't agree on. He got up as she approached and kissed her cheek. There was a bucket of Perrier-Jouet champagne by the table and Tony was looking very pleased with himself.

He poured a glass for each of them. He was quite gray by his ears and he still wore his hair longish, though it was receding at the temples. His jaw was wide and firm, giving him a look of great resolve, which was, in practice, more often just bad temper. His gaze was level, his dark brown eyes as clear as ever. He had a long straight nose, shaggy eyebrows, and looked like he belonged on a horse, a cowboy in an advertisement. A Ralph Lauren man in a worn corduroy jacket and a cotton polo shirt that had been washed twelve thousand times: Tony Rader, her ex.

He lifted his glass, clinked the rim of hers.

"Happy birthday, Nat," he said. His eyes twinkled.

She knew her face looked blank, her lips parted as if a question was forming.

"I knew it," he said, sipping his champagne. "I knew you'd forget. It was bound to happen, you used to come close, but this year you just forgot! Glad I lived to see it!" He seemed high on something, the way he'd get when his nerves were strung too tight.

"My God, Tony . . . you're right. What am I? Thirty-seven? I must be—how could I actually have forgotten?" She took a healthy swallow of champagne and felt it go straight to her head. Passing her nose it made her sneeze, and she heard him laugh.

"You forgot because you've got the worst case of tunnel vision in the world. You never think about anything but work, you don't worry about birthdays, yours or anyone else's. So you forgot. So I remembered for you. Sitting out there on the Island in the fog, seeing the shape of Manhattan kind of blurred, I got to feeling funny. About you, I mean. Lonely for you. Lonely for your face and your self-centered approach to life—"

"Watch it, buster."

"You don't scare me anymore, Nat. Don't even try." She laughed. "Dummy. And thanks for the flowers."

"Flowers? I didn't send you flowers. I bought you a Tiffany bauble. But no flowers." She could see his face clouding over: only she could notice it, probably, but she'd had lots of experience. She could see the old possessiveness, the jealousy burning in the irises of his eyes. The flowers pissed him off.

"If it wasn't you, it had to be Lisa. My secretary. Or

Julie. They both know my birth date." She wondered if the lie sounded anything like the truth. The light in his eyes dimmed a bit. "Anyway, what were you saying about Tiffany's?"

"Don't look so surprised," he said. Clint Eastwood never sounded petty but he was already beginning to pout. "Even writing my kind of garbage I occasionally get paid—"

"Come on, Tony. Remember, this is supposed to be fun." She forced herself to smile brightly. "I want my present!" She was mildly disgusted with herself for doing her excited-little-girl number, but anything was justifiable to avoid one of Tony's moods.

"And you shall have it." He handed her the baby-blue box.

"You really shouldn't have—well, I'm pleased that you did, anyway." Her fingers were fumbling with the ribbon, finally slipped it off the edge. There was a baby-blue flannel pouch inside and she lifted it out by the drawstring. She looked up hesitantly, asking herself: Why? What was the point? But also remembering all the years when there had been a point, when why was a question you never had to ask. She pulled it open and slid her fingers in, touched something warm and smooth. She emptied it into her palm; it was silver, caught the light from every direction: a diamond-shaped egg of silver with a silver chain. She was trying very hard to keep her lower lip from quivering, fighting back even a single tear. What was the point? But it was such a beautiful thing. . . . It was warm in her palm and she closed her fingers around it, looked up at Tony and his handsome, silly, weak face.

He swallowed hard, smiling at her. "I just saw it, you know, and your birthday was coming up . . . like they say, it was you, Tiger. It's a replica of the Tiffany diamond in silver." He shrugged. "Wish it had been the diamond itself . . . Happy birthday, anyway." He cleared his throat. "Don't ask me why, I just miss you sometimes. You're just so damned busy, you filled the air with the beating of your wings—I miss all the little flurries sometimes, that's all."

"Oh, shut up, Tony," she said, hugged him, felt his mouth against her ear. *This is ridiculous, she thought. We're divorced. We know it's better this way. We can never go back and I wouldn't go back for all the diamonds in South Africa! But it's so sweet.* . . . She blinked and wiped her eyes, hoping he hadn't noticed.

She needn't have worried. He worked the conversation back to the flowers, who might have sent them, dancing around the edges of whom she might be going out with, sleeping with. If he'd have believed her, she'd have told him how long it had been since she'd slept with anyone. But that would have been wasted breath. They drank their way through the champagne, glancing off several of the old arguments, the little blades of frustration that whittled at them until they weren't a couple anymore, just two different people.

Natalie made a last-ditch effort to point the conversation in a happier direction. "So, the work is going pretty well." She had hung the silver pendant around her neck, and now hefted it in her small hand. "Must be," she said, winked.

"I don't know. I hate writing that porno crap—how many ways can you say 'cock'? How many ways are there to describe doing it? It's like making your living sweeping out a whorehouse—"

"But your other stuff? The novel?"

"Christ, you really think anything's ever gonna come of that?"

"Yes, I do. You're a good writer—"

"Well, there are those who think I'm a hack, and they, sweetheart, big-time agent, are right. I had a little problem today, Nat. . . ." He lit a cigarette. His hands were shaking: she hated herself for not wanting to watch, for not caring about his problems anymore, for being there to accept gifts but not being there to care. She felt like shit and she hated him for making her feel that way about herself. It was all so mixed up in her mind: the more she thought about it, the more confused she became.

"I was at Prime Books; you know the crap they do. The crap I write. Well, I went to see Engebretson, this hairball editor—I mean not your A in citizenship, this guy—and he rejects this load I sent him a couple weeks ago. Too much characterization, too much plot; he says, 'What we need, Rader, is more of the old in and out,' . . . and he sticks his forefinger through a circle he makes with his other hand. Christ, what a crud this guy is. So I flipped out—" He watched his ash fall into his champagne. He rolled his eyes. "I grabbed this prick by his spotty little tie and yanked him up out of his chair.

91

I pointed out that I thought I was going to have to kill him right then and there! Hyperbole, for Christ's sake—but he was buzzing building security, and these guys showed up, looked like cop rejects, linebackers, and we had a chat and they escorted me out to the street. . . . Fine. But this goddamn Engebretson rejected the manuscript! I mean, what the hell's going on, Nat?" He fished the ash out of his glass but it came apart and he reached over and sipped from hers.

"You're just too fine a writer for that kind of work—"

"So what good is it doing me?" He laughed, shook his head, ground out the cigarette. "Ah, fuck it, Nat. You couldn't sell that book—the old book. Maybe that was an accurate assessment of old Tony's work. Maybe I should just face up to it." He looked off across the room, which was filling up. The smoke hung in a thick cloud.

"What do you want me to say? You've got to take the time off from writing the stuff you hate and pay attention to the work that's important to you. You've got some money. And if you don't, you're a fool if you don't borrow some from me—I can certainly afford it and I've told you a thousand times—"

"I don't give a shit what you've told me, Nat."

"Well, if you don't want my help, I wish to God you'd stop bringing your little dead birds and putting them at my feet. What can I do? What change can I effect? What's the point?"

"Maybe I just wanted you to commiserate with me over a glass of champagne on your birthday—"

"You're such a liar, Tony. You really are. Once you heard someone sent me flowers, you lost it, you just lost it—your concentration, your generosity, your ability to behave, your . . . sanity!"

"Nat," he said, standing up quietly, "the last thing I need from you is a lecture on my lack of sanity. The check's taken care of. You might as well drink the last glass." He turned back once he was a few feet away. "Happy birthday, Tiger." Then he just faded away in the crowd.

She sat quite still, her hand between her breasts, holding the silver diamond. He was right, she was an unholy bitch. Sure, he was right.

Wasn't he?

She wasn't quite sure how long she sat there. She sat quite still, thinking about Tony, replaying their conversation, wishing he hadn't attacked the editor. . . . She wasn't particularly upset. Just a little numb.

She thought the waiter had come over to her table.

But when she looked up she saw Jay Danmeier looking down at her.

Chapter Ten

"I've been watching you."

"Jay, I can't believe you don't have something better to do—"

"A debatable point. But, nevertheless, I have been watching you." He sat down where Tony had sat, shot his cuffs, crossed his legs, and straightened the crease. "You look more or less like I feel, a bit of a lost soul. Am I close?"

"I don't know." Natalie shrugged. "My circuits are somewhat overloaded at the moment." She smiled wearily. "You are not the lost-soul type, however."

"I skipped "21" tonight. I must be off my feed. Just walked on home, not feeling up to par. Maybe I'm getting old, who knows? Full of memories I'd just as soon forget. There was nothing in the fridge, it's my housekeeper's night off . . . so I took to the streets, wandering, bereft." His crocodile smile had lost its usual gloating aspect. He took a black pigskin case from inside his jacket and slipped out one of his cigars, clipped the end, smelled it. "I hadn't been in here for years, since the old days. Thought I'd drop by, look at the drawings on the walls. Then I saw you and Tony and, well, things didn't seem to be going awfully well and I figured I'd just watch. Like the little boy with a view of the girls' locker room. Dreadful fellow that I am." He lit his cigar and she smelled the smooth, pungent aroma, liked it. "What was the present for? It's very pretty."

"Just celebrating memories." Her hand went to it again. "I guess it's a night for memories." Jay ordered a split of champagne and she took a swallow, wondering if it was a good idea. "You didn't by any chance send me flowers today, did you? To my home?" She watched him shake his head.

"Should I have?"

"Somebody did. But didn't sign the card."

Jay smoked, scowling. "I don't like these little oddball things happening to you, Nat. Not since the man with the gun—"

"You're too jumpy, Jay. Forget it."

"I've got a couple of reasons for not forgetting it." He wasn't kidding: it was interesting how much more appealing he was when he wasn't being *the* Jay Danmeier. She liked him in his serious, quiet mode.

"What kind of reasons?"

"Well, for one thing, that cop, MacPherson, stopped by the office just after you left. He wanted to see you but said it could wait. He spent some time in the hallways looking at the framed dust jackets. Got me to talking about birds. Looked through my binoculars—

there was something going on in his mind that made me uneasy. I did a little checking on him once he left."

"You checked on a cop? What's gotten into you?"

"I thought I remembered something about him, that's all. My memory's pretty damned good. So I called a mystery writer I know—Victor Stallybrass, you've met him in the office—and asked him. Well, I had remembered something about him all right. You told me he didn't seem very coplike?"

"Yes, something like that." She bit her thumbnail, an instantaneous gesture, concluded almost before it began. What was Jay getting at?

"Turns out he's got good bloodlines. His father was a cop, too. Mark MacPherson. Almost forty years ago he cracked a case here in Manhattan that set people talking for years—you don't recall that Franklin P. Adams–Dorothy Parker–Bob Benchley–Alec Woollcot bunch, of course, but there was another columnist, very big in his day. Guy named Lydecker, Waldo Lydecker. He tried to kill a girl who jilted him, but shot the wrong girl. Mark MacPherson pinned it on him and married the girl who had jilted him. Beautiful girl, Laura Hunt, wound up owning a big ad agency. Our MacPherson is their son." He leaned back, puffing, surrounded by smoke. "I hope he's as smart as his daddy. It's his mother's genes that keep him from being the prototype cop. Anyway, he made me nervous, looks like an English professor. . . . Look, let's get out of here. Get something to eat."

It was beginning to sleet and they found a quiet little Szechuan restaurant nearby. Natalie felt as if she was just being swept along, low on emotion, almost out of gas. She couldn't have argued with Jay if he'd decided to sell her into white slavery. The fight with Tony—the sorrow and ugliness in the memories and in her reaction to him—had taken everything out of her. She wasn't really even Natalie anymore. What, she wondered, had MacPherson wanted to see her about? And who was sending her yellow roses?

Jay ordered fried dumplings and a large bowl of cold sesame noodles. Natalie insisted on drinking tea and picked at the edges of the food. Then there was moo shu pork and garlic shrimp. She couldn't resist. The food was too good, and using chopsticks was like a course in basket weaving to calm the criminally insane. Short of a lobotomy, Szechuan food would get the job done.

She found herself telling him about the unpleasantness with Tony and the burglary of her apartment the night before. She almost told him about the man at Scandals who had approached Julie about her roommate, then thought better of it. Jay was nervous, something eating at him. It would have been a bad idea to aggravate his state of mind.

"You said you had two reasons for not forgetting my mystery gunman," she said instead.

"That's right. People with guns scare the hell out of me. I never told you about my wife, did I? My first wife?"

"No. I didn't know your present wife wasn't your first wife."

"Christ, my present wife!" He shook his large, craggy head. "I hardly ever think of her as my wife anymore. . . . Anyway, Diana was my first wife. Long time ago. I was working in the story department at MGM, thinking I wanted to be a movie producer, and I met the daughter of a really big producer. Diana. I fell madly in love, we got married, and her dad put up the money for a house in Brentwood. Hell of a house, huge lawn, pool, tennis courts, a greenhouse. We had a son, Paulie." He stopped eating, laid down his chopsticks, sipped hot tea. "By then I had decided I wanted to be an agent. I was working for one of the top shops out there, mainly with literary properties. It began to look like I had found my niche, as Wodehouse would say. Then, one night I had a meeting about a new property—Christ, it was Vic Stallybrass, come to think of it—I'll never forget that night." He sighed pensively, his eyes faraway. "I got home and my wife, Diana—y'know, it's funny, like I'm telling a story about somebody else—she was dead on the stairs coming down from our bedroom. Paulie was dead, too, both of them shot. Burglars. Guns. They had panicked and killed two people they didn't have to kill. . . . I don't even remember the next few days, then the weeks are sort of blurry, and finally I was here in New York becoming the man you see before you covered with garlic shrimp." He smiled self-consciously. "You can understand why I don't talk about it much. And you can understand why people with guns spook me. I'm worried about you until this thing gets settled . . . whatever the hell that means, Nat."

"I don't know what to say, Jay. It's so utterly awful."

"Yes, it is. Life sort of gets that way. But it was a long time ago, thirty years. . . . Funny, I started this agency with the insurance money. So, Diana got me started here in New York. She'd have enjoyed this life—at least, if I remember her correctly." He caught her eye and nodded. "Yeah, you do forget. That turns out to be the saddest part of all, the forgetting. You think she'll live in your mind forever, she'll be with you until you die, and little Paulie, too. Well, surprise, Natalie—it's not true."

Ten years later he had married Helena, an English heiress, and she now ran the London office of the Danmeier Agency. The marriage had become a business relationship, which was fine with both of them. They loved each other but not as man and wife, not anymore.

"So, now that I'm baring all my secrets," he said, "I might as well make myself clear on something else. You know how I feel about you. I want you. I'm curious about you, I know what you're like in the office, I've kissed you, and you've kissed me back, Natalie, and now I want to know what you're like in bed, all that sophomoric stuff that makes so much sense however old you are. Any of this surprise you?"

"No." She touched the back of his hand. "You haven't exactly been a shrinking violet. I've thought about the same things you have, I've wondered, but I'm frightened, okay, frightened of being alone for the rest of my life and frightened of making the wrong kind of commitment. I've got one huge mistake behind me and sometimes I think I'll never find the guts to choose again. But what I can do is like you, and hope you can be tolerant of me. We know each other differently now than we did at lunch today. That's exciting to me, whatever else may happen between us later."

"Well, let me tell you, I'm not going to keep pestering you, Nat. I can live without you and be happy. Maybe I'd rather live with you in my life. Maybe I'd be happier—"

"Maybe, maybe not," she said softly, smiling, tapping fingernails on his hand.

He nodded and grinned, accepting the uncertainty.

He hailed a cab on the corner and as she leaned up to peck him good night, he held her tight and kissed her. A real kiss. If the cab hadn't already been standing there, she wasn't altogether sure what might have happened.

Natalie sat before a single leftover log she'd managed to get burning and tried to pay attention to an unpromising manuscript. The Saint-Saëns Organ Symphony was playing on the tape deck the burglars had left behind. She had read for about an hour when her brain gave a last surge of rebellion, fuzzed the lines of type. She couldn't shake free of the tragic story of Jay's wife and son . . . the sudden nastiness of the quarrel with Tony . . . the realization that this was how, at thirty-seven, she had celebrated her birthday—with discord, tragedy, the attentions of a man about whom her feelings were too ambivalent to define, a cop with a weird background and the bearing of an Ivy League professor, the shadow of a gunman across her life, and those damned, ominous, sinister, anonymous yellow roses in the vase before her. . . .

The memory of the scene with Tony bothered her. Why had she been so unsympathetic? What was it at work in her? What was she afraid of? She felt as if she was vulnerable to contamination. Other people's weaknesses might become hers and then, somehow, inviolate, independent Natalie would be irrevocably lost. . . .

What a lot of crap! She determinedly grabbed the telephone and called Lew Goldstein. While she waited out the rings her hand went to the silver diamond, caressed its warmth. There had to be an explanation for her behavior. Tony hadn't done anything so awful. He hadn't done anything awful at all. He had remembered her birthday. Lew's answering machine came on at last and she hung up without waiting to leave a message. Just as well. Pointless to bother Lew. . . .

She was too wide awake to go to bed. As if sensing her confusion and frustration, Sir came bounding down from the bedroom, throwing his tennis ball into the air and chasing it with utter abandon.

"Poor old Sir," she remarked to him, "you're not afraid to go for a walk, are you? Good idea, Sir?" He threw himself ecstatically against the front door, rattling his leash, which hung from the doorknob. Natalie slipped into her old sheepskin jacket, hooked his chain through the loop on his collar, and set off. It was safe: there were still strollers on the street and Sir would protect her. Fierce fellow that he was.

Chapter Eleven

Guilt about her treatment of Tony was still with her when Natalie woke up. It was underlined by the first sight of the birthday present hanging by the mirror. After she'd made her single cup of coffee she sat looking out the window into the slushy, half-icy backyard and dialed Tony's number on Staten Island. He was an early riser, if he'd gone home last night; otherwise he might have stayed with Garfein. The Staten Island house belonged to his aunt who enjoyed having a man around the house; it was perfect—meaning rent-free—for Tony and kept him away from all the hanging out he used to do with his pals.

She let it ring. Tony had been upset when he left the bar last night. She knew his habits: once back to the big old house he might very well have decided to stay up all night, working in the barn on his stained glass. He was pretty good at it, had even shared studio space years before with a guy in Soho. Since their split-up, he'd gone

103

back to it, building elegant stained-glass windows of his own design. He treated it as his therapy, told her it had been his way of closing himself off and hiding from the end of their marriage.

There was no answer and she finally hung up.

Lisa had laid out her pink message slips and Natalie sifted through them before getting her first office cup of coffee. Nothing overwhelming. Dr. Goldstein had already called and would call back. . . . A thought flickered across the edge of her mind: had he sent the flowers? She wasn't sure why the question kept nagging at her: maybe just because it was a loose end. The thought of speaking with Lew again filled her with something like relief. He was so reasonable, always had been.

Jay stopped by her office in mid-morning and stood in the doorway massaging his jaw with his hand, acting like he wasn't quite sure what to say. She smiled brightly, hoping to God their evening together hadn't for some— for her—unimaginable reason plunged him into one of his moods.

"Look, Natalie," he began, then saw her smile and grinned. "I appreciate your willingness to listen to my little trip down memory lane last night. I don't normally go on like that—"

"You were terrific last night," she said, feeling like Mary Richards talking to Lou Grant on a rerun.

"I was?"

"Well, pretty terrific. You were very nice. And you listened to me, too. I'm glad you were there."

"Just remember. I could be there whenever you wanted me. Get it?"

"Got it."

"Good. Say, your friend MacPherson just arrived in reception. You know, he dresses awfully well for a cop." He went away and she buzzed Lisa, told her to send MacPherson on in.

He was wearing a gray herringbone jacket and black slacks, a blue button-down shirt and a rep tie, all very preppie. He gave her that remote, level-eyed look and sat down with the wall of books behind him. Looking around him at the stacks of papers and manuscripts and folders that had long ago begun their steady encroachment onto the floor, he didn't quite seem to approve. She asked him what she could do for him, determined not to be caught in her friendly-puppy persona.

"It's more a question of what I can do for you, Ms. Rader," he observed. "Once again I'm afraid you haven't been confiding in me. That disappoints me. However, others are more concerned about your welfare, apparently, than you are."

"Would you translate all that, please? And why don't you just leap right in and call me Natalie?" She'd forgotten his first name: was it Danny? But she hadn't forgotten Jay's story about his father and Laura Hunt and Waldo Lydecker.

"I called your husband after speaking with you the other day and confirmed that he had told Mr. Garfein about your experience with your laughing gunman. We proceeded to chat, Tony and I, and he seems to understand the possible seriousness of your situation.

He then called me this morning, said he'd seen you last night and that you'd mentioned a burglary at your home. And your fears that someone might be following you. I wonder if you'd like to tell me about any of these recent . . . incidents?" He took out his notebook again and went through the slow ritual of uncapping and poising his fountain pen.

"Yes, it's true, I did mention some things to Tony." She was irritated by his continuing interference in her life: she didn't like him, anyone, talking about her life without her knowledge. Actually, she barely remembered saying any of it to Tony: she must have done so in the interstices between shreds of argument as they had worked their way through the champagne and old battles. She told MacPherson about her paranoid fears of being followed; she recounted the story of the burglary; then figured the hell with it and told him the story of Sir running away on the FDR walkway and the man grinning in the shadows and the appearance of Lew Goldstein.

"And who is he?"

"A very dear, longtime friend. A psychiatrist. He was out for a walk. I was lucky."

"Lucky," MacPherson mused. "How well do you know this Dr. Goldstein?"

"That's a rather puerile question. I said he's an old friend. Nothing lurid, nothing earthy between us, which is what I assume you—"

"Exactly what I meant."

She sighed. "I'm trying not to lose my temper with you," she said, "and right now I'm not succeeding. I resent your prying into my private life. I merely saw something weird happen out my window—I'm not the criminal, I don't need to be investigated—"

"Excuse me," he said calmly, "but I'm not prying. Your husband called me, not I him. In any case, my concern is not only with keeping you out of harm's way but with the men you know." He shrugged. "I don't know what I'm looking for, I'm just looking. For the odd incongruity, a stray anomaly which might tell me something, give me some answers—"

"To what questions?" she interrupted.

"Is someone following Natalie Rader? Is the man with the gun worried about your presence? Might he try to do something about it? Is your burglary related to the rest of this? You see, you find yourself in an entirely unprotected position. He knows who you are, where you are—he can ascertain who your friends and associates are merely by observing you. You, on the other hand, are living in a paranoid's fantasy world. You know nothing about him besides the fact that he saw you. Consequently, we need to read the situation as closely as we possibly can." He looked up from his notebook. "Do you follow me?"

"You're scaring me all over again."

"Your husband is concerned that—"

"My former husband—"

"He has added to your troubles. He feels badly about shooting off his mouth to Garfein. It seems to me that his concern is reasonable and well placed. Wouldn't you agree?"

"Look, I don't want to let this get to me any more

than I absolutely have to." She was holding her voice steady but her hands were balled into fists in her lap. "Anyone in my position might be nervous. But if someone wants me shut up, there's already been plenty of time to do something about it. No one has. What I'd like to know is why you keep pushing at this. It seems to me that it just isn't amounting to much . . ."

She watched him shut his notebook and put his pen away. He stood up and put his hands in his trouser pockets, went to the bookshelves and took down a volume. "Good book," he said, waving it at her. "Did you represent it?" It was a prominent war correspondent's memoirs, *Back to Normandy*.

"Yes, I did. What has that got to do with anything?"

He shrugged. "Nothing. It just caught my eye and I liked the book." He slid it back into the shelf, kept looking along the spines. "Why do I keep pushing at this?" he said softly. "I suppose because we got a report back on the gun. It's worrisome, actually. We'll handle it, of course, but—" He turned back toward her. "It is worrisome."

She felt her breathing mechanism tighten. Her stomach knotted. "What do you mean?" Her voice came out so soft she barely heard it.

"The gun you saw thrown and which we subsequently retrieved from the construction site was used earlier that rainy afternoon to commit a homicide. About three o'clock, as best we can tell, somebody pulled that particular trigger in a cooperative on Central Park West. Couple blocks up past the Dakota. Very nice view over the park. And a woman named Alicia Quirk got most of her face blown off."

Natalie heard herself gasp.

MacPherson went on in his flat, professorial tone. "Ms. Quirk was not a good citizen. She put up money to produce particularly vile porno films, performed in them for kicks. But she was mainly a drug dealer, specializing in coke. Her clientele was made up of actors, musicians, singers, and the idle rich they seem to attract, most of them Upper West Side types. A smattering of Chelsea and Soho, you know the drill, I suppose. Alicia was bored, rich, about your age, even looked rather like you, very pretty actually, kinky as hell and pretty well known . . . but no threat to the mob, no reason for the big boys to snuff her. She was in the scene for fun, for sex, for the rush of controlling people's lives. But apparently there was one chap she couldn't control. Goodbye, Alicia."

Natalie swallowed, trying to moisten her mouth so she could speak. "So what would be the next step?" Her mind was racing, trying to fit herself into the puzzle. She'd never thought about murder in any but abstract terms. Now . . . last night Jay telling her about his wife and son; today Alicia Quirk. Murder was real.

"Well," MacPherson said, standing at the window, looking down at the scene where it had all begun to go crazy for Natalie, "we've done some checking on Ms. Quirk's movements. She spent a lot of time at a club called Lulu's on Forty-sixth, an aftertheater joint, popular place with actors and whatnot. Burgers, spaghetti, beer, not a bad joint. She saw a lot of this singer down there, Susannah Something. Maybe they were lovers, maybe not." He shrugged. "She did a lot of business, dealt out of the ladies' room, for all I know—I imagine it's too much to hope that you've ever been there?"

"The ladies' room at Lulu's?"

"Just plain Lulu's would suffice."

"No, I've never been there."

"Well, in any case, since our man didn't plan on having you see him dispose of the gun, it must be irrelevant—your ever having been there, I mean."

"It's too far out of my way." Natalie was biting her thumbnail. "Why is Lulu's so important?"

"It was Alicia Quirk's métier, that's all. We figure the guy who killed her, the guy you saw, probably knew her there. After all, the joint was her office."

As a consolation prize for MacPherson's upsetting visit, she arranged to meet Lew at four-thirty at the Algonquin, his choice. When she got there he was waiting by the registration desk chatting with the desk clerk. He disengaged himself, gave her shoulders a quick squeeze, and led the way into the lobby cocktail lounge. The late-afternoon mob was still fifteen minutes away and they got one of the tables with a genteel, elderly couch where they sat side by side. He draped his trench coat and hers over a chair, ordered a pair of gin gimlets, and surveyed the room.

"Thanks for humoring me," he said at last. "The Algonquin's old hat for you but I don't often get this far downtown. I like to pretend I'm an author at last, drinking in my natural habitat. Is that Irwin Shaw over there?"

"Afraid not," she said. "Sorry."

"Well, I'll keep an eye peeled anyway. So, how are you feeling today? Any dizzy spells? Upset tummy?"

"No, really, I'm just fine, Lew. No ill effects."

"Well, that's fine." He handed her a gimlet, clicked his glass against hers. "Confusion to our enemies," he said, watching her over the rim as she took a long sip. "So, you're supposed to be telling me all about what's been piling up. Remember?"

She nodded.

"Come on, Nat, you look worn out, pale, not terribly perky . . . and you've got me just a little worried. You're battling with some demons and maybe I can help." He waited for an answer. "It *is* my job, sport." He sat back, waiting again, letting his gaze wander across the lobby.

She took a sip and set the glass down too hard, splashing her hand. "Oh, Lew. I hate to be making a big deal out of this stupid thing. I—"

"Rest easy," he said. "I'm the one who's dragging it out of you."

"Remember how it was at Northwestern? I never was able to keep anything from you . . . and now I just feel that everything is closing in on me, ever since I looked out my window that night. And," she felt a flush of anger, "I resent it. I resent the way it's all affecting me. Everything that happens to me seems so strange—it's all in my mind. I mean, I don't even *know* it was the killer laughing at me on the other side of the door!" She bit her lip and ate some peanuts and caught her breath.

"But it's a pretty good bet, isn't it? And what difference does it make who was laughing? Once Garfein put it all in the papers, the guy knew it was you." He crossed his neatly pressed trouser legs, patted her arm. "You just called him a killer? But you don't really know that, do you?"

"No, no, he's a killer!" Her voice had risen, and a man passing their table paused momentarily, registered what she had said, raised his thick eyebrows, and went on to a wingbacked chair adjacent to their settee. She heard him banging the bell on his table. She thought she'd recognized him, probably an actor in his turtleneck sweater and expensive hairpiece, leather jacket. It occurred to her that she should point him out to Lew, the celebrity watcher.

"You *know* he's a killer?" Lew said.

She nodded, finished her drink, pointed at the empty glass. "I really could use another one," she told him. Lew waved to a waiter. The tables were filling up. "Yes, this cop, MacPherson—he's part of what's bothering me, actually; he's just too snotty for words, such a smartass—this MacPherson dropped in on me today with the good news. The gun was used in a murder earlier that day. He shot some awful woman. . . ." The words were rushing out, spilling. "A porno actress, Lew, a cocaine dealer, he blew her head off, oh shit. . . ." She felt tears welling up, hated herself, let her voice trail off.

Lew touched her arm again, handed her the fresh gimlet.

"What a world," he murmured.

"And then Jay told me this awful story about his wife and son being murdered—"

"Danmeier? What the hell is this?"

"Thirty years ago. Oh, it's just awful, and for some reason it's all just landing on me right now . . . Tony and Jay and that creep the other night in the shadows. . . . Oh, Lewis, I don't want to talk about this anymore, okay?"

The noise level was rising as the lobby filled. The man in the wingbacked chair lit a cigar and the smoke drifted toward her, strong, rich, overpowering. She choked back a cough. He banged his bell again. His weekly *Variety* fell on the floor and he reached down to pick it up. *God, I'm making a scene,* she thought, *and this bastard is lapping it up.*

Lew was saying something but she couldn't hear him, saw his lips moving. "What?" She cupped an ear.

"Dr. Drummond," he said. "Alex Drummond, a colleague of mine. I think you might have a chat with him. I'm not suggesting treatment, Natalie, so don't look like that. But you could lay out some of this stuff and he might help you get a bit of perspective—"

"I don't need a shrink," she said. "I need a few days of vacation."

"Sure, sure, but you are under a lot of stress, aren't you? Well, Alex is a good man—"

"No, thanks."

"Get serious, Nat." He leaned forward. "Look, I

113

know you won't call him. Right? So let me have him give you a call—you can say no, but you'll like him. Very serious, no nonsense, a solid guy. Okay?"

"Give it a couple of days, though. Please, Lew. I'm okay—"

"Of course you're okay, no one's suggesting you're not. I mean, you're a nut case but you've always been one of those."

She gave a liberating laugh. "Okay, it's a deal." She picked up her drink. "To Dr. Drummond!"

"Listen, we shrinks gotta stick together."

When they left she noticed that the actor must have gotten his earful and moved on. Only his *Variety* remained, and Lew hadn't seen a single famous face.

Waiting for a cab she had a thought.

"That's it!" she exclaimed, feeling much better. "It was you, wasn't it?"

"Me what?" He was gesturing wildly at a Checker.

"The flowers. You sent me the flowers on my birthday. Yesterday—"

"Give me a break, Nat. You know I never can keep things like birthdays straight. . . . Here's your cab." He pecked her cheek. "Now be nice to Drummond, okay? Make me look good. And call me if you get to feeling lonesome."

She looked back at him as the cab pulled away. Why couldn't he have sent the flowers? She was running out of candidates.

Chapter Twelve

Naturally she was in the shower, with Sir sitting in the bathroom doorway watching her shape through the shower curtain, when the doorbell began buzzing with a hellish insistence, as if the Prince of Darkness waited without and knew damn well she was in there somewhere. She finally yanked back the curtain, threw her wet robe over her soaking body, cinched the belt, and went to the intercom. "Who is it and this better be good!" she shouted.

"Miss Rader? It's me again. Dante's Flowers, delivery for you."

She recognized the voice, the same little guy with the cigar who'd brought the last bunch of roses.

"All right, all right." She buzzed him in through both locked doors, heard him in the hallway. She looked through the peephole. Sure enough, same guy, same black cigar. A New York character. Somehow he was managing to whistle and smoke his cigar simultaneously. She undid the lock and opened the door.

The deliveryman fell back in amazement. "You was in the shower—I'm sorry. But then," he went on philosophically, "you don't get flowers every day, right? Well, you seem to get 'em damn near every day, doncha? Listen, you're gonna catch your death standing here— where do you want 'em? This thing weighs a ton—must be a coupla dozen. . . ."

She backed up and he came in tentatively, as if he was afraid she might think he was trespassing. He carefully left the door open. "You wanna get a vase or something? What is this, your birthday?"

"No, no, I don't know—"

"Just popular, right?" He followed her down the stairs and around the corner into the kitchen.

"Up there," she said, clutching her robe, water dripping from her hair into her eyes. "Could you reach that vase on top of the cupboard?"

Still holding the long, heavy box, he climbed up on the utility stool to reach the vase. She shook her head and like a dog sprayed water, saw the droplets hit his trouser leg and speckle his black shoes. "I got it," he grunted, backing down the steps.

"Listen," she said, "were you in the shop when these flowers were ordered? I mean, did you see the person who sent them?"

"Beats me. Probably not." He sucked the wet cigar, shook his head. "I'm out on deliveries all day. Delivered flowers to Mrs. Robert Redford the other day. Makes you think . . . There should be a card inside." He was going up the stairs.

She followed him, found two dollars on the table,

and gave them to him. "Thanks for lending a hand and not being a maniac," she said.

He chuckled. "Thank you for not being a maniac. You do something friendly for somebody, nice lady like yourself, and you never know if they're gonna think you're some kind of pervert—jeez, what a world, right?" He was out the door, in the hallway. "Well, enjoy your flowers. I seen your others are still holding up real good." He nodded and she closed the door, locked it.

Sir was watching her expectantly, suddenly tugged on his leash hanging from the doorknob.

"Don't be an idiot," she said. "I'm dining chez Linehan."

She went back down to the kitchen with a vague sense of dread. She opened the box. Twenty-four red roses. There was a plain white envelope, tiny, and a card inside.

You're my kind of girl.

Dammit! No name.

Had she told MacPherson about the flowers?

Judging from what she had gathered from Linehan about his financial condition and from the address, she wore a heavy sweater, turtleneck, and wool slacks. The sheepskin coat. On her way out she noticed the red light on her answering machine, something she'd forgotten to check when she'd arrived home in her usual frantic rush. She played it back.

"Natalie, this is Danny MacPherson. Do give me a call. Please, home or office. Thanks."

She looked at her watch. Too late. She was always

late, running behind schedule. *I'll remember,* she thought. *It'll be an early night. I'll call him when I get home.*

All the way to the Linehans' her mind clicked back and forth, from Alicia Quirk with her head shot off to the goddamn anonymous red roses to Lew and his Dr. Drummond. . . .

The cab dropped her at a dark, sooty brick building on Sixth Street near First Avenue. The street level was given over to a pair of India-Pak restaurants and the lobby was dimly lit, the walls stained with spots of stuff she didn't want to speculate on, and there was no elevator. She wound her way up the stairs to the third floor, smelling the restaurants and generations of families who must have cooked every imaginable cuisine over the past century. Art, she reflected as she knocked on the door, would flourish anywhere, indestructible. Particularly if your name was anything like Rory Linehan. Late of Belfast.

He proved to be rather older than she'd expected. He came to the door wearing an ancient fisherman's sweater that was a good match for the lobby walls. Heavy shoulders, hands the size of bricks, a pipe with a broken stem jammed into the corner of his mouth, a fifty-year-old man with oily gray hair over his ears and a face like a Niagara of broken blue and purple veins, like worms crawling across his face. He called her "dearie" and waved her into "this hovel we call home. Moira's roasting a stray cat in the kitchen, she'll be with us all too soon." His voice was deeper, wetter than it had sounded on the phone.

Natalie summoned up a load of small talk, sat down on a couch, nearly crushing an angry black cat in the process. The animal hissed, flashed her a nasty glance, and stalked off to join several others in the general vicinity of an enormous cat box full nearly to overflowing. The living room was furnished sparsely, reeked of cat, the lingering aroma of Irish whiskey, and thousands of hours spent smoking joints. She'd never smelled anything like it, felt it sticking in her nostrils and throat, like dry fur. She thought, *Remember, art for art's sake* . . .

Moira, younger, with the heavy sensuality of a disappointed whore on her face, appeared wearing jeans and a cardigan sweater, heavy breasts riding low, unbridled, nipples bulging. She brushed her faded red hair back from her tired, freckled face and nodded to Natalie. She was holding a bottle of Bushmills in one hand. Her fingernails were cracked, the bright red paint that matched her lipstick chipped. "Rory, get her a glass. She'll be wanting a dram."

Linehan fetched a glass, came out of the kitchen wiping it with a paper towel. Moira splashed a great deal of whiskey in its general direction and he handed it to Natalie; the outside was slippery with drink.

"To success," he said, and they drank. Moira smiled bitterly, made a laughing sound, and went back into the kitchen. "Light of my life, my Moira, stuck with me through thin and thin. When I met her she was a serving wench in a pub, best tits in Belfast." He kicked a cat out of the way and lowered his thick frame into a rocking chair. A black-and-white television set was humming in the corner, the picture snowy and blurred almost out of focus. A children's Christmas show, maybe "Rudolph the Red-Nosed Reindeer"; she couldn't be sure. Linehan was talking but she couldn't really follow the thread of his observations. His brogue came and went, he left out words, and she eventually realized he was either drunk or stoned or both. They didn't converse: he talked and she listened. And the words kept pouring out, opinions about publishing and New York and cats and Moira and Northern Ireland and the fucking Brits and how hard it was to be a writer in this rotten bloody world and on and on. . . .

She sipped at the whiskey, which was warm and, coupled with the smell in the room, was making her feel slightly nauseated. Her mind wandered away, to Jay's warnings about what he thought of Linehan's book and the kind of man he might be, to the realization that the atmosphere in the apartment was not only supercharged with a kind of malevolent energy but with a rough sexuality she couldn't ignore. It made her think of animals mating. She had no frame of reference for it, no experience like it to draw upon. But the thought stuck in her mind, unavoidable, like the cats and the smell, like the remembered moans of rutting.

"So you like my bloody book, do you?"

"Very much," she said. "I was very excited about the chance to handle it. And very pleased with the response from the publisher. In the present publishing climate, you really have done very well for yourself—they'll be wanting to talk to you about your next book." She was lost, trying to carry on a normal conversation with a man who was clearly coming from another planet. He looked down his broken nose at her, eyes squinting, a caricature of mistrust, canniness. Nature had given him a perpetual leer.

Moira was suddenly standing over her, dribbling more Bushmills into the glass. Then she turned away, splayed a hand on her hip. "Very excited, are you? Very excited about twenty-five hundred dollars? Now, that's a wee bit hard to believe—himself there," she pointed at Linehan with the bottle, "he says you got a million for some kid's book, some dumb kid. . . ." She looked accusingly at Natalie, wiped back the red hair again, her eyes a curiously dull gray. She finally went back to the kitchen, where she could be heard muttering to herself. Natalie felt as if she'd been slapped, felt her cheeks flush at the attack.

Linehan was holding up the copy of *Publishers Weekly* open to her photograph. "No story about what you did for me, is there? And here we are opening our home to you!" He threw the magazine at a cat, emptied his glass. His wrecked eyes bored into her. He scratched his crotch angrily, as if it had dared to offend him. This was crazy and her face was now on fire.

Natalie stood up. "I think I'll be going now," she said, scooping her coat from the chair where it had been flung. She headed for the door.

With astonishing alacrity, Linehan leaped from his rocking chair and interposed himself between her and the door. His empurpled face was working, almost as if he was on the point of tears. "Now, now, you're not going anywhere. We've not had our dinner yet and you wouldna want to spoil our evening, would you?"

"I really don't care—"

She felt his huge hand clamp down on her arm, twisting the flesh. She flinched back as the pain shot along her forearm.

"Well, we care, don't we, Moira? We invited you to dinner and dinner you shall have!" He grinned. "You're just not used to our ways, dearie; we're a rough and ready pair, Moira and me. No pulling of punches allowed. Now just come back and sit down." He pulled her back to the couch. He belched. "'Scuse me. A breach of etiquette—mustna tell wifey. When she married Rory she married above herself, poor girl." His voice had dropped to a moist whisper, was close to her ear. He let go of her wrist and she sank back down onto the couch. "Wouldna want to shatter the last of poor Moira's illusions about old Rory." His voice trailed off. He went to the dining table, which was stuck into the corner opposite the cat box, pulled out a chair, and straddled it backward, leaned his chin on his crossed arms. He was sweating. Smiling at her.

Moira came back to the kitchen doorway, smoking a badly rolled joint as if it were a plain cigarette. Then she nipped it off between thumb and forefinger, threw back her head, and sucked the smoke in. She held it out toward Natalie, who shook her head. Moira laughed harshly. Finally she said, "Dinner is served. Rory, get out here."

Natalie went to the table, closed her eyes, and prayed that it would all be over soon. Dinner had once been a chicken, far too recently by the taste of it. Underdone baked potatoes. Half-cooked brown-and-serve rolls. She ate what she could. Her brain was just cutting out. Moira smoked two joints during the course of the next hour and the relationship between husband and wife seemed to deepen into something very like wickedness.

Rory got going on the smallness of his advance and Natalie made the mistake of trying to explain the realities to him.

"Fuck all that, dearie. That doesna mean shit to me—Moira made me write the book, it's a piece of crap, I wrote it for the money—for the money! Understand? And what do I get? Bloody nothing, just nothing. . . . What's the point? What did I prostitute myself for, piece of crap—goddamn it, Moira says write it, write it, play the game, make some money for a change! Mother o' Mercy, make some money!" He began to cough into his napkin, couldn't speak. Natalie looked away.

Moira went on the attack: "You're such a hot agent—I say you're a whore, you're all whores, agents and publishers and editors and critics, all whores, all fucking each other. You fuck that kid? The million-dollar kid?" She smiled shrewdly, as if she had stumbled on the truth. "You want to fuck Rory here? Go ahead, you can have him if you can get him some real money . . . fuck the literary world! Christ." She threw her fork at a cat, who looked up and went to hide under a wooden chair.

"I'm going," Natalie said abruptly, standing up, her chair falling over backward and clattering on the bare floor.

"Cunt," the woman hissed.

"You're insane!" Natalie was screaming suddenly. She felt like an unlucky Alice, stepping through the looking glass into the nightmares of Hieronymous Bosch.

Linehan lurched to his feet, grabbed at her, but she twisted away. Moira sat watching, dragging on the joint, knees spread loosely like her bright red mouth, the wise-crazy shrewdness putting light in her eyes for the first time. Natalie slipped, reached the couch, and heard Linehan fall heavily behind her, the air knocked out of him with a rushing sound, as if he'd been punctured. He was on his knees in the middle of the room. His chest was heaving beneath the soiled sweater; he had the copy of *PW* in his hand and was shaking it above his head.

Natalie was fumbling with the door, realized the chain was on. Her hands were working frantically, slipping. Moira had begun to laugh again, like a doll who gave a bad imitation of mirth when a string in its back was yanked.

"How about this!" Linehan roared hoarsely. He ripped her picture out of the magazine, shredded it again, then again. . . .

Finally the chain was off and she bolted into the hallway. She went down the stairs as quickly as she could, stumbling, grabbing the railing, finally breathless and out the front door into the street. She stood gasping in the cold air.

She walked toward Second Avenue, not thinking, just putting one foot ahead of the other. She stopped at the corner, feeling like someone in an isolation booth, watching the world go past. Not a part of it—alone. The

life, the energy field she'd just left, the perverse
sexuality of Moira curling her mouth around the word
fuck as if she could bring it to life with her lips
. . . What was going on back there now? She knew, she
knew what was happening, on the floor among the cats
and the rank odors—

Then she began to laugh.

At herself. At the Linehans.

At all of it . . .

Chapter Thirteen

Inevitably Jay showed up at her office once she got settled down to work and had put the Linehans as far out of her mind as possible. He came in, his binoculars hanging around his neck, and went to her window, ever searching for a better angle.

"The thing is," he murmured, "these peregrines seem to love construction sites. It must be the exposed girders, places to sit down and have a look at all of us earthbound creatures." He knelt, tilted his head to see what he could see. "So," he went on, radiating a new scent of cologne she didn't recognize, the binoculars riding the bridge of his nose, "have a nice evening with your favorite author?"

"It was different," she said, smiling to herself. She was delighted with her unexpected ability to shift the ghastly evening into perspective so quickly. And easily, for that matter. She was already seeing it as one of those bizarre turns on which a raconteur like Jay could dine out for months. If enough really trying and peculiar and unsettling things happened to you in a short time, she supposed, you were able to rank them in terms of priority. As far as her own life went, the past ten days were quite without parallel.

"Different," Danmeier repeated in a silky monotone. "Now what could that mean?"

"Less sophisticated than you would enjoy. More my milieu, lots of booze and dope and uncooked food and a dozen cats using the living room for a toilet. Moira was a vision and Linehan—Rory, that is—looked like he couldn't quite remember who'd thrown up on him most recently. Dylan Thomas effect."

"Very funny." He lowered the binoculars. "Be serious, Natalie. He's a client of ours. What was it like, really? All sort of Irish and everyone quoting Yeats and Wilde?"

"Not exactly. Let's see—seriously summing the evening up? Let's just say it was grand through thin and thin. Loved him, hated her—I don't know, Jay." She smiled sweetly across the desk at him. "Once they began defacing my picture in *PW* I left. . . ."

"Sometimes," he sighed, "your sense of humor is lost on me." He got up from where he was kneeling and took two mints from the dish on the corner of her desk.

"How was Clive Morrison?"

He rolled his eyes, frowning. "He brought his mistress with him. God. He spent more time with his hand on her leg than he did talking to me. Randy old bastard." He sucked the mint. "So, despite your feeble attempts at wit, I was lumbered with a truly ghastly evening. Consider yourself fortunate. Ah well, one never knows—I spent most of the evening longing to exchange places with you." He shrugged and went back to his office.

Friday night.

Natalie was used to spending Friday evenings at home, alone, worn out from the week, glad to settle down with a new record or a book to read for pleasure or a trashy movie on television. She would sometimes order in a pizza from the Original Ray's. Or soak the evening away in a hot tub. Or write letters. Or make a careful plan of the weekend, allowing time for all the necessary errands—the laundry, the cleaning, the seamstress who altered this and that, the shoe-repair man, the trip to Gillies for her favorite coffee—as well as visits to the Whitney or MOMA or the Metropolitan for a certain show. She'd check the Weekend section of the Friday *Times* for the hours at which movies she particularly wanted to see were being shown. She might arrange to have Sunday brunch with a female friend from outside the world of publishing. Friday evenings were precious. Friday evenings were for Natalie. For throwing the tennis balls for Sir, maybe for a leisurely walk to reacquaint him with the block on which he lived. Friday evenings she began to unwind and recover from the week. . . .

But tonight was different. Almost unprecedentedly, she wanted company. She wanted someone to talk to and she realized how few were the possibilities. Tony would misinterpret a suggestion that they meet—even if she wanted to see him—and in any case he was probably out on the island. Or busy. And Lew . . . poor Lew, she'd burdened him enough.

She ran through her list of girl friends and couldn't get excited. What was the matter with her? Was she becoming such a recluse?

Julie, of course. But it was Friday night and Julie was bound to be laying waste her various watering holes of choice. Still, there was always the chance for a miracle. She looked around the apartment: none of the stolen items had yet been replaced. So Saturday was already planned for her. Unless she didn't really give a damn, for the moment. Perhaps she needed a day in the museums. . . .

She called Julie. A miracle. Home and no plans for the evening. "Sure, order a pizza and I'll be down in fifteen minutes."

Waiting for her, Natalie wasn't sure what she wanted to talk about. It would come to her.

"And you worry about me when I go out for an evening!" Julie's deep, throaty laughter erupted in the stillness. She licked tomato sauce from the huge pizza slice that flopped around in her hand with a life of its own. "I mean, last night you saw the seamy side!" She laughed again, her great wide mouth grinning, showing more teeth than was possible.

"I've been thinking about it," Natalie said, leaning back, sitting on the floor looking at the brick wall where the television set used to be. "There was a stagy quality about it, like I had walked into a theater and found myself in a play I hated. It was both more and less than real, sort of intensified—do people really act that way?" She took a drink from a can of beer and bit off another chunk of pizza. "They even had names like people in a play—Rory and Moira. Who's named Rory and Moira, anyway?"

"What are you saying? That you think they put on the whole little psychodrama for your benefit? And once you escaped they had a good laugh and brought out the Louis Quinze table and chairs and dumped the cats out the window?" Julie snorted indignantly. "No way. These were real loonies. People don't pull practical jokes like that in what passes for life. No way."

"No, I don't suppose." Natalie leaned forward and poked the logs in an attempt to coax some flames out of them. "But there was something else going on in that room, something between the two of them. There was so much energy—I don't know how to explain it but that's what made me think of the theater, it was like the energy I've seen on a stage." She shook her head, knowing she wasn't making much sense. "Horrible as they were—and they were horrible, I promise you—there was an electric current running between them. It was exciting—it excited me, I was sweating and my heart was pounding. . . ."

Julie looked at her appraisingly. "You were excited, weren't you? I mean, *excited*—"

"That's what I'm telling you. And when I left them I felt lonely . . . and frustrated."

"You're talking about sex, aren't you? You were

sexually excited by the situation and then sexually frustrated afterward—am I getting this right?"

Natalie nodded. "Yes, you're getting it right. It couldn't have been *about* them. But all the talk about fucking and my being a whore and did I fuck the other writer—" She shivered at the memory, disgusted. "But I was aroused *by* them somehow. It was something in the air—look, do I sound like a raving idiot?"

"No, I'm just trying to think." Julie munched another wedge of pizza. "I've felt the same thing. In a way. In a bar or a room full of people I really don't like, a setting I don't like—when I leave, when I'm alone—and glad to be alone—I get, you know, that feeling. It's just there. Sure, in the air. But then, that's me . . . your case is much simpler." She chewed away, smiling.

"You think so?"

"Of course. You *are* lonely. Lonely for a man. It's been a long time, Natalie."

Natalie felt herself flushing. "Haven't you heard of the new celibacy?"

"Of course. I may even confound medical science by deciding to adopt it, but that has nothing to do with simple desire. Celibacy does not remove desire, Nat: it's not surgery. You've been alone with your vibrator too long—" She laughed loudly.

"I don't have a vibrator!"

"That's your problem! Get one!" She couldn't stop laughing.

"You're missing the point. Stop dribbling pizza— the point is, I'm talking about the feeling that I needed warmth, some human companionship. Not a vibrator, for God's sake."

"Well, don't forget Sir." At the sound of his name, Sir came edging toward the box of pizza and Julie gave him a chunk.

"Okay, don't be serious." Natalie had almost lost the point herself and was beginning to giggle.

"Look, it's so simple. You're finally past the divorce trauma, you've had your delayed reaction to the sense of failure you felt after investing so much of your life in Tony, after trying to help him get his book published. Now you're getting ready to reenter the real world and find a man. Simplicity itself—you make such hard work out of everything, Nat—"

"But that's not the way I feel. I don't want another person underfoot, someone I've always got to consider whenever I want to do something."

"Then why bellyache about being alone?"

"Damned if I know." She grinned. "Maybe it was a momentary aberration?"

"Bullshit, darling! But why don't you just sort through the men in your life. There's Tony, of course. I mean, it's never over till it's over—"

"It's over."

"I'm not so sure. There's still something there, something you're trying to sort out. Maybe you still feel responsible for him, how should I know? But he's not a goner, yet. Then there's Jay Danmeier. From what you say, he's quite an imposing guy—"

"He's married, Julie. And he can be a real pain in

the neck, believe me. An ego the size of Rockefeller Center and all the vulnerability that goes with it."

"First, you didn't say you were looking for a husband. And second, he's obviously nuts about you. You can have him any way you want him—as a lover or a husband. Believe me, I know these things. He's a sitting duck, Nat. And—" She took a deep breath and a long drink of beer. "And then there's Lew, your old pal who's probably been crazy about you since college. Poor bastard. On the whole, that's not bad for a start. Three live ones." She leaned back, rubbing Sir's ears and smiling smugly.

"You named three men. These are not relationships, just men. Men I know. And they're all out of the question. An ex-husband, my boss, and an old friend who is strictly that. Not a chance." She felt helpless: there was no getting past Julie's own kind of logic, no making her see the differences.

"Only because you won't let them be relationships. Who knows, maybe you're not ready yet. But you're never going to find out if you keep everybody at arm's length. Lighten up, Nat, have a little fun. You take it all so seriously."

"How else am I supposed to take it? I'm thirty-seven, I'm caught in the great female time warp—I want my career, I love my work, really love it. And a lot of the time I feel pretty sure that I want children and the meter's running, faster and faster. And I can't bear the thought of setting out with a sheet of requirements to find a man who matches up . . . I don't simply want to *breed.* I guess I want to fall in love. And you can't make that happen, Julie, you can't force it. So how else can I take it? It *is* serious, for God's sake."

Sir looked up at her with a piece of pizza crust dangling from the corner of his mouth. He swallowed and it dropped onto the floor where he discovered it and ate it.

"It can be fun," Julie said, yawning. "Surely you remember fun?"

"Vaguely."

They both laughed.

Natalie went to bed early, right after Julie left. She was preoccupied with the content of Julie's observations: there was enough truth in what she'd said to nibble away at Natalie's resolve to live alone, to concentrate on getting her own life under control before further complicating it. Spontaneity was out, as far as Natalie was concerned. At least for now. Impulses had to be curbed and their places taken by plans with some thought behind them. She had to give Julie credit for seeing to the heart of things: the idea of the failure she felt at the end of her marriage, for instance. So often people thought that it was your lost mate you were moping over when in fact it was the loss of the relationship and all the effort you'd put into it—not the specific person. You mourned for the give and take, the familiarity and ease, and deep in your heart you were afraid that you could have saved it had you been a better human being. . . .

She lay in the darkness listening to Saint-Saëns First Symphony, wishing for the moment that she had never heard of the Family Linehan, never experienced the bizarre, unsettling evening.

The telephone rang.

It was MacPherson. Immediately she remembered the message on her machine, began to fall all over herself, apologizing for not getting back to him.

"Hey, Natalie," he said, calming her, "it's okay, really. I know you're busy. And I'm feeling overly protective for a cop. Anyway, I just got to wondering if everything was all right—if there's been any more scary men in the shadows. So, how are things?"

She told him about the evening with the Linehans, making a manic comedy of it.

"Ah, the literary life," he said. She'd never heard him laugh before. "It makes a good story. By the way, have you told anyone about the Alicia Quirk murder? The tie-in with the gun?" His voice had lost its amusement but the supercilious edge was absent, too, which was a relief.

"I told Lew Goldstein . . . and I mentioned it to Julie Conway just an hour or so ago—why? Wasn't I supposed to?"

"Oh, I don't know." He paused. "I guess I just don't think it should become common knowledge, people talking about it in social situations . . . you don't want the connection between you and the gunman and the murder suddenly turning up one morning in Garfein's column. You want the guy with the gun to just forget about it. The best thing would be for him to figure the gun just disappeared under several tons of cement. Then he'd believe he's safe." He sounded thoughtful and marginally worried.

"I'm sure you're right," she said. "But I've told only the two of them. And I'm all they have in common, so they won't be going on about me to mutual friends. No, I think we're all right."

A few moments later he said, "I had another reason for calling you, ah, Natalie. An apology. I'm not sure how to go about this—"

"Indecision suits you," she said, smiling to herself.

"How did you know?"

"Sticks out a mile. Almost human. Even friendly. Certainly not as detestable as I'd thought—"

"Clever you! Well, the point is, I'm sorry for giving you such a hard time. I've been under some pressure here in the world of evildoers, but that's no excuse. For some reason, you make me nervous and I come on nasty. Tough-cop routine. You're dangerous . . . or something."

"I'm dangerous and I make you act silly—how's that?"

His laughter erupted over the telephone. "Nice. A little simplistic but nice, very nice. Cuts right to the core. I'm trying to keep my silliness under control—and how dangerous you are only time will tell. Well, I'm glad I caught you at home."

"Have you got a band playing in your apartment?"

"Usually. But not right now. That's Stan Kenton's Christmas album. It's the only Christmas music I ever really get into. My folks didn't ignore Christmas but they didn't make a big deal out of it. Where do you stand on the Christmas issue?"

"Christmas, my God—I haven't even thought about it yet. I guess it's—what? Two weeks away—wow. I may skip it this year and just settle into a nice comfortable depression. I always think of that song about the snow is snowing, the wind is blowing, but we will weather the storm . . . and Mel Torme, the chestnuts roasting on an open fire. And I always get sad."

"Remember that part of *All About Eve*, where they drive up to that house in the country and there's the big snowstorm and Bette Davis can't get back to do the play and Eve has to go on in her place—"

"Doesn't Hugh Beaumont or somebody sabotage the car?"

"Hugh Marlowe. Look, have you got your tree yet?"

"I guess I wasn't going to get one."

"Well, I'm going to get one tomorrow. The Deaconess Hospital always has good ones in their lot. Your neighborhood—look, you want to go with me?"

"Sure, why not?"

"Precisely. Let's get an early start. I'll come by at ten tomorrow morning. Okay?"

"Absolutely." She had almost hung up when she pulled back the mouthpiece: "MacPherson? You still there?"

"Yes, what is it?"

"Have you sent me any flowers in the past few days? Roses?"

"No." He waited. "Good idea, though. I wish I had."

"See you in the morning," she said.

She went to sleep, happily for a change, wondering, *What next?* Of all the men she and Julie had considered, the cop had never crossed her mind. But then, why would it have? Until a few minutes ago, he'd been a cop . . . not a *person*.

She woke to the sound of shovels on the sidewalk outside her bedroom window. It took several minutes of listening before the implications of the sound struck her and she leaped out of bed, ran naked to the window, and peered through the curtains. The street was thickly coated with snow, several inches of it piled up on cars and sidewalks and trash cans. Cars moved slowly past, the sound muffled. She felt a little-girl's excitement at the change, the newness of the world outside, as if it were a fresh chance somehow, a clean slate she hadn't yet smudged with her mistakes.

She was up and into her jeans and heavy sweater when MacPherson arrived at ten on the button. His face was red from the cold and his hair was dusted with snow. She fixed him a cup of coffee and they stood in the living room looking out at her courtyard with the evergreens drooping under the heavy snow and the lawn furniture on the way to disappearing. The snow fell thickly, tufts clinging to one another as they floated through a windless sky.

She couldn't get the image, the metaphor, out of her mind: it was as if the snow was falling, covering up all the bad things she'd experienced lately. A fresh chance . . . It was hopelessly silly even to think in such terms but she couldn't help it; she let herself feel rescued, freed from worry.

MacPherson was making the switch from cop to whatever he had in mind—and she wasn't altogether sure—with considerable ease. He mooched around the apartment, sipping the hot coffee, inquiring about the collection of tigers, looking through the tapes and recordings, admiring the art and the spaces the burglars had left behind.

She found herself listening more than talking, watching him in a way she hadn't before, wondering what his life was like. He made little jokes, smiled quickly, showed a sense of irony and enjoyment at the snow and the season. She let herself be swept along by him, didn't bother to *try*. She just allowed the morning to happen: the choosing of a tree and then learning that he had decided it was to be her tree rather than his because he was determined to have her celebrate Christmas. She smiled, nodded, knowing he was inserting himself into the holidays—her holidays. Which, she knew, wouldn't have existed without him. It's all right, she told herself. Let it happen. It was fun. Slowing down, not forcing everything through on her own, letting someone else take over for a while. She had been fighting it for so long, had looked upon it as some kind of defeat . . . yet there was no defeat in this, no defeat in standing outside the hardware store holding on to the tree, which was full and round and cheery and only three feet high, while he went in and bought her a stand to put it in, a box of lights and tinsel to decorate it. She was smiling broadly, then laughing as he came out laden with packages, which he gave to her, and began his struggle to embrace and carry the sweet-smelling little tree.

Back at her place they moved a table and put the tree on it with the windows behind, framing the tree with the snow falling in the courtyard. She watched him set it into the stand, then helped him string the lights and arrange the tinsel almost a strand at a time. While she finished the job he went to the kitchen and she heard him banging around in the cupboards. By the time she was done he had butter melting in the omelet pan and a bowl of eggs and milk and a mound of freshly slivered cheddar. He was smiling and humming happily to himself. She watched him make the omelet and she ground some fresh coffee and carried the mugs into the living room. They sat on the floor before the fireplace, where a couple of last night's logs got a big fresh one going quickly.

"Delicious," she said.

"I've made enough of them. Just call me Cholesterol Man." He looked up at the tree, twinkling brightly on the table. "Looks good. You really know how to decorate a tree."

"Very funny. The first tree I've had in three years."

"Dammit, we forgot to get mistletoe—"

"Ah, the last resort of the terminally shy," she said.

"Listen, it's a fact of life. No one has ever been rejected while standing around underneath the mistletoe." He smiled gently at her, almost wistfully, and she realized she was feeling a kind of spontaneous warmth she hadn't known in a very long time. She couldn't remember the last time she'd acted on impulse.

She leaned across their empty plates and kissed him softly. She felt his lips smiling.

"Mistletoe, while useful," she whispered, "is hardly necessary."

"Apparently not. You're showing wonderful initiative."

"You're the one who's made the effort," she said, leaning back against the table leg, watching the fire. "It's very sweet of you—the tree, all the doodads, the omelet. Very thoughtful. But you've far exceeded the simple apology for being such a shit . . . or is this part of NYPD public relations?"

"Oh, it's the famous MacPherson Touch all right, but . . ." He seemed at a loss for words, unable to find the right lightness, the little joke.

"I understand it runs in the family."

"What does that mean?"

"Your father must have had quite a touch, too."

"Ah. You mean Laura. Mom, I should say. Quite a pair, those two." He said it fondly.

She sat quietly, relaxed, curious. "I can't remember the last time I spent such an enjoyable Saturday. It's been . . . well, fun, MacPherson."

He looked at his watch and asked her if he had time to light up a pipe before leaving.

"Of course. It's my free weekend, nothing hanging over me."

"Wish I could say the same." He pulled a tartan plaid tobacco pouch from his hip pocket and filled the pipe. He lit it and she smelled the clean smell of tobacco, not some awful perfumed gunk. "I've got to head out to Glen Cove to see my parents tonight, spend the day, come back tomorrow night. I don't mean to say I'll mind being there—Dad and I play chess and he beats the hell out of me at darts and the three of us go for long walks and there'll be some people over for dinner in the late afternoon. My mother is a fanatical Giants fan so there'll be a football game or two on television all afternoon—very homey, nice, easy . . . but this weekend I wish I were staying in town." He puffed, looking at her openly: the curve of her thighs in the tight denim, the boyish figure beneath the sweater, her eyes. She felt his gaze like a soft, insistent touch.

"Why? Sounds like an idyllic visit—"

"It is, but just badly timed. Seeing you today, like this, makes me wish we could just haul out and go to a movie late in the afternoon and have a bite to eat and . . ." He shrugged. "Well, listen, I'd better be going." He stood up, stretched. "With all this snow I must be Long Island bound. Natalie, thanks for the use of the hall. I had a marvelous time and I'm sure I'll be replaying it all the way to Glen Cove." He knocked his pipe out against the bricks in the fireplace.

She followed him up the stairs. "I love my tree," she said, looking back.

At the top of the stairs he turned and took her by the shoulders. "I hope I see it again. It's partly mine."

"Indeed it is. You're welcome anytime."

He leaned forward, kissed her very lightly, and said, "Be careful. Don't go out alone. I don't want anything to happen to you, understand?"

"Yes," she said. "I understand."

Chapter Fourteen

Natalie spent the next hour busying herself around the apartment, straightening and fussing and trying not to think about Danny MacPherson. After all, there was no sane reason to assume that merely because he regretted having treated her badly and had tried to make amends . . . no sane reason to make any more out of it. Absolutely no sane reason. But . . . but that kiss . . .

She put *Tosca* on the stereo and vacuumed the stray shreds of tinsel from the carpet, played with the logs in the fireplace, and watched the afternoon darken and finally close down over the snowy courtyard. No sane reason—but she could feel his lips on hers, his hands on her shoulders, she could still hear his laugh as he struggled down the street with the Christmas tree, still saw him at home in her kitchen with the omelet pan. . . .

God! She was acting like a child with a sudden crush! What could be cornier? The nasty cop turns into a pussycat and falls for the lady in distress. Absurd. Still, he was awfully well dressed! She laughed aloud and Sir's ears pricked up. One thing struck her as particularly odd: what had she thought she was doing, *kissing him?* But then, nothing normal had happened in days. Nothing . . .

She was throwing Sir's soggy orange tennis ball when the telephone jarred her out of her reverie.

It was MacPherson.

"Natalie," he said, his voice a shade flatter than when he'd left, as if he wasn't quite so sure of himself or was having trouble about their day together. "I have a suggestion, that is if you're not entirely tied up this evening. Are you free, by any chance?"

"Let me hear your suggestion and I'll tell you."

"Very wise, I'm sure. My idea is a simple one—let me buy you a hamburger and a couple of beers." He sounded nervous, asking for a date. The kiss, the touching, had changed everything.

"You lost me somewhere—what do you mean?"

"You know, little patties of ground meat, fried and then put inside a bun, fries on the side, beer's a grain beverage and you're over the drinking limit—"

"Sorry. But I'd never be seen in public with a man so insufferably coy. Anyway, what happened to Mom and Dad in Glen Cove?"

"If I didn't know you better, Natalie," he chuckled softly, "I'd take this as a rejection. Glen Cove will have to wait until tomorrow, snow or no snow. However, I shall proceed—sorry to say but these hamburgers I speak of are entirely in the line of duty. A policeman's lot. I'd like you to meet me at Lulu's, the late Ms. Quirk's home away from home, and under the guise of eating hamburgers we can take a look at the crowd. I grant you it's a long shot, but—well, you never know. If you would happen to see a man who reminded you in any way of your gun thrower—well, we'd at least have a starting point. Right now we've got zip so far as tracing that gun goes." He paused and she heard him saying something to someone else. She wondered if he had gone to the precinct house upon kissing her goodbye. Now he was trying to be a cop. "Well, what do you say, Natalie? There's nothing to be afraid of—"

"Who said I was afraid?"

"A normal mortal might have a passing concern for her personal safety when getting involved in a murder investigation."

"I'm already involved," she said. "Will you have a gun?"

He laughed unexpectedly. "Armed to the teeth," he said.

"All right," she said. "It's my duty as a citizen, right?"

"What an attitude! Way to go." He was mocking her but she didn't really mind. She was glad for his ironic, slightly sour sense of humor. "Eight-thirty." He gave her the address on Forty-sixth. On business, he seemed further away from her, which was probably for the best, but she felt a moment's sinking disappointment.

She called Julie on the off chance and found her in.

"You want to come with me and play detective tonight?"

147

"Nancy Drew is well behind me, dear," Julie said.

"I'm serious. I got a call from MacPherson, he wants me to meet him at Lulu's and look for the man with the gun. Lulu's was Alicia Quirk's place of business, she dealt coke and used it as her headquarters. MacPherson seems to think the chances are pretty good one of her clients killed her—maybe I'll see somebody. Don't say it, I know, I never saw the guy's face. But there might be something that'll ring a bell. . . ." Her voice trailed off: it all sounded so hopeless and lame. "Come on, be a pal."

"What's this MacPherson like?"

"Kind of a smartass. Nice-looking, I guess. Not my idea of a cop, but then what do I know? You'll make mincemeat out of him." She paused, unhappy with what she'd said. "He can be sweet, too. He bought me a Christmas tree today. . . ." She didn't want to give away her feelings—whatever her feelings were. But it would be interesting to get Julie's reaction to him.

Julie jumped on the little she'd said. "He what? A Christmas tree? That's not in the cop's manual, my dear girl."

"I know. I know. I'm not sure what's going on. Come down about eight."

"We'll sort it out. As for Lulu's," Julie said disparagingly, "it sounds like a dive."

"Sure does."

In the cab Julie exclaimed, "Oh, Nat, I forgot to tell you—oh, God, I don't know if I should. . . ." She gave Natalie a worried, quizzical look, her wide mouth angled sharply in a frown. Her gold earrings twinkled in the passing lights of traffic.

"You mentioned it—don't be a jerk!"

"Well, maybe I was wrong—no, I wasn't wrong—"

"What is it, Jules? Don't make me crazy, please."

"Today, I was out getting my cleaning and some flowers at the shop up on the corner. I came out and started home and there was this guy walking ahead of me, trench coat, collar turned up, snow in his hair, and I thought I knew him, there was something familiar about him. When he got near our house he went across the street, just stood there watching the house, like a man waiting for something. Or someone . . . I couldn't take my eyes off him, and the gross part was—I recognized him, I *knew* him. . . ." She turned and looked out the window.

"*Jules!*"

"Well, I don't know his name—okay, it was that guy I had the problem with the other night. You know, Nat, the one who was so interested in my 'roommate'—you." She turned back, shaking her head. "Why—tell me why—I don't just keep my mouth shut?"

"Because seeing that guy made you worry about me—because you're my friend, you idiot. What did he do?"

"It was spooky, he just watched until I went into the building. Then I looked back—and he was gone! Spooky!"

Natalie shrank back inside her coat. What was she supposed to do? All she needed now was some jerk cruising bars and bothering her. If she thought about it at all, she wouldn't be of any use to MacPherson. She was beginning to feel like Scarlet O'Hara, putting everything off till tomorrow. Resolutely she straightened her spine.

"Now," Julie said, rushing on, "what's going on with your cop? Who does he think he is, buying you a Christmas tree?"

Natalie had never seen Broadway in the immediate aftermath of a snowstorm, with a few flakes still blowing over the city and the incredible brightness of the lights on the marquees reflecting in the glassy whiteness. The glare and blur were almost blinding when they got out of the cab at the corner. The pulsing crowds had diminished, entered the theaters, and she and Julie picked their way through the deep ruts and paths toward Lulu's. The Great White Way was living up to its name, the sordid reality hidden for the moment. It was all an illusion but spectacularly welcome. Julie grinned at her, soaking up the excitement the storm had somehow conveyed to a scene they both knew so well. A Santa Claus stood ringing a bell on the corner. A group of Salvation Army singers caroled to the tinkly blare of a couple of trumpets. It all struck Natalie as a scene from a Frank Capra movie, and for the moment it displaced the ever-growing mountain of worries and fears that seemed to be building up over her, threatening to break loose in an avalanche at the next loud noise. Like the pounding of her heart. But just now she was all right, she wasn't alone, she'd had a nice day. She even had a Christmas tree with lights and tinsel. . . .

Lulu's sported a small neon sign in the window, a

dark doorway down a couple of steps from the street, just across Eighth Avenue. MacPherson was standing in front, stamping his feet, blowing into already gloved hands, deep in the recesses of a British warm.

Natalie said, "Okay, where's your gun?"

MacPherson gave her a pained look and introduced himself to Julie. He took their arms and ushered them inside. Lulu's was low-ceilinged, dark with blue and red lights creating a kind of intimate gloom. A long bar ran along the wall to the right, old and scarred wooden tables filling the remainder of the main room and overflowing into a smaller anteroom. The bar was crowded, but a couple of tables were still empty and the waitress seated them and took a drink order. The walls were covered with framed photographs of various Broadway stars both current and long gone. Several huge framed posters were lit from above, the joke being that they were all great box-office disasters. *Kelly, Frankenstein, Little Johnnie Jones*, on and on, a rogues' gallery of squandered fortunes.

Natalie was warming herself with a spicy Bloody Mary when MacPherson set down his mug of beer, lit a cigarette, and squinted at her through the smoke. "Any new ideas, Natalie, since this afternoon? That I don't already know about?"

Julie spoke up: "I've got one you should know about—"

Natalie flinched. "Jules, *please*—"

"Let the lady speak," MacPherson said. "That's the only way I ever hear anything about this case—from your friends. You were saying, Miss Conway?"

Julie told him about the man in the bar who had turned up watching the house today. "Think about it," she said. "Maybe he's been sending the flowers—I mean, it's the sort of weird thing that kind of guy might do."

"The flowers are beginning to bother me a bit," MacPherson said. "You've checked everybody you know—this Danmeier character with his binoculars, your old analyst chum, your ex-husband. And you can't think of anyone else? Any rejected suitors?"

"I haven't dated anyone in a long time."

He smiled at his beer, as if the fact satisfied him. "You know," he mused, "I wonder about that watcher today. What time did you see him?"

"Between noon and one, I suppose."

He nodded. "Natalie and I were decorating the Christmas tree. He may have been watching off and on for a while . . . he may have known we were in there together. Think about the past, a man you knew well—"

"I hate to disappoint you, but there certainly isn't anyone from the past. And anyway the man with the gun was sheer coincidence, no ghost from my past could have planned it—making me go to the window at just that moment—"

"No, of course not. But we could be dealing with two unrelated but intersecting arcs of your life, wasting our time trying to make them connect when there's just no connection. I've gotten into traps like that before and getting out can take forever. Well, hamburgers, ladies? Fries? Another round?"

"Cheese on mine, please," Julie said. "You know,

I've seen most of these shows—the big losers." She grinned, winked at MacPherson. Natalie tried not to smile, said a prayer for the cop.

"Who made sure you saw all these flops?"

"Big losers." Julie giggled.

"All we need is one more big loser. Who sends roses." He turned back to Natalie. "What is it about you, anyway? All these nice men buzzing around the edges of your life. All they do is confuse the issue. It's funny. None of them threw the gun. None of them sent the roses. None of them stood outside that door laughing. None of them burgled your apartment. . . . So, I ask you—" He took a long, slow drink of beer, wiped his mouth on a napkin. "Why do I keep coming back to them? I wish I knew."

"Well," Julie said, "they do keep turning up, don't they?"

"They're not involved in my gunman thing. That's obvious."

MacPherson nodded. "But Goldstein is following you the night your dog runs away. Your ex-husband inserts himself into the case by talking to Garfein and then making nice-nice with me. Danmeier just happens to wander into the Bemelmans Bar, he just happens to be watching you out the window with his binocs. It sort of hangs together but I can't see what it means."

The hamburgers arrived and they ate slowly, looking at the gathering crowd. Natalie tried to light on a face, a shape, a coat, anything she might recognize, anything that might remind her of the gunman. It was a losing battle.

At one end of the long room, perhaps twenty feet from where they sat, there was a small stage with a microphone stuck in a stand, a piano, a couple of stools. After they had been talking and eating and scanning the crowd for an hour and a half, the lights dimmed slightly and two guys came out and began fiddling around with the piano and a saxophone. The lights dimmed some more and a tall girl with long blond hair and a lean, lanky figure, wearing a blue dress and a cameo choker, came out and began singing over a smattering of applause. Her voice was strong but soft, as if there were an endless supply of decibels she had no need of. She didn't confuse the issue with lots of pointless patter, just sang with the piano and the sax behind her.

She sang "Blue Moon" and "Back Home Again in Indiana" and "But Baby It's Cold Outside" and "These Foolish Things" and "Have Yourself a Merry Little Christmas."

"Through the years," she sang, "we all will be together, If the fates allow . . ."

Natalie watched Julie humming along to herself. Julie's eyes glistened, as if filling at the lyric.

MacPherson leaned across and whispered in Natalie's ear, "Goddamn Christmas songs always make me want to cry. Promise not to tell anybody." She nodded. "This girl, Susannah Durrell, she was Quirk's . . . whatever, girl friend? Pal? I've talked to her about the murder, she's tried to help, but Alicia kept her dealing well apart from her girl friend." He shrugged. "Anybody look familiar to you?"

She shook her head. "It's hopeless. I just didn't see his face."

Susannah was singing "Fools Rush In."

> *"Romance is a game for fools*
> *I used to say . . .*
> *Then you passed by and here am I*
> *Throwing caution to the winds . . ."*

The onlookers were pretty well mesmerized by the singer. Natalie glanced again at the faces but she knew it was no good. She smiled to herself. Romance doubtless was a game for fools. . . . From the corner of her eye she saw MacPherson turn slightly to watch her. She shivered, pleasantly, looked at him. What had really been going on with the Christmas tree, the kiss?

> *"Fools rush in where angels fear to tread*
> *And so I come to you, my love,*
> *my heart above my head,*
> *Though I see the danger there*
> *If there's a chance for me*
> *Then I don't care . . ."*

Natalie felt him squeezing her hand. "Are you okay, Nat?"

She nodded.

It was eleven-thirty when MacPherson acknowledged that it wasn't going to work. He told Natalie not to worry and not to feel badly: it had been a crazy long shot. He thanked Julie for coming along, it was his pleasure, then put them in a cab, said he was going back to Lulu's. He had a few more questions for Susannah.

In the cab the two women rode in silence. Natalie couldn't get the song out of her mind.

> *"Though I see the danger there*
> *If there's a chance for me*
> *Then I don't care . . ."*

Julie said, "Okay. He's okay, Natalie." Then she winked and Natalie felt a momentary warmth, contentment.

Chapter Fifteen

Sir was bounding around on the other side of the door when Natalie said good night to Julie and went into her own apartment. She was baby-talking him, feeling him wriggle at her ankles in what was, even for him, an excessive joviality and excitement. She hugged him in the darkness, glad to be home, weary from the long day but still wide awake, ready to watch a movie on the tube or read . . . and the lights wouldn't go on.

She heaved a mighty sigh. "Shit, shit, shit! Sir, did you blow out the lights?" Somewhere in the wiring system there was a glitch no one had been able to find. Three or four times a year it blew the fuses and she had to fumble around in the darkness, inevitably spilled the fuses, wouldn't be able to find the flashlight . . . why tonight?

She felt her way down the stairway to the living room, across the width of the room, and down three more steps into the brick-walled kitchen, muttering the entire way.

"What's going on, Sir? It's all dark, isn't it? Now where's the flashlight?" She rooted around in a utility drawer and came up empty. Where was the damn thing? "Remember the Audrey Hepburn movie, Sir? The bad guy opened the refrigerator to use the light inside. . . ." She stepped on one of Sir's tennis balls on her way to the refrigerator and swung the door open. As she turned to go back to the utility drawer, she saw something wrong in the living room. A trick of the light maybe. Or had Sir knocked something over? She went to the steps, looked into the shadows, her eyes accustomed now to the dim light from beyond the huge windows.

And then she heard herself scream.

The cry choked her and once it was gone she found she couldn't repeat it, all the vocal mechanism had frozen, and she stood helplessly for endless seconds staring into the living room.

Across the room, in a silvery shaft of moonlight reflecting off the snowbanks in the courtyard, she saw a man's leg crossed over a knee, the shoe slowly tapping in the air.

All the muscles in her throat constricted but she couldn't make a sound, stood shaking, feeling her legs weaken. The foot just kept slowly keeping time. A trench coat was folded across a chair.

She stumbled backward, feeling along the counter-top for the row of Heinkel knives in the rack, her arms weak, fingers trembling, her brain shorting out in fear and shock.

Sir was scrambling around her feet and finally she was able to speak. "Sir, get him, Sir . . . oh no . . ."

Afraid to take her eyes away from the foot in what looked like a polished boot, she found the knives at last and grabbed the biggest handle, yanked it from the rack, and stood in the doorway. She heard herself moaning, not words, just the sound of someone in pain, wounded too often.

His voice was surprisingly hesitant, as if he was as unsure of himself as she was frightened.

"Please, Mrs. Rader," he said from the shadows, "don't come at me with that knife. That would just be stupid, and besides, you might stab me, and then think how we'd both feel. Really, think before you try to kill me. Okay?" She heard him swallow hard, heard him moisten dry lips.

"What do you want?" She could barely raise her voice above a whisper.

"Look, before we get to that, you'd better close that refrigerator door, it's a terrible waste of energy. You can't be too careful about stuff like that these days."

"You're crazy," she whispered.

"No, it's just that I want to talk, and having that door open pouring energy into the kitchen is a dumb idea. Believe me, Mrs. Rader, I'm not going to hurt you—I'm in more danger here than you are." He laughed softly and she felt a chill.

Still holding the knife, she went back across the kitchen and closed the refrigerator door. She was getting back her breath and had stopped shaking. Back in the living room, she stood watching him in the moonglow from the snow. He hadn't moved, his face was still in darkness.

159

"Look, Mrs. Rader, you can relax. I have to talk to you. Come on," he wheedled, making fun of her, his manner gaining in confidence, "just relax and grab a chair. I'm really sorry about being here like this but . . . well, I've been watching you and when you went out I thought I'd just come in and wait for you. See, I've got this story to tell you. Come on in, sit down."

She had stepped through the looking glass and she knew it, saw it happening, saw herself leaving the world of normal reason and sanity and entering this . . . other place. It was like looking up into the grinning face of the man in the shadows. She felt almost reassured, almost at home with the bizarre voice coming from the corner. He hadn't moved since she'd first seen him: he just spoke quietly, pleaded with her, tried to convince her that she should hear him out. She should have been holding the knife on him while she called the police . . . or she could just as easily have run up the stairs into the hallway calling for Julie. But she didn't. Instead, still holding the knife, she went farther into the darkened living room with the snow glistening beyond and the pink glow of the city in the night sky—she went in and sat down on the couch across from her visitor. He seemed supernaturally calm, as if he had once known her a long time ago.

"All right," she said, "I'm sitting down. I've still got the knife—"

"You've got a hell of a fierce dog, too. He kept bringing me tennis balls, one after the other, until I got the idea and threw them. Great dog, Mrs. Rader. Really." His innocent-sounding voice, the ordinariness of his remarks set the fear working in her again: she'd heard that same kind of innocent control, the determination to be pleasant and undisturbed whatever the circumstances. She'd heard it from certifiable crazies, the loons you ran into while living your life. . . . She felt Sir come in and curl up at her feet.

"What have you got to say?"

"First, let me apologize for the melodrama here tonight. I'm going to try and explain myself if you'll give me the chance. There's nothing wrong with your fuses, either. I ran all over the place pulling the plugs—I had to have darkness, I can't let you see me. Try to understand—if I could let you see me, well then, I could just have called you and met you somewhere." He crossed his legs in the other direction and she tightened her grip on the knife, flinching, half-expecting a lunge, an attack.

"Look," he went on, "I'm just your typical New Yorker, no matter how hard that is for you to believe right now. My main interest in all this . . . mess, I guess . . . is that I don't want to get any more deeply involved than I am. I'm just a regular guy—you know how it is, I'm like everybody else, lonely as hell most of the time, alienated from the impersonal city, sexually frustrated but I hate the singles' scene—" He laughed again, softly, as if she weren't there. "I've got a good job, I make pretty good money, the recession doesn't really bother me much. You hear what I'm saying? I'm just an ordinary person, somebody you might even like if we met somewhere in the normal course of life. . . .

"And now, suddenly, I'm getting a lock-picking kit from a guy I met at a Giants game one time, I'm breaking into your home here, I'm running around like an idiot throwing tennis balls for your dog and unplugging lamps, scaring myself half to death . . . and then I naturally scare hell out of you, which was not the point of this whole stupid exercise. But I had to talk to you and I couldn't let you see me—that's damn hard to do—"

"No it's not. You could simply have called me."

There was a long pause. "Jesus, I swear to God I never even thought of that." He paused again, considering what might have been. "Still, it's better to talk like this. I've got a fairly weird story to tell you, I think convincing is easier in person—"

"Look," Natalie said, feeling as if the control of the situation was passing to her, "why don't you just leave me alone? I couldn't care less why you threw the gun away, why you had the gun, what you did with it . . . and I obviously can't identify you—so just stop following me. Forget about me—"

"Well, all of that is sort of why I'm here. I mean, it is why I'm here." He cleared his throat like a reluctant after-dinner speaker. "I don't think you have any idea how hard this is for me to do. Breaking and entering aside, just venturing out to meet somebody—well, sort of socially—it's a big step for me—"

"I wouldn't say," Natalie observed, almost smiling, "that this is a social engagement."

"Not for you." He laughed softly. "But like I said, I'm a really lonely guy, quiet guy, I have to talk a lot in my job and be a gladhander type and pick up a lot of tabs—but on my own I'm a loner. And I like it, pretty much. I go to concerts and museums and once in a great while I have a date. But basically I don't seek contact with people. I get plenty of that in my job. Look, I don't mean to bore you with all this. I just wanted to put you in the picture, because you don't have any way of knowing what's going on and I'm sure you've been worried—"

"Listen, you got rid of the gun—you're in the clear!"

"There you go, that's the whole point. It wasn't me, I wasn't the guy with the gun. Oh, God, no, I didn't have a gun—"

"Then who are you? Why are you here?"

"It's about my . . . well, he's my roommate, actually. No, really, I can imagine what you're thinking and I don't blame you, but I'm not kidding. It was my roommate, he did the number with the gun—what you saw that day." He sighed. "I'm a nervous wreck, do you mind if I smoke?"

"No, go ahead. There's an ashtray right there." She watched the match flare, only caught the planes and shadows of his face, saw the glitter of his glasses. "Would it be all right with you if I turned on the Christmas-tree lights?"

"Oh, sure, I guess so." She knelt on the floor and felt around for the plug and the extension, fitted them together, and the soft glow of red and blue and green lights flickered on. "I still can't see you, if your anonymity is so important."

He laughed softly, ruefully. "Oh, it is, it is."

"Back to your roommate," she prompted. She was getting to the heart of something, felt a weird elation. He might be telling the truth. He certainly sounded confused and honest enough to have gotten himself into such a ridiculous situation.

"Ah, my roommate—he's not such a bad guy, actually, though I don't really know him terribly well. About six months ago, we met at a party on some guy's boat, I had to go for business reasons. Anyway, that's irrelevant. We've got a loft down in Chelsea, he's pretty good with tools and did a lot of the work on it himself—his jobs are pretty irregular—"

"What does he do?"

"Oh, I can't tell you. I've got to play this pretty close to the vest. Anyway, we're a couple of not-very-swinging bachelors, like those jerks on 'Saturday Night Live' years ago. Which is how I usually spend Saturday nights, watching the damn television. I don't know, maybe you can't relate to all this loneliness stuff, the life I guess you lead—"

"Are you kidding?" She laughed, somehow enjoying this strange Woody Allen kind of conversation. "I'm just as lonely as you are. You get used to it, don't you?"

"Anyway, my roommate got mixed up with some very odd people. He got into all sorts of weird shit that scared me half to death. I mean, you know . . . cocaine, sexual stuff, home movies, the works . . . and he found out some things about some drug dealers and hoods that he wasn't supposed to find out—I don't know what, he talked about snuff movies and getting little girls for big shots to use, the worst stuff you can imagine. So, anyway, these people started threatening him . . . they weren't the kind of people who spend much time kidding around, y'know?" He took a deep breath and ground out his cigarette. She felt sorry for him.

"Do you know who these bad guys were?" She blinked away the image of the dead woman, Alicia Quirk. . . .

"Christ, no. I tried to divorce myself from the whole business—I thought about just moving out, I didn't want to be there when they came for him with the muscle. And my friend was getting pretty scared and one day he came home with a gun, see. He said he was going to be ready for these bastards."

"It sounds like a movie," she said.

"Well, now the gun's gone, he told me he threw it away. He was really weirding out on me, doing lots of cocaine, he had more around the loft than he'd ever had before. I didn't know what the hell was going on. Then he reads this thing in the newspaper, that Garfein guy's column, he shows it to me and he's got this dumb, scared grin on his face and he tells me that it was him that you saw throw the gun away. He said he looked up and saw you in the window and he doesn't know what to do, he's scared shitless that you saw him well enough to recognize him—"

"But wait a minute," she interrupted. "What if I could? When would I ever see him again? What are the chances?"

"Well, that's sort of the point—I guess I'm going to have to tell you this part." His voice was shaky: he sounded like her little brother years ago confessing an indiscretion to her, afraid of giving something away but having to tell someone. She wanted to pat his hand and tell him it was all right, she'd take care of things for him. "See, you might very well recognize him on TV. He's an actor, he's worked in a couple of soaps, a couple of TV movies, he works off-Broadway every so often . . . and he does TV commercials. He did one for some kind of motor oil and one for a life-insurance company and one for maple syrup, he's a good actor, got a very ingratiating quality about him, and he looks different every time you see him. Anyway, he thought you might see him and something would click in your mind and you'd tell the cops that he's the guy . . . so he's been following you around, trying to figure out what he should do about you. . . ."

She saw his shoulders shrug heavily and slump. He leaned forward in the chair. When he spoke again his voice was still shaky. "He's so scared and I've been worried about him, worried he might go off the deep end and then . . . then, for Christ's sake, I started getting worried about you. I mean, if he thinks you can identify him, then I don't know what he might do. Let's face it, he's not the most rational, the stablest guy in the world, and you're just an innocent bystander and what if he decided he had to do something about you?"

Suddenly she realized he was crying. He was afraid and she knew what he felt, the vulnerability to a situation, a person, he couldn't control. He leaned forward with his elbows on his knees, his face in his hands, his head shaking. "God, I'm sorry, but I'm just an ordinary guy and this whole thing has been driving me nuts . . . my heart gets to pounding in the middle of the night and I can't sleep when he's not in his room and I just wander around that loft wondering what he's doing. . . . Please, forgive me, you must think I'm a real creep, but I didn't know what else to do—"

She went to him and knelt in front of him, took his hands in hers, and started to tell him that she understood, that she'd also felt the awful, consuming anxiety that ate you up and reduced you to a sobbing shell. He nodded, wiped his eyes with one hand. "Here I sit, thirty-one years old, crying my eyes out—fuckin' idiot!" He tried to laugh. "And then I break in here and scare you—somebody ought to lock me up!"

They both laughed.

"Well, Merry Christmas," he said.

She stretched up and kissed his cheek, not thinking what she was doing, or why, just reacting, empathizing with the man. Softly he took her face between his palms and kissed her lips and she felt the sudden surge of desire, returned his kiss, opened her mouth and drew him inside. She wanted him and she heard herself breathing too hard, heard him whispering in her ear, telling her what he wanted with a sudden, driven urgency, and then she had him in her hand and was stroking the wetness, inflaming him, feeling his fingers at her nipples, stroking her through the material, tugging gently as they hardened, feeling the heat and the flood between her legs.

It had been so long, she'd kept it out of her mind for such a long time, and now there was a stranger who was as fearful and confused as she was, a stranger who wasn't telling her how to handle her fears but was wrapped up in experiencing his own, and she wanted to take him inside her and feel his tension and frustration and strength driving into her and she wanted to tell him not to hold back, to let himself go . . . but she couldn't do it. She turned away, her face wet with tears of frustration and anger turned inward against herself, and lay sobbing, her knees tucked up to her chest, trying to disappear. "I'm sorry," she whispered. "I'm so sorry. . . ."

She lay panting on her back, watching the blur of lights on the Christmas tree. His breathing rasped in her ear, then he turned and lay on his back next to her.

"Man," he whispered hoarsely, "I just don't know what to say . . . I didn't mean to do this. Really. I'm the one who's sorry—"

"A sorry pair," she said, wiping her eyes. "If you recall, it was my idea. I hate women who do that. . . ."

"Don't be silly." He shook his head. "Crazy, it was just crazy, that's all."

Her mind was operating sluggishly. Slowly she sat up, put an arm up on the couch. Felt the cold steel of the knife blade. It brought her back to reality for an instant, then she shook the facts of the matter out of her mind, and stood up. Shaky legs. She wasn't thinking about what had just happened. She couldn't afford to: all she could do was sit down, feel Sir leaping up into her lap. She wanted to go to the bathroom and dry between her legs, it was a warm flood of stickiness, her inner thighs were slippery and damp. She was sweating. . . .

But she felt no fear of the man now. He lay on the floor, then stood up with his back to her. She watched him zip his pants, pick up his tweed jacket and put it back on. Just a guy, nothing special, no name, no future, so . . . so how did it differ from lying in bed with her hand between her legs, massaging her clitoris until the whole thing swept over her and left her weary, exhausted?

He sat back down. She wasn't even trying to see his face anymore. She didn't want to see his face. It just didn't matter.

"You said you've been following me?" she asked at last.

"No, not exactly. My following is sort of a by-product. I've been following my friend. He's been following you. I've been making my mind up, wanting to tell you what's going on, but you wouldn't believe what hard work I've made of it. The thing is, I don't want to get him into trouble, with you or with the cops—I mean, I don't know that he's done anything wrong. Anyway, I was going to tell you the situation and warn him off . . . but now—well, now he's disappeared."

She wasn't paying close enough attention. She heard the last word and it snapped her back: she'd been thinking about what she should tell MacPherson and suddenly she'd heard—

"Who's disappeared?"

"My friend, Mrs. Rader. That's who we're talking about—"

"What do you mean? He's just gone?"

"Oh, I suppose he's out there somewhere, but I don't know where, it's been a couple of days . . . I can't find him, anyway. What I'm afraid of is, see, he's a movie

nut—he lives and breathes movies, hangs out at the
Thalia and the Regency and the Carnegie, sees all the
revivals . . . and I've got a feeling that this whole crazy
thing with these people and the drugs and the gun and
you, I've got a feeling that it's all become a kind of movie
in his eyes—I guess I'm afraid he might do something
melodramatic." She could see him in profile, looking
into the lights on the tree. "But don't worry, I'll find him.
You'll be okay."

"I hope you're not offended," she said, "if I tell you
that I don't find that terribly reassuring."

"I know, I know," he said.

"I'm going to tell the police what you've told me—"

"Well, you can do what you think best. But really
you don't know all that much, do you? No names . . ."

"All right. But shouldn't we stay in touch? How can
I get hold of you?" Her mind had begun to turn over
furiously: once he was out the door she might just as well
have had a hallucination. MacPherson would believe
her, she supposed, but what did she actually know? How
long would it take to track an actor through clues to
commercials he'd made? Or search through Chelsea
lofts?

He was looking down at her. "I don't know how to
say this without seeming rude as hell, you've been so
nice to me, so understanding, but the idea of involvement—any kind of involvement—in this, or with you,
scares me. Really scares me. So let's see how this all goes
down in the end. I can always get back to you, call you at
your office like real people do . . . but not until I find

him and get him straightened out. Is that all right with you?"

He looked down at her, reached out and stroked her cheek, and she felt the whole balance tipping back toward him. She nodded.

"I'll be in touch," he said, and she heard the smile in his voice, reassuring her. "In the meantime, let's just sort of think it through, think what's the best thing to do."

He leaned down and kissed her forehead. He ruffled Sir's ears. She followed him slowly up the stairs. When he opened the door he was taken by surprise by the light in the entryway. He blinked, shielding his eyes, and for an instant, her own vision impaired by the sudden brightness, she saw his face.

The door slammed and she heard him go quickly through the outer doors.

But she'd know him if she saw him again.

She wouldn't forget the face.

Chapter Sixteen

Natalie had the foresight to look at the situation squarely once she was alone but yet not worry about the weirdness of what had just happened to her. She took two sleeping pills, put Saint-Saëns on the tape machine, and got Sir situated snugly on the bed with her. She was not going to lie awake in the middle of the night working herself up into something full-blown and neurotic and disgusting. If she had to think about what had happened, she could bloody well think about it in the cool light of morning, distanced from the event. And even with the sleeping pills she had to fight off the tapping, crawling fingers of anxiety that tugged her toward the rim of the pit. Then, blessed sleep . . .

Her subconscious had been at work while she slept.

When she woke and came to some awareness under the shower, she found that she believed what the man the night before had told her: for a time, before sleep came, she had thought he had no roommate, had in fact been describing himself. That had only made him more human to her . . . but on the other hand it had made him crazy. If he had been talking about himself, then he was well around the bend. But now he seemed honest, seemed anything but dangerous. Frightened, shy, romantic—even sensible in a strange way. Strange: talk about an understatement . . . but honest.

She was less worried about the nameless man than she was about her own behavior. About what she had wanted from him . . . By the time she'd made her coffee and toast and was sitting in the living room looking out at the gray light and the high banks of snow, she'd begun to shake and feel a thread of nausea running through her. What had she been thinking of? She had wakened with her period and some cramps and she wasn't quite succeeding in rising above the facts of life. In fact, her hands were trembling.

She plugged in the Christmas tree and watched the lights snap on. Twenty-four hours before, she had not had a tree, had had no plans for one, no plans for Christmas. Her mind turned from the tree to thoughts of MacPherson coming by, taking over, seeing to things, and she found herself smiling. Calming down.

Sir had ambled down the steps and begun sniffing and digging at the carpet. For a moment Natalie watched him curiously, wondering what on earth he thought he was doing. Then she realized and couldn't take her eyes away. He had found the spot where she had lain the night before. . . .

"Sir!" she snapped at last, poking him with her foot.

He slinked away, giving her a dirty look over his shoulder.

She looked at the place where she'd lain, slowly shaking her head. She hated having done it, but maybe she was beginning to realize why. The pressure of the past ten days, the lack of a warm sexual component in her life, the excitement and fear at finding the man in her apartment—it wasn't quite as crazy a thing as it had seemed. *Yes, it was, Natalie*, she thought, crazy and—far more importantly—horribly dangerous. What in the name of God had she thought she was doing? He could have killed her, he could have become violent and left her hurt and beaten. . . .

Jesus H. Christ, Natalie! Better not start making excuses for yourself at this late date—you behaved like an idiot. Well, almost. She wished she could stop her heart from beating irregularly, stopping and starting and fluttering in her chest. She wished she could get things under control.

Which was how it went through the morning. Sir went out in the courtyard and decorated the snow and flopped around, pursuing squirrels he would never catch. She nibbled at her toast, debated calling Julie but knew she'd wind up telling her about the man and that was the last thing she wanted to do. She put Villa-Lobos's *Bachianas Brasileiras No. 3* on the stereo and just sat staring into her garden, drinking coffee, listening. Alone.

Absolutely alone. Trying to replace her thoughts of the night's intruder with calm, smiling reflections about MacPherson, the unlikeliest cop . . .

* * *

She was still sitting watching the sun trying vainly to burn through the heavy gray sky of afternoon when the telephone jarred her out of the pointless, worn-out daydreams.

"Mrs. Rader," the voice said, "I'm Captain Arthur D'Allessandro. NYPD. I'm assigned to Internal Conduct Services, which is a fancy way of saying internal public relations—making sure we're not vulnerable on the PR front. We're doing a routine check on Sergeant Mac-Pherson, who I believe has been working with you on a matter—that is right, isn't it?" He sounded as if he was filling in a form.

"Yes," she said. "MacPherson."

"If you're going to be home this afternoon," he went on, "I'd like to stop by and just interview you briefly. You'd be helping us out, Mrs. Rader. Could you manage that?"

"I suppose so. I don't quite understand why, though—"

"I'll fill you in when I get there. I'll be there in half an hour. D'Allessandro's my name. We appreciate it."

It was a drag and she wasn't in the mood to have anybody stop by, but she couldn't have said no, refused to cooperate. Internal Conduct Services! Whatever that was supposed to mean. She pulled herself into her jeans and sweater and made a fresh pot of coffee. Waiting in the living room, she vowed to have the stolen things replaced during the coming week, get some Christmas shopping done, make some plans for the holiday season. But presents for whom? Plans to do what? There were all the usual invitations, ways of filling the endless holiday evenings and keep from feeling left out . . . but nothing she wanted to do, so few people she really cared about seeing. She wished she had the nerve just to get out of town, go to a country hotel in Massachusetts or Vermont and take along some good books, meet some people who were new . . . whoever might be staying in a hotel over the holidays. She smiled to herself at the thought.

Captain D'Allessandro seemed to have come right from a television cop show. He was shortish, stocky, with thinning hair, heavy black-framed glasses, a leather coat that squeaked when he walked, the kind of swagger common to short men who had gained a position of some authority and power. He was chewing gum back on his molars.

She took him downstairs to the living room and got him a cup of coffee while he opened his leather coat, took off his scarf, and settled on the couch. "Lovely place you got here, Mrs. Rader, just very lovely. Like a movie. Jack Lemmon or Tony Randall, a New York pad in the early sixties. Very nice, very tasteful. Ah, that's fine, I like it black and hot, like the old joke. Thank you very much, very nice."

"I don't mean to be snotty," she said, "but can I see your badge?"

"Oh, you certainly can, Mrs. Rader. My mistake, you should get a refund." He grinned, chewed away at the gum, and began fumbling for his wallet. The coat creaked. He found it, a black leather folder, dropped it on the carpet, leaned down to get it, his face reddening.

177

"That's all right," she said. "You look like—"

"A cop," he said, sitting back up. "I know." He flipped open the wallet and looked at the badge. "Gotta pencil? Take down my number. It's 7614. Write that down." He looked at her.

"I'll remember," she said, smiling.

He repeated the number. "Adds up to ninety, okay?"

"Fine. Now what can I do for Internal Conduct Services?"

"Right. I'm sure you're busy, let's get right to it. Sergeant MacPherson." He sighed. His face was troubled and he rubbed his chin with thick, black-haired fingers. "First-rate man, don't misunderstand anything I have to say here. First-rate, no question about that. The thing is—listen, you realize that I'm dealing in strictest confidence here—the thing is, we've had a few complaints about Sergeant MacPherson's personal conduct in the course of his investigations. Groundless, I'm sure, but we have to check them out. Innocent till proven guilty, of course. But we gotta check—"

"What are you talking about?"

"Well, the complaints have all come from ladies. Get it?"

"No, I don't get it."

"Ah, well, you know what I mean, you're a woman of the world, out there in the business world—"

She laughed uneasily. "I don't know what you're talking about. I can't make it any clearer than that."

"Overly familiar. Familiarity. Unwarranted."

"With the ladies?" she prompted. "You're joking."

"As I say, we've had complaints from some women he's met during the course of investigations. No proof, mind you. Just allegations. Calling them up for dates during an investigation, insisting on maintaining contact with them once an investigation is concluded, pursuing them too energetically. Now me, I figure a lot of these women give a guy encouragement whether they know it or not, he's a good-looking guy, likes the ladies—what else is new, right?" He shrugged, opened his hands in a gesture of resignation. "I'm just here to ask you if you've had any experience with Sergeant MacPherson you would characterize as overly familiar or suggestive?" He looked embarrassed. "What can I say? It's a dirty job but somebody's got to do it."

"I'm amazed," she said.

"Try to think of it as consumer relations, Mrs. Rader. Like we just want to know if you're satisfied with the NYPD product—"

"Yes, I'm perfectly satisfied. Is that clear enough? MacPherson has turned out to be sensitive to my situation, very involved in handling it effectively—I think I've irritated him by my reticence to rely on him . . . but he has certainly behaved in a professional manner at all times. I can't imagine what else I could say."

"Well, remember, his performance of his duty is not in question. However, we've got a report he's seeing you socially during the course of an investigation. Now say he tried to cop a quick feel—" He raised a palm, shook his head. "I'm sorry, I'm sorry. Say he tried to make an improper advance of some kind—you'd tell me, right?"

"Whatever you call it in the police manual, he hasn't done it. Get it? Zip, zero, he gets my vote for Cop of the Year. Now, if that's it, I've got to get going, Captain—"

"Listen, that's just great, Mrs. Rader. You've been a big help. Believe me." He put down his coffee and stood up, buttoning his coat. "I'm sorry I had to barge in here and subject you to this. And," he winked, "pardon my French there a second ago. It's funny, though. A guy gets a rep like MacPherson's and it follows him around. With some guys it's brutality—they look at some punk sideways and suddenly it's brutality. Years ago, when I was in narcotics, I used to have these little conversations with dealers down on the East Side, take 'em aside into an alley and leave 'em standing there spitting out Chiclets, but I never got a rep for brutality. I know lots of cops, screwing their way through the precinct—half the burglary calls they get are phony, just babes wantin' a cop for their dance cards—and nobody ever reports them. Then a guy like MacPherson—whammo, and it follows him. You never know. You can't trust anyone, Mrs. Rader. Like the business with my shield—now you got the number, y'know."

He stood by the door tucking his scarf into the leather coat. She could smell his spearmint gum. She watched him swagger out, a funny little cop. Familiar. It had to be because he was so much like a TV character. Somebody not real.

So concerned about his shield, making sure she had the number. Not very efficient.

She never had seen the shield.

And who had been watching her with MacPherson? Who had reported them to Internal Conduct?

Once the evening of her quiet, lonely day had come, she was feeling as if she could deal with the sexual encounter of Saturday night. Beyond the sexual encounter, however, waters were murkier. She'd replayed the weekend again and again: the day with MacPherson and the story the anonymous man had told her about his "roommate." She knew she should tell someone about the latter, but whom? She simply didn't want to blurt out the sexual content, and the rest of the story struck her as sufficiently out of kilter to require some further reflection on her part. And the description of MacPherson she'd heard from D'Allessandro was festering in the back of her mind.

She was quite sure that the last person in the world she wanted to talk to that evening was MacPherson. Of course, at nine o'clock, he called to tell her he was back from Glen Cove and ask her how things were going. She searched his voice for the sound of the womanizer, the leer for the woman who was so lonely and frustrated she was falling for him . . . but she hated it, didn't want to believe it—still she kept hearing D'Allessandro going on, the gross implications, the creak of his coat, the sound of his chewing gum cracking.

"I'm sitting looking at my beautiful Christmas tree. There's one big log burning in the fireplace. I'm drinking a Scotch and water. I'm reading a manuscript—"

"What are you wearing?"

She recognized the question: from the past, from

men who had cared for her, wanted to visualize her while they talked. But suddenly it seemed an invasion, full of innuendo. She shivered. "Nothing special."

"I'm sure. Leather tunic, boots, and a whip?" He laughed softly.

"Not exactly. Scruffy old terry robe with a coffee stain, a granny nightgown dating approximately from the time of my granny, and white gym socks."

"Anything interesting befall you since yesterday afternoon?" He sounded almost as if he expected something, as if he knew. . . .

"No, nothing at all."

"Good." He paused, said, "Are you all right? You sound funny—is someone with you?"

"No. I'm fine. I told you what I'm doing. I'm going to bed very soon." She knew he was right: she sounded so remote, even to herself. Damn D'Allessandro! "How was your day?" she added halfheartedly.

He yawned. "I'm bushed. Had to suffer through the Giants losing on a field goal with three seconds left—my mother nearly had a stroke. Then the drive back in the snow took forever plus fifteen minutes. You're okay, though? Everything all right? No mysterious men following you around or showing up with guns?"

She tried to laugh it off.

He wasn't entirely satisfied. "You really do sound just a little off, Natalie."

"Oh, you're just being a suspicious cop. Or you're getting too close to me, know me too well. Maybe you'd better concentrate on some other ladies in peril who need Christmas trees."

"What's bothering you, Natalie? That doesn't sound like—"

"Really, it's nothing. Just drop it, okay? Got my period today and the cramps are sort of rotten, that's all. Menopause, where are you when I need you?"

He laughed. "You'll just have to wait another decade or so, I'm afraid. Look, I'll give you a call tomorrow. And call me if you have anything that's bothering you. And get a good night's sleep."

"All right."

"We're going to make some headway this week. Hang on. You got that?"

"Don't worry. I'll call if I need help. I promise."

He told her to sleep tight, and she hung up the telephone with a weary sense of disappointment. Her head was suddenly splitting.

Chapter Seventeen

It was still dark when she awoke at six, but half an hour later, when she had left the bathroom and gotten dressed, made the coffee and seated herself by the window, the sky was gray with just a sliver of pink to the east where the sun was threatening to make an appearance. She turned on WNEW to hear Ted Brown, her own personal "morning man." She smiled rather fixedly as she made a list for the day, which she was somewhat disconcerted to discover included a television appearance on one of the five afternoon chat shows—half-news and half-nonsense. On this program, she recognized, Natalie Rader fit firmly into the nonsense portion. She wished Jay hadn't insisted that she accept the invitation to go on and be trendy, hot, and full of crap, which was of course precisely what they—the TV people—wanted. Still and all, she concluded her list with "TV at 5" and looked at the day from a fairly aggressive posture. Very determined to advance on the week with stately, controlled resolution.

Quite unexpectedly, as she was deciding to get to the office by seven-thirty for some peace and quiet before the telephones began their constant bitching, there was a knock at the door. She opened it to find Julie in her bathrobe, a Band-Air on her left cheekbone and looking generally as if she'd gone a brisk fifteen with Sugar Ray Leonard. One eye was well blackened, there was a bruise on her forehead, the Band-Aid on her cheek.

"What in the name of God happened to you?"

Julie charged into the room swearing under her breath and stomped down the stairs into the kitchen, where Natalie heard her banging a coffee cup. She reappeared, went to the table by the window, and stood staring at the Christmas tree.

"What the fuck is that?"

"It's called a Christmas tree. What happened to your face?"

"When did you get it?"

"Saturday. It's MacPherson's doing. I told you . . . and I'm not going to ask again, Julie—"

"You're right. MacPherson. God, I'm losing my memory! The romantic sergeant . . . honest to God!"

"Your face, Julie! It's seven o'clock in the morning and I want to know about your face!"

"Oh, that old thing . . ." She sat down and began to cry, gritting her teeth and biting back the noise as tears coursed down her cheeks. Natalie went to her, knelt beside her, took her hand, murmured to her until the tears had subsided.

"Now let's have it," she said softly, patting the cold hand and giving her a handkerchief from her purse.

"An adventure. One of *my* adventures. Stupid, so stupid really. Christ, it was a hellish day, Nat, it really was a hellish day. Yesterday I met a guy at Scandals. Turned out to be the wrong man—stupid, so stupid. You've always warned me. Scoop—you were right. But, as you might guess, he seemed like such a nice guy. Quietly dressed, good taste, sort of preppie but about forty or forty-five. Nice conversation. I went back to his place with him. Very nice, good pictures, reassuring furniture, no glitz . . . but once home on his own ground he struck me as a little spooky. I don't know why—I've tried and tried to think it through and I can't sort it out. But I got to thinking no, I'm not going to bed with this guy. If he likes me, it won't make any difference, and if all he wants is a fuck, then I'm not interested anyway—turning over a new leaf and all. But when we'd had a couple of drinks and listened to some music and chatted and I said I had an early day coming up and really should be going home—then he went sort of vaguely crazy. Well, not vaguely. I tried to leave and he turned out to be a tough guy. Thus, my kisser. I finally got him in the nuts with a paperweight." She smiled and winced at the memory. "And away I went." She dabbed at her nose with the handkerchief. "I got a cab, and the driver, he was a nice young guy, pointed out to me that I was bleeding, a bloody nose, and insisted on taking me to Lenox Hill Hospital." She sighed at the absurdity of the situation, made fists. "Emergency room, yet. They huffed and puffed and fixed me up, I talked them out of an overnight stay and police reports, God knows what else, and the cabbie brought me home." She sniffled. "God, it was all my fault, I suppose. . . ."

"It was what?"

"My fault. I'd had a lousy day, believe me, one bitch of a day and I probably was bugging the guy—"

"This is not a question of your fault," Natalie said, managing to keep her temper. Only just. "It's not a question of bringing something on yourself, not a question of bugging some idiot—it's a question of assault and battery!"

Julie kept talking, alternately crying and laughing at what seemed to strike her as a bleakly, blackly comedic situation. "But listen, forget the punchout. That's nothing, old stuff. I had some tests last week and . . . oh, shit!" She sniffed, wiped her eyes. "Yesterday morning, Sunday, I called my doctor in the morning—poor bastard—and made him raise hell with some people at a lab somewhere about some tests, but they weren't biting. So I yelled and moaned at him to get some kind of an opinion and he finally told me yes, I'd say you've got it, Miss Conway, you have almost certainly got it!" She broke off, blew her nose, wiped at tears.

"What? Got what? Cancer? Oh, God, Jules, you haven't got cancer—"

She began to laugh through the sobs. "Herpes! Not cancer, *herpes*! He said it was an epidemic, told me to find consolation in that. Me . . . herpes, for God's sake. And here I was with this guy, he said he used to play with the New York Philharmonic. Under Bernstein . . . and there I was, worried that I might give

188

this virtuoso herpes! I was probably acting nuts, I don't know. And he beat me up. Oh, Natalie, what the hell's going on?"

Natalie held her on the couch for an hour, comforted her as she would a child. Finally the crying was over.

"Look, the guy didn't kill you, which he might well have done. And you had an angry doctor you were bugging on a Sunday morning make a guess at something only lab tests will show—you don't know if you've got herpes! So just relax, calm down, and we'll deal with it when we know. And if you don't stop saying it was your own fault, I'll personally kick you out in the snow. Look, let me call in to your office for you. You just sit here and recuperate and watch TV or whatever you like to do— take a day off, do Valium, do whatever you want. When I come back tonight I'll bring cold lobster and we'll talk it through. Okay, Jules?"

"Oh, Natalie . . ."

"Pals, kiddo. It'll be okay. More or less."

They laughed.

Natalie was horrified by the whole stupid mess, but she was hiding it, drawing strength from trying to help out, from giving strength. There was no point, no point in telling her about the man on Saturday night, about D'Allessandro's revelations.

Everything seemed to be coming apart, just spinning out of control.

Rory Linehan was waiting for her at the office. So much for her stately, controlled resolution.

"Ah, my dear Miss Rader," Linehan said, struggling to his feet. He was wearing a shabby corduroy jacket with a plaid shirt and striped tie. She wasn't sure if she was actually smelling Bushmills or if it was a particularly nasty trick of memory.

"Feeling better, Mr. Linehan?"

He looked puzzled. "Why, I'm fine—"

"Not the last time I saw you," she said.

"And that's what's on my mind, dear lady. Perhaps we could discuss—"

"Why don't you just apologize and be on your way?" Natalie could hardly believe what she was saying. It felt good.

Linehan shuffled his feet nervously, ran his fingers back through his slick gray hair. "Now, now, no point in holding a grudge." He flashed a deathly grin, a man who needed a drink. She thought briefly of E.T. Here was an Irishman, alone, a million miles from home and afraid— he'd have sold his sainted granny for a double shot of Bushmills. He looked at Lisa behind her desk, licked his puffy lips. "Ah, could we go into your office?"

"Lisa," Natalie said, "I'm really pressured today." A lie, she supposed. "So give us ten minutes and buzz me."

In her office she sat down and stared at him, waited. She felt all the anger and impotence and frustration bubbling within her, everything she'd been storing up. She nearly laughed, watching him: if he'd had a forelock he'd have tugged it. Should she squander it on him?

"About the other night," he began. He rubbed his red nose like a man caressing his last valuable possession. "It was all in fun, we're hoping you understood—p'raps we sometimes go too far, Moira and old Rory. Money worries, Christmas coming, a wee bit too much to drink . . . all in good fun." He gasped a laugh.

"It was despicable. Let's just forget it—a bad idea all around. Now, I really have lots to do—"

"You're still my agent?"

"For the moment, yes."

"Now looky here, there's no use in threatening Rory Linehan." He shuffled his feet again, like an actor in a bad play well on his way to running out of gestures. "It was all Moira's fault, always is, long as I can remember—"

"Please, Mr. Linehan, just leave. There's no need for this scene."

"I'll be the judge of that." He coughed, rubbed that awful exploded nose again. "There's explaining to be done—"

She shook her head. "No, there really isn't."

"I just want you to know, it's Moira. She's got terrible problems, and, well, maybe you and I could have a drink someday and get to know each other." He spoke like a schoolboy reciting a memorized piece. "Just the two of us." His face was gray, like a bum's stubble. He looked shaky and she didn't want him to faint. She got up and opened the door.

"Anything is possible, Mr. Linehan. Thanks for coming by." She waited, holding the door, looking at the floor while he thought it over and finally went into the hallway.

"I won't bring Moira. Just the two of us." His eyes

were dull and wouldn't come back to life until he got his fist around a drink. "Till then," he said.

She watched him wander down the hall, touching the wall with one hand, turn the corner, out of sight.

What was that all about? She went back to her office, closed the door, suddenly drawn to the window with its view of the construction site where it had all begun, where things seemed to have started going crazy.

But of course it hadn't begun with the sight of the man with the gun. You never really knew where anything had begun unless you took it all the way back to the beginning, being born and looking around for the first time. Neither had it begun with the breakup of her marriage and the collapse of nerves she'd experienced in the aftermath. No, it had all begun a long time ago. She didn't suppose she'd ever really understand it, and maybe it was just as well that way. . . .

The rubble of Moira and Rory Linehan's life had set her on a retrospective course and she found herself thinking about her mother and father. It had been a messy relationship that she had observed and withdrawn from all through her childhood. It had been possible to be close to both her parents, but never when they were together. Together they seemed to form a third creature, curled in upon itself, feasting on anger and frustration and closing out the little girl who would lie in bed listening to the raised voices, clapping her hands over her ears, pretending she was the heroine of *Rebecca*, who last night had dreamed she'd gone back to Manderly. . . .

She'd been through enough self-analysis, acres and

acres and years and years of it, she'd traipsed back and forth past the effigies of her mother and father, talking, talking, talking, crying until she couldn't cry anymore. Maybe it had begun then, buried in the fears of her childhood, maybe that was where everything began and maybe the shrinks were right on the money. And here she was, thirty-seven, still wondering, still striving to understand and solve and move on.

She remembered her mother. Elizabeth. She, too, had been small and dark but had lacked the sturdiness of Natalie's hips and thighs. She had been a slight, almost wispy woman with shining dark eyes deep in the sockets, long black hair that had streaked with gray when she was still a young woman. A fondness for cameos, anything set in burnished, glowing gold. A thin voice that seemed to come softly from her forehead . . . Stylish, always dressed in the best, the most expensive, always ready for a shopping trip, always bandaging over the wounds, her own wounds, with an application of money. She used to tell her daughter, "Never marry a man who can't keep you in good shoes. Everything else will follow, dear, if he doesn't mind the shoe bill." Elizabeth: a weepy, neurotic woman, pretty, sharp-featured, lovely hands with exquisite rings and bracelets, wholly dependent on her husband, hysterical if she felt she'd been caught in a mistake or a failure or any act she imagined was unladylike—the worst sin. Putting up a shiny, moneyed front to disguise her frustrations, her sadness, her despair.

Side by side they stood, in her memory, Elizabeth and Ray Mitchell. Ray, looking like Jimmy Cagney, short and dynamic and busy, always incredibly busy without a moment to spare, full of expectations—of himself, of Natalie, of Elizabeth. Bustling, full of energy, surrounded by other men like himself. Work, golf, work, duck hunting, work . . . Self-centered, successful, almost unaware of the feelings of others, utterly confused by his wife's desperation and dissatisfaction with their marriage . . .

Side by side they stood like two sad-faced figures on a crumbling, dried-out, fly-specked wedding cake, until the lady began slipping off, running away from home for days at a time, no way to find her, and coming back— what had the doctor said, that night so long ago? Ah, yes, *a wee bit under the influence*. . . .

In the end she did it with Glenlivet, a quart of the best, and about forty sleeping pills, according to the doctor, and poor Ray had been quite broken up about it. He'd taken a month down in Pinehurst with his chums consoling him.

And Natalie, far away at Northwestern, had come back for the funeral, which had been carried off under something of a cloud, what with the rumors behind the explanation of a sudden cardiac arrest. Then, Daddy off to Pinehurst with his golf clubs and Natalie back to school, never having cried.

"Hang on, Tiger," he had said. "She was a troubled woman with a mighty load of anxiety. Forgive me, but maybe she's better off now. At rest, you know."

He had kissed her goodbye at the big house in Rye and patted her fanny and the limo had taken her to LaGuardia.

Two years later, having chipped to within four inches of the pin—his cronies seemed to find that awesome, what a way to go!—he had keeled over in a sandtrap on the seventeenth. A real heart attack.

Anxious Mommy. Daddy playing to an eight handicap.

Gone.

She was brought back from the past by Lisa buzzing her. Natalie punched line two.

"Mrs. Rader, I'm dreadfully sorry about intruding on your workday. This is Alex Drummond . . . I'm a friend and colleague of Dr. Lewis Goldstein. He may have mentioned that he'd referred you to me, or me to you, anyway you get the point."

"Of course, he told me. You're on my call list—"

"Well, I had a free moment and thought I'd go the extra step at Lew's urging. And, of course, we're having trouble with our telephone line this morning, incoming calls are being routed to a woman in Brooklyn. I'm lucky I'm not particularly paranoid. You did want to see me, according to Lewis." He was all business, just short of brusque.

"You must be a wise man, Dr. Drummond."

"Oh, I am, off and on. But how did you know?"

"Because with my schedule I'd probably have put off calling you—"

"You're certainly under no obligation, Mrs. Rader. I'm doing Lewis a favor, that's all."

"You remind me of a song. Something about rushing in where angels fear to tread—"

"I'm afraid I don't know the song. Ought I to be alarmed?"

"Fools rush in, where angels fear to tread," she murmured softly, remembering the smoke and the blue light on the singer, Susannah Something, at Lulu's, eons ago. ". . . And so I come to you, my heart above my head, though I see the danger there . . . something, something, something." She laughed.

"No danger here. Unless you fall off the couch."

"Analysts should have seatbelts. Couchbelts."

"Well, to the point." He seemed uncomfortable with the chitchat, unlike Lew, and she felt as if she'd been babbling. "Lewis suggested we might have a talk soon. I'm sorry to say this is a bad week for me. The painters are doing the office, I've rearranged appointments. . . ." He sighed. "But, forgive me, none of this is your concern, is it? If you could come down to my office tomorrow at ten we can try to cope with the fumes."

"Sure, why not?" She didn't bother to consult her diary for the morning.

"I will have to ask you to be prompt, Mrs. Rader. I have a lecture at eleven. I'm on Tenth Street, just off Fifth. Do you have a pen?" He gave her the address twice and warned her about the telephone problem again.

The anxious psychiatrist, she thought, grinning.

Then it occurred to her: would she have to tell him about her Saturday-night visitor?

Oh, Christ.

As she hung up she knew she would have put him

off had it not been for D'Allessandro's story about MacPherson. The fact was, she felt not only disillusioned but betrayed. By MacPherson. The illusion he had created, smashed by the intrusion of reality. *Betrayed and, admit it, Natalie—bereft . . .*

Chapter Eighteen

She had just finished an agonizing conversation with an editor at Harper & Row, desperately trying to rearrange an author's payment schedule without revealing just how hard up the poor bastard was, when Tony's call came through. She sighed, put her stockinged feet up on the file drawer, and leaned back, wondering why she was glad to hear his voice. He'd been such an ass the last time she'd seen him . . . or did she have that backward? She vaguely remembered feeling guilty afterward at not having been more sympathetic to his problems. It was hard to keep everything straight.

"Look, Nat, I want to get back on your good side," he said. "I know I behaved like a prick up at the Carlyle the other night. I had a lot on my mind and it was your birthday and I wanted it to be nice for you, and you know me, I fucked it all up—anyway, I have got—repeat, *got*—to see you pronto. Like now, for lunch. Don't bullshit me about being busy, you told me you've cut your lunch schedule back to nothing. So, let me buy and make up for being a jerk. Really, Nat, I promise to be good."

"Okay, okay, lunch it is." She touched the Tiffany silver diamond dangling between the points her nipples made in the sweater.

"Orsini's, then. Meet me at Fifth and Fifty-sixth in half an hour."

A light snow was falling, the flakes clinging to her black, double-breasted coachman's coat, staying in her thick black hair. She could hear the brass quintet from a block away, and when she got to the appointed corner she looked up at the players on the ledge set back a couple of stories above Fifth Avenue. They were wrapped in mufflers and surrounded by Christmas lights with the Trump Tower rising jaggedly above them. New York wrapped up in a single image: the world's most expensive piece of real estate and the clear, crystalline sound of "God Rest Ye Merry, Gentlemen" floating among the swirling snowflakes, drifting like tinsel on the shoppers below. My God, how she loved it, how she loved her awful, wonderful city. . . .

Tony took her by surprise, touched her arm, looked down at her with that carefree smile that hallmarked one of his customary moods. He was wearing some kind of *Raiders of the Lost Ark* fedora and a heavy Burberry trench coat with the camel-colored liner. He looked handsome and chiseled and happy, but nothing could ever erase the vacant spaces behind his features, the lack of depth or density or weight, whatever it was he lacked. Still, he looked cute and sort of silly in his hat and his snazzy coat, and it occurred to her just at that moment that he was wildly out of place in New York, had always been. He was pure Los Angeles. All these years he'd been a displaced person and neither of them had ever realized it. He wasn't quite real in a real city like New York. In Beverly Hills, on Rodeo Drive he'd have fit perfectly.

Orsini's glittered quietly behind the simple Fifty-sixth Street door. All mauve and pink and loveseats rather than chairs, fashionable, full of East Coast movie executives and rich, lovingly overdressed women. Tony couldn't wipe the smile off his face once they were at their table. He ordered an overpriced white Bordeaux that was very good, indeed, and toasted himself.

"To my escape from Staten Island," he said. And they drank.

"To my aunt and all her snotty cats," he said. And they drank.

"And to my great and much-deserved success!" And they drank.

"Would you be good enough to elucidate?" Natalie interrupted, laughing. "Along the lines of this success?"

He insisted on getting the ordering of lunch out of the way and then he leaned toward her, kissed her ear. "Tiger," he whispered, "I've actually done it. The mother lode, pay dirt. I, my darling, am quite suddenly in the chips." He leaned back, grinning at her. "Home free."

"Well, I'm sure I'm very happy for you." She went on with her wine while he just kept grinning. "All right, stop looking like an idiot and reveal all—got lucky on the lottery, I expect—"

"Nat," he went on seriously, "I put aside my big, lumpy novel. Well aside. And for the last six weeks I went to town on an old idea plucked from a notebook. Years old. Something scary. Wrote it in four weeks. Four weeks, Nat! Gave it to Ed Riker, my agent—doesn't quite move in your circles, of course—and he went to town with a bloody vengeance. He loved the book, said it gave him goose pimples—I told him he was an easily frightened little pansy, which he admitted he couldn't honestly deny. . . . However, he insisted it, the book, had a certain something. Deals with a big old house, my aunt's actually, which is haunted by something really nasty—I mean not my aunt's, of course, the one in my book, and it is pretty scary—"

"Title?"

"*Spooks.*"

"Oh my, I do like that quite a lot."

"Well, the long and the short of it is that Donner and Clay is doing it and they made a paperback deal up front, which is two hundred grand for dear old Tony, the penurious scribbler, and over the weekend we got another hundred for the film rights—not an option, but an outright sale to somebody by the name of Claude Davies, who is determined to become a producer. Made his money in fountain-pen clips or something. Anyway, that all adds up to three hundred thousand . . . and I'm going to LA right after Christmas to meet with Davies. . . . Nat, Donner and Clay want to do another deal for the next one and I'm working on the outline—"

"More ghosts?"

"But of course! Don't you love it?"

"I do, Tony, I really do love it." She was on the verge of tears. "I'm so happy for you." She clasped his hand tightly. "You were right—much deserved."

She didn't pay much attention to the rest of lunch and the conversation for which Tony assumed happy responsibility. She felt an enormous flood of warmth toward him, a kind of love, too. But more than anything else she felt the last ties, the last bonds of responsibility for his welfare, being severed. She could smile at him now while she let him float away into his own life. A life without her. While he was celebrating one thing, she was celebrating something else—his independence, his liberation from everything she had come to represent in his eyes.

Outside the restaurant she hugged him. "Enjoy it all, Tony. That's the important thing. Enjoy the hell out of it!" The snow was gathering on the brim of his dashing hat. "I'm so happy for you."

She walked off alone, knowing he was standing quietly watching her go. She looked back and waved, and on his face she believed she saw the beginning of a realization passing like a shadow across his face.

She blew him a kiss and he nodded slowly.

Natalie was guided by the elbow to a tiny makeup room where a girl with bad skin and a bandanna holding back her hair patted her face and pronounced her camera-ready.

On to the Green Room, where the leatherette

couch was scarred with cigarette burns and was losing gray stuffing. There was a pot of coffee plugged into the wall, styrofoam cups, powdered creamer, and something posing as sugar. Flattened plastic straws were provided for stirring. She demurred at the bright, smiling suggestion that she might need the coffee and settled down on the couch to watch the monitor. The show went on with a fanfare and several stories about people living in the streets as Christmas approached. A fire had killed a family of three in Brooklyn. Natalie passed the time chatting haltingly with the other guests: a psychiatrist who was going to talk about how to keep from committing suicide during the holiday season; a football player coming off a serious knee operation who would be chatting about the agony of missing his team's games and working for the United Way; and an actress who was going into a Broadway hit talking about her film career, which had collapsed, as far as Natalie knew, about twenty years ago.

And then it was her turn. During a commercial she was led into a shabby conversation pit, planted in a swivel chair, equipped with a tiny lapel microphone, and introduced to a woman who seemed to have no idea who she was. She kept staring at a sheaf of notes that Natalie sincerely hoped were about her. Apparently they were, because once the little red light went on above the camera lens, the interviewer snapped a dazzling smile into place and asked her to tell our viewers just what it's like to be the hottest, prettiest agent in the publishing business.

The questions followed in the same wildly humiliating manner and she did her best to field them, explaining a bit about how auctions worked, trying to keep observations about her personal appearance to a minimum. She had no idea how she was coming off but she was sure the ribbing would last for months. In the back of her mind she was damning Jay Danmeier to a particularly fiery corner of hell when she heard the interviewer, good old Betty, talking about something else—the bit in Garfein's column about the man with the gun. "Tell us, did they ever find the man with the gun? Or should I say, did the man with the gun ever find you?"

"Oh, God," Natalie said, "isn't that awfully old news by this time?"

"We can't help wondering, though. What happened?" Betty was just sitting there, suddenly very serious, staring at her.

"Nothing happened," Natalie said at last. "I didn't see the man's face, of course. So he has nothing to fear from me—"

"I see. Well, I guess you have to say that, don't you?"

The question hung between them and Natalie decided just to smile back and wait it out.

"Well, turning for a moment to your personal life—"

"Seems to me we're already there." *Smile sweetly, Natalie.*

"Here you are, the hottest agent, and your husband writes novels under a whole bunch of names, can't get anything published as Tony Rader. Can't you maybe help out?"

"Well, Betty, in the first place, he's my former

husband. And he's a very good writer who makes his living writing in a very competitive field." She longed for a machine gun to further explain things to Betty. "And no agent can force the publishing industry to do what she wants, not for her husband, not for anyone. An agent tries to cope with the fluctuating state of the marketplace, understand it, deal with it. In Tony's case, he has a very good agent of his own and I'm glad to report that he's doing very well. Perhaps you'll be interviewing him one of these days."

And then it was over and Betty was shaking her hand and dashing back to the anchor set. Natalie's previous keeper returned to the scene of the crime and led her away. "Now wasn't that fun?"

"That woman should be kept in a cage," Natalie said.

"Oh. She is a pussycat, isn't she? Men just love her."

Back in the Green Room, she was struggling into her coat when she caught something on the screen from the corner of her eye. "And now, Joan Brandon, live in Chelsea at the murder scene." The image on the screen changed to a blond, windblown woman who was clutching her microphone and seemed out of breath. "There has just been a shooting in this loft, David, and the police are here now, they've just brought the body down and put it in the ambulance." The camera panned across the front of a building with snow blowing across the scene. "We've got Sergeant Dan MacPherson here." Joan moved in on MacPherson, held the mike before him and asked him just what had happened. MacPherson's face wore its supercilious, faintly unconcerned look. He brushed his hair back against the wind. "We don't really have much to say yet, Joan. We were told there was a body here—anonymous tip, of course—and we came down. Sure enough, there was a body, and we're just beginning to get a line on things. We'll try to have a bit more for you later tonight—"

"Then we'll be talking to you on the eleven o'clock news?"

"You sure can try, Joan." He ducked away, out of the picture, his smile lingering like the Cheshire cat's.

"You heard that, David. A murder in a Chelsea loft, not much else yet that's definite. Back to you, David."

Natalie grabbed a cab and headed home in the darkness of early evening. Snow blew across the streets and the wind was icy, cutting.

MacPherson. A murder. A Chelsea loft.

She forced herself not to think about it, not to make all the connections that frightened her. But she wondered if MacPherson was already planning a Christmas tree for some lucky new lady in jeopardy. . . .

Julie's face was much improved and she had a Bloody Mary ready when Natalie got home. The swelling was almost completely gone, makeup had done quite a lot for the eye and the cheek bone, and she was wearing a long wool robe and a smile.

Natalie changed into her own robe, curled up on the couch before the fire, and slowly put away the Bloody Mary. Julie wanted to know about her reaction to the questions Betty had sprung on her, adding that despite a look of stunned surprise Natalie had carried off the whole thing pretty well. They each had another drink and Natalie dragged out three tired bits of cheese and some stone-ground crackers. They munched their way through the Jets game on "Monday Night Football," Julie cheering loudly for her art-loving lineman.

Natalie had a third drink to keep her anxieties at bay, waiting for the news, which finally came on half an hour past midnight, once the stupid game was over. Julie was yawning and gave Natalie a good-night kiss of thanks for helping her through the hideous day. Before leaving she looked back at Natalie: "My gosh, I didn't tell you— the herpes thing? Well, I don't have it! I think you were right, the doctor was just pissed off at my bugging him. Anyway I called him again today and he'd just gotten the report back—I'm okay."

Natalie sighed deeply, looked up shaking her head. "Thank God," she said. "So be warned, all right?"

Julie nodded, held up crossed fingers and left.

Turning her attention back to the television news, she heard the anchorman say, "Next, after these words, a brutal murder in Chelsea. Stay tuned."

She poured the last bit of the pitcher of spicy Mary into her glass, sipped at it, waited. The anchorman switched to a reporter in the studio, an intense-looking woman with huge glasses. "Sometime today, the time hasn't yet been fixed, a network television sales executive was murdered in Manhattan's Chelsea district." The screen filled with a pan down the street and up at the building she'd seen earlier on the monitor at the studio. "It was here, in a fourth-floor loft, that Bradley Nichols, a thirty-one-year-old television executive, lived and—

today—died at the hands of an unknown assailant." The screen now filled with a close-up of Dan MacPherson, his breath hanging in clouds before him like steam from a struggling engine, talking with the woman in the huge glasses. A voiceover continued, "We spoke with Sergeant Daniel MacPherson, who is in charge of the investigation." The voiceover ended, was replaced by conversation, a wintry wind in the background. "What can you tell us now?" she was asking. "Are there any suspects?"

"Well, Anne, the victim was stabbed repeatedly—do you hear what I'm saying? Rage. We're talking about rage. And all we really have to go on now is the information that the victim did apparently have a roommate. Naturally we'd like to talk to him. And we're talking to other people in the building, people at his place of employment—we're right at the beginning of this thing, Anne, but the kind of killing it was, the manner in which it was carried out, makes it very high on our priority list." He wasn't smiling. Then his face was gone and the camera was on Anne, back in the studio.

"We do have a photograph of the victim. . . ." She waited, staring at the camera. "If we could just show that—there it is." A black-and-white photograph appeared, a smiling face, innocent and happy. "Bradley Nichols, brutally murdered in Chelsea today. We'll keep a close eye on this one as it develops." She turned back to the anchorman. "You know, Bill," she said in the spirit of conversational, one-big-family news, "MacPherson, the cop I was just interviewing, has headed up several murder investigations in the last few years and he's always helpful, very professional, and, you know, good copy, candid. But I've never seen him quite so tight-lipped as he was tonight. When he said that this killing was done in rage, let me tell you—though he wouldn't go into details—he wasn't kidding."

The screen again filled with the face of the victim, then slowly faded away as they went to a commercial.

There wasn't a shadow of doubt in Natalie's mind.

On Saturday night she had held Bradley Nichols in her arms.

Four o'clock in the morning and Natalie was beginning to wonder if the clocks were broken, if the night would ever end. Her breath stuck jaggedly in the center of her chest, like a stake between her breasts, and her face was damp with perspiration. She hardly noticed Sir grumbling and shifting at the foot of the bed. But she couldn't shake the sound of MacPherson's voice.

Rage. We're talking about rage. . . .

Then she saw Bradley Nichols's frightened, vulnerable face, heard him crying softly in the darkened room, in the dim glow of reflecting snow. She felt again the pressure of his mouth, a stranger's kiss, and she wondered what had happened to him . . . what the rage had done. She tried to push him out of her mind but it was no good, he was with her now, the memory of him and his fear of his crazy roommate. . . .

My God, a tear squeezed from the corner of her eye, there was no epitaph, nothing left of him. Rage . . . rage had claimed him.

The night was tearing apart and she couldn't stop it. Her psyche was a graveyard, it seemed, had become one since chance had placed her at the window and made her look. And now it was coming to life, the graves were opening, the night seethed with her own fears and the images she couldn't wipe away. Murder. And blood. Alicia Quirk's face disintegrating, poor Bradley dead of someone's rage, and who would be next? It was a middle-of-the-night question and too easy to answer—

Rain spattered against the bedroom window, lashed at the crusty snow. The tips of the evergreens in the window box tapped at the glass like survivors in water, clinging to the wreckage and weakly reaching for safety, begging to be noticed. She made a face. Her thoughts sounded like something she'd read in a very bad manuscript. She blotted her damp cheek and forehead on the sheet. The streetlamps cast shadows bisected by windowpanes across the rumpled bedspread.

She gritted her teeth and tried to focus her thoughts, but it wasn't working. She was heading into an anxiety attack and she knew the territory. She'd been there before. Through the breakup with Tony, confronting and acknowledging the failure, the waste of seven years.

And this was a honey, building up along the walls of her bedroom, pushing in on her like seeping gas from vents she couldn't find, nastier than she remembered. A classic. She knew how an anxiety attack worked, recognized its every angle, but that didn't make it go away. It had to blow itself out, a typhoon in her brain, snapping at her nervous system. She hated it, resented the way it penetrated her real self, violated her and demeaned the woman she knew she was.

Resourceful, tough, able to deal with what came along. All those aspects of her self-image she had so carefully put in place . . . with no provisions for dealing with murder. Goddamn it!

She had been in bed for nearly four hours. The pretty flowered sheets, blanket, and spread lay in a twisted welter all around her, soaked with sweat. It was building. She felt the gnawings of hysteria. Nausea. Heart pounding. Eyes flickering around the room like a caged, terrified animal's.

She willed herself to switch on the bedside lamp, blinked against the sudden glare. Sir's eyes popped open nervously. She picked up her old copy of John Fowles's *The Magus*, a mammoth hardback like an anchor that might hold her attention in place. She'd read it three times over the years, knew it held a secret she'd been trying to pin down all her life. The dust jacket with the eerie horned creature's head was tattered. Page after page with bent-down corners. The spine had broken long ago. She wanted to call MacPherson and ask him if he'd read it, what he thought about it, get through the night with his voice at her ear, calming her, talking her down like someone in the control tower in a movie. But she couldn't call him, not now, not anymore . . . not after listening to D'Allessandro.

She opened the book at random, tried to force herself to read, but the lines of type blurred, melted into single black bars stretching aross the page. Her hands were shaking so badly that she couldn't support the weight, couldn't hold the book upright. But she kept trying.

And then she broke.

Crying out, in a spasm of strength and frustration, she slammed the volume shut and hurled it blindly across the room.

It hit the mirror over her dressing table. The glass seemed to explode in movielike slow motion, spraying across the table and floor. Hair dryer, perfume bottles, nail-polish bottles, bits of jewelry scattered, floated through space, Sir off the bed and headed for the hallway . . .

She untangled herself from the bedclothes, ripping a button from her pajama top, and ran into the bath-room. In the brightness of the tube of light over the sink she stood gagging, fighting it off, then knelt over the toilet bowl. The tile was cold and hard under her knees. She felt the sting of a piece of glass in the sole of her foot. Then the unstoppable surge in her belly, and she vomited, her slender back arching, knuckles white on the cold porcelain.

Finally she sighed, exhausted, slumped against the toilet. Sitting on the bathroom floor she caught a glimpse of herself in the full-length mirror next to the scale.

The color had drained from her dark complexion, some strands of gray in the thick black hair plastered across her forehead caught her eye, she rubbed her tilted nose and swallowed back the sourness, blinked at the reflection of herself stripped of defenses, so easily hurt, so cornered just now.

Her mind wandered sluggishly. She'd never looked

at herself in the moments after making love, as the orgasm lingered and slowly faded, but she thought she must look then much as she did now. Mottled and pale and so terribly vulnerable.

She wiped her face on a towel and flushed the toilet.

In the living room the light of the night was filtering through the huge window facing the garden. The leafless trees were turning to ice in the rain. She went to the door leading to the garden, flung it open, and flipped the switch on the outdoor lights.

Snow was piled on the remains of the geraniums in the big terra-cotta pots. The white metal furniture had become a row of hulking, round mounds of snow.

Standing in the doorway, wearing only her pajama top, she felt the cold wind harden her nipples beneath the cotton. She wiped her eyes, sniffled. She had to get through the night and she had to be a big girl. She had to pull up her socks, the way her father used to tell her. *No more, Natalie. Cry yourself out and throw up and scare hell out of Sir, but get past it. Life won't stop for you. You've got to hang on, so get it out of your system now. The hell with all of them—MacPherson, D'Allessandro, Bradley Nichols . . . just move on, get it together and move on. . . .*

Chapter Nineteen

Somehow she managed to get through the night without Valium or even a sleeping pill, but she was exhausted once the day began. Sir looked at her reproachfully and she had to clean up the mess in the bedroom. And she couldn't get the face of poor dead Bradley Nichols out of her mind. He'd been there most of the night, like a haunting dream, along with her memories of how he'd seemed Saturday night. Nervy, shy, afraid, sad, lonely, yearning . . . She could still hear the things he'd said, his description of his own life, the story about the roommate she'd decided was in fact he. Maybe she'd been wrong after all.

Once she'd gotten to work, she put in a call to MacPherson first thing, not altogether sure what she was going to tell him but knowing that tell him something she must. Of course he wasn't there and she left a message. He should return her call as soon as possible, it was urgent.

Jay was taking a morning at home so she didn't have to put up with his expected critique of her performance with the odious Betty on the television pyre the night before. Lisa hadn't seen it since she was still at the office, but her boyfriend had passed judgment: "Said you were smashing and made a fool of the silly cow."

She took a cab down Fifth Avenue, got off at Tenth Street, and found Dr. Dummond pacing the newly shoveled sidewalk in front of the address he'd given her. It was a narrow brownstone with an unobtrusive nameplate by the shiny black-painted door a few steps below street level. Elegant neighborhood, chic at the Topside of the Village. He watched her coming toward him.

"Mrs. Rader? Dr. Goldstein gave me a very accurate description. I'm Alex Drummond." He was stocky, fifty or so, in a black overcoat with a velvet collar, his gray hair combed straight back from his forehead, rimless spectacles, and a slight pink flush. He had a bulbous nose that struck her as a clownish comment on the otherwise somber, grayish presentation. The nose gave him the edge of a Dickensian creation. He shook her hand, squared his shoulders, jammed his hands into the pockets of his coat, pulling it tight across his solid girth. It was hard to picture him as a friend of Lew's. Drummond had the look of a banker, a stuffy lawyer. But then, Lew hadn't recommended him as a chum, but as a good doctor.

Now he took her arm and steered her away from his office. "The painters," he said. "It's insufferable in there. Let's just take a walk. The exercise will do me good. If you don't mind . . ."

"You're the doctor," she said.

"So I am." He blinked, his eyes given a roundness by the glass discs, shining darkly through the glass. He kept his mouth clamped in a thin, determined line. Like a father who spent his days counseling endless numbers of his children, accustomed to dealing with their countless and unpredictable problems. He walked neither fast nor slow, but merely determinedly. "Now, Mrs. Rader, Dr. Goldstein has told me only that you've been under a good deal of strain lately, that—to be absolutely blunt—you may need some calming down, some reassurance, before we even contemplate anything beyond that. This is not the sort of thing I would normally embark upon, but Dr. Goldstein has not inconsiderable persuasive powers. Perhaps, if you could give me some idea of what it is that's troubling you . . ."

She laughed nervously, her mind racing, watching Drummond from the corner of her eye, thinking about the possibility that MacPherson might even now be returning her call, seeing the face of Bradley Nichols in the blank windows of the stately brownstones they passed. Then she let herself go, starting with the sight of the man with the gun and rushing at breakneck speed through the rest of the story until she reached Saturday evening, coming home from Lulu's. She stopped abruptly, out of breath.

"Go on, Mrs. Rader. What then? Sergeant Mac-Pherson spent much of the day with you, you enjoyed yourself, you became the proud owner of a Christmas tree . . . you spent the evening at this Lulu's—and now you seem unable to continue with your story. Why is that, I wonder?" His voice droned, a monotone, as he marched on. They were rounding a corner, a dark church brooded in the cold, rising wind.

"It's nothing," she said. The chill stung her cheeks. She fumbled in her mind, pushing what had happened with Bradley Nichols back into the darkness. Shame, frustration, disgust at her own reactions: what difference did it make? "Something upsetting happened the next day. . . ." She was having trouble winding the key that would make her talk.

"Yes. Upsetting! I can see that, Mrs. Rader." He stopped at the curb, a red light. Snow was piled in darkly crusted mounds beside them.

"What can you see?"

"I can see that you're crying."

"Oh, Christ," she said.

They walked toward Washington Square. The arch seemed to be holding up the low gray clouds. The trees were black and tortured, like Giacometti sculptures.

"Let's rest a moment," he said, led her to a bench. The drug dealers were clustered together discussing the state of the economy, ignoring them as unlikely consumers.

She sat down, took a bedraggled tissue from her pocket and blotted away the tears.

"What happened Sunday?"

"Look, I'm just being foolish—"

"I doubt that, Mrs. Rader."

"I was upset when I was told by a cop investigating MacPherson that he has a habit of combining business with pleasure when it comes to women involved in cases he's working on. . . . Oh, please, there's no point in going on about this, Doctor, it's so silly." She sniffed. "And humiliating—"

"You found this fact about MacPherson distressing." He looked off across the expanse of snow, at the traffic and the quiet buildings facing the square. "Because you had—what? Begun to grow fond of this man? Because he had been nice to you? Bought you a Christmas tree and made you an omelet?"

"You think I'm an absurd neurotic woman, don't bother to say it—"

"Hardly, Mrs. Rader. That's not what I think at all." She saw him slowly shaking his head.

"What do you think, then?"

"I don't have any kind of clinical opinion, obviously. I'm reacting as an observer, not a doctor. And I think this—you are very tense for the perfectly sound reason that you have in fact been under a good deal of stress. Anyone, Mrs. Rader, would be showing signs of wear and tear at this point. Couple that with the fact that you found Sergeant MacPherson an intelligent, appealing person who obviously reacted the same way to you . . . and that you then discovered that he might not be quite what he seemed—what could be more normal than some tears? Neurosis is hardly indicated, Mrs. Rader." Finally, the firm mouth smiled, ever so slightly, and she let herself slump back on the bench. "But," he said slowly, "I have the feeling there is still more to the story. Am I right, perhaps?" His face was reddening in the chill wind.

"The man with the gun," she said, bit her lip, stopped.

"Yes? The man with the gun?"

"He killed someone else. Last night . . . his roommate."

"I don't understand." He blinked, curious. "I thought this man was anonymous, unknown. How could you know he killed someone besides this woman, this Quirk woman?"

"Well, I suppose I'm the only one who knows it's the same man—"

"Good heavens!" It was the first sign of emotion he'd shown, and she smiled involuntarily. "You've lost me, Mrs. Rader. If I may ask, how can you know such a thing? You say you never saw this mysterious man's face, so how . . ." He offered a shrug of incomprehension.

"Look, take my word for it, Dr. Drummond, I *know*. The fact is, I met the man he killed last night . . . his roommate. This roommate, Bradley Nichols, came to me—"

"This murder, this is the one I saw mentioned on the news last night? Is that what you're talking about?"

"Yes, yes." She nodded impatiently.

"But you're the only one who knows about the roommate, the killer? That he's the same man?"

"Yes. I've got a call in to MacPherson."

Dr. Drummond looked at his watch. She remembered his lecture. He stood up. "Mrs. Rader, let me tell you that in the first place, I feel that you're holding up very well, considering the circumstances. You're doing just fine. I wouldn't even prescribe a Valium." They were walking across the packed snow toward the arch and Fifth Avenue. "But I would very much like to stay in touch with you over the next few days. Believe me, you're not cracking up, not overreacting. You're handling the whole thing with considerable grace . . . but do check in with me if you have a moment's unease, if you'd like to talk about any of this." He looked at his watch again. "Now I have to go be terribly authoritative for my students." He allowed himself another small smile. "Let me give you a number where you can call other than the office. The painters informed me they'll be a few more days. It's incredible." He wrote his number on a small notepad, using a thin gold pencil. "Don't lose this. And please stay in touch." He was holding the door of a cab for her when he said, "Don't worry about the business with MacPherson. I'm sure it will resolve itself. Goodbye, Mrs. Rader."

She looked back as the cab pulled away and he was standing in the snow watching her. His restraint and austerity, like a stage uncle, had reassured her, made her realize there was sanity out there after all. She was already looking forward to talking with him again.

When she got back to the office she put in another call to MacPherson and left the same message. She then tried to work on a variety of projects, fielded a couple of calls from business pals teasing her about her television appearance.

In mid-afternoon MacPherson called. He didn't sound like himself. His voice was tight, almost as if he was angry with her, someone, the world.

"I've got to see you," she said. "I've got to talk to you about this Bradley Nichols murder . . . are you there?"

"What about it?" he asked pettishly.

"He came to my apartment the other night. He said it was his roommate who threw the gun away, the man I saw . . . he said his roommate has been following me. . . . Say something!"

"We know all this already, Natalie."

"What are you saying? What do you mean? How—"

"We know he came to see you." He paused.

She felt herself beginning to hyperventilate, heart pounding.

"We know everything about Saturday night, Natalie."

Chapter Twenty

"This is a little tricky, Natalie."

MacPherson's office was grim, long ago painted shades of pale green and battleship gray, so long ago that the grimy overlay had blurred them to something like a single unhappy color that reeked of desperation and sorry midnights. It was cop institutional, as far as she could tell from the movies she'd seen, and its effect made her slightly nauseated. Inexplicably, a plastic Christmas tree a foot high sat on one corner of his desk, a cynical reminder of the season out there in the other world. A coffeepot sat on a bookcase heavy-laden with files, manuals, odds and ends. There were two cups, one with a rainbow decal, the other with the heart logo proclaiming the owner's undying love of New York. The coffee standing in the former looked like paint thinner. MacPherson ushered her into a straight-backed chair and sat down behind his desk. "Tricky," he repeated. He looked at his surroundings. "No wonder I liked looking at your office. Cops' offices have to look like this, by the way. Regulation. Crazy world but . . . You don't look so good, Natalie. Water? Coffee?"

She shook her head. "I resent the way you handled our telephone conversation just now. You're back to treating me as if I'm the enemy—"

"Not true," he said. "I treat you inconsistently and that's because I personally want to think of you as a woman I like very much. But professionally you're a situation, not a person. I keep forgetting that because you're very appealing and very vulnerable—and if I lose my objectivity about you, I'm not going to do you much good as a cop." He took a deep breath while she remembered all the things D'Allessandro had said. "So I treat you inconsistently. Sue me."

"But you scared me on the phone." She crossed her legs and clasped her hands tightly in her lap. She had kept her coat on. She couldn't seem to get warm.

"If that scared you, I suggest you fasten your seatbelt. You ain't seen nothin' yet."

"Stop saying things like that—"

"Now listen to me!" MacPherson leaned forward across the desk and gave her a meat-eating, predatory look. He seemed even more distant than usual and she was startled by the firecracker explosion of his voice. "Somebody's got to scare you because you sure as hell aren't taking this thing seriously—you haven't treated it seriously since the day you saw the guy with that fucking gun!" He swallowed and threw himself back in the chair and scowled at her. "I've had to find out everything through other people and I wonder, what's going on here? Don't you give a damn or what? Haven't enough weird things happened to you? Christ, you baffle me. You really do—"

"The situation baffles you," she corrected him. The impact of his anger left her breathless.

"Why don't you stop being a smartass and explain to me why this guy visiting you Saturday night wasn't worth telling me about? Jesus, Natalie, you knew the gun had been used to commit a murder and this guy told you whose gun it was! That makes his goddamn roommate a very likely murder suspect—and you don't tell me a thing! That's a crime, for Christ's sake, do you understand that? Do you understand anything at all?" He shook his head angrily and lit a cigarette from his case.

"I'm sorry," she said quietly, watching her hands squirming in her lap. "I have taken it seriously . . . but I've been trying to keep it under control. I didn't want to become any more frightened than I already was . . . I didn't want to lose my ability to function. I'd rather be dead." She felt as if she were dropping the words like coins into a wishing well, hoping he would understand.

"Well, you may be closer than you think!" Shouting—MacPherson finally sighed down to the bottoms of his Guccis and nodded. "Okay. I won't send you up the river this time. But you've got to pay attention to me—"

"I am, please believe me. But I've got to ask you one important question—how do you know anything about the man Saturday night?"

"Look, let me sort of work my way around this one in my own fumbling fashion. And this is not a story you're going to like much, Natalie, but listen closely. Are you ready?"

She stuck out her lower lip, she felt herself doing it, an involuntary gesture of determination from her childhood. "Yes."

"The man who was murdered, the thing you saw on television, was Bradley Nichols. TV-time salesman. Nice, quiet guy according to his neighbors. And he had a roommate, a guy named Barry Hughes. Not around much, kind of a night person . . . well, we've found out quite a lot about Barry. I figure it was Barry himself who called us and told us we might find something of interest in the loft—used a funny accent, sort of heavy Viennese, according to the officer who took the call. Real joker, Barry. Anyway, we went to the loft and it wasn't a pretty sight and I'm going to tell you about it because it's important that you know, that you get the point. . . ."

"I saw you on television," she said. "You said it was rage. . . ."

"Rage is an understatement. Bradley Nichols looked like the pieces to a jigsaw puzzle—"

"Oh God, no!" It hit her like an electric charge and she jerked away, turning her head. She saw his face in the flash of the hallway, heard his voice with the lights of the Christmas tree beside him, saw him roll over beside her, remembered the heat of her own desire. . . .

"Bradley was all over that loft. I've seen a lot of godawful messes but I've never seen anything like this." His voice droned on insistently. "If the *Post* gets hold of it they're gonna scare the shit out of half this city. It was a wildly, insanely sexual crime. Bits and pieces of this guy's apparatus everywhere, a testicle dropped in a shot glass. Nice homey touches. The tip of his penis in an ashtray . . . I mean, not nice—"

"Please stop, please, please, just stop—I'm going to be sick—"

"All right. But you do get the point, don't you, Natalie? This is serious—has that sunk in?"

She nodded.

"Barry Hughes did it, Natalie. We've got more bloody handprints and fingerprints than we know what to do with. So, let me tell you a bit about Barry Hughes. He's an actor—not just a guy who calls himself an actor, but an actor-actor. He's done some commercials, some soaps, some off-Broadway and off-off. Actors Equity and the Screen Actors Guild provided us with some information. And we've spoken with his parents. They live up in Buffalo, they're on their way down here now—poor people, poor helpless people with a son who's a homicidal maniac. Barry has been something less than a model citizen, it seems, for quite some time.

"He did two stretches in mental institutions but responded well to treatment. He 'bothered' women a few times and got into some small-time trouble, but rape wasn't involved—he just exposed himself to women in movie theaters, suggested they might like a ride on the old joy stick, suggestions the ladies involved had the good sense to decline. Which brings us to the movies, a very big thing in Barry's life. A real movie freak. Constantly role playing based on his favorite old movies, used to drive people crazy, he'd stay in character for days, almost completely blurring the line between the movies and reality." He stubbed out his cigarette and peered warily into the coffee cup with the rainbow. "Jesus, there's something growing in here. Anyway, we got most of this from the parents."

He leaned back again, lit another cigarette, and picked up a tiny computer game from the table in front of him. He stared at it, pushing buttons, watching something happen.

"What's that?"

"Baseball game. Takes a lot of concentration. Quiets my nerves when I'm about to get upset. Trick I learned from my father. He used to be a cop, too. Everything about this case makes me nervous—"

"You still haven't told me how you knew about Saturday night."

"We're coming to that and that's where it's going to get a little tricky. You're going to have to trust me, realize I'm just doing my job. Can you do that?"

"What do you want me to say? I'll try? Okay, I'll try."

"The late Bradley Nichols kept a diary, Natalie, and we found it. All splattered with blood. A mess. But Bradley was a very determined diarist, he got it all down on paper, his whole life. He treated the diary like a close friend, told it everything that mattered to him, and I suppose that's what a diary's for. He confided all his fears about Barry, his getting into the cocaine scene and some of the sleazeballs he dealt with—he even mentions Alicia Quirk, which is good for us. He writes about the sexual stuff Barry found so intriguing. You get a picture of one guy, Bradley, liking another guy, Barry, but finding out so much crud about him that it scares him . . . *and Bradley was scared of Barry*. He was scared of Barry's friends, scared that Barry was into something he shouldn't know so much about—which made him scared of Barry and scared for Barry. And he writes about how Barry seems to be playing his life like a movie for days at a time. So one day Bradley goes out and follows Barry and it's the day Barry kills Quirk, only Bradley doesn't know that. And he's following Barry when Barry throws the gun away—it's all in the diary." MacPherson stood up, went and shook the coffeepot. "If I faint," he said, "tell them I was drinking coffee reheated for the third time, okay?" He flashed a quick, cold smile, then went to stand beside her, holding his newly filled cup. With his other hand he patted her shoulder.

"Was I in the diary? Is that how you knew?"

"All right, back to the diary," he said. He went to the single window, stared at it. "Hmmm. They've painted over my view of the alley and the garbage cans. I wonder when they did that to my window. Well," he shrugged, "maybe the paint is better than the view. The diary. Bradley wrote down how Barry and he had read the piece in Garfein's column. And how he found one of Barry's notepads with the name *Natalie Rader* printed hundreds of times, over and over, the pencil point tearing through the paper. . . ."

He settled back down behind the desk.

"Then we come to Saturday night. He tells us how he went to your house, how he managed to get inside, how foolish he felt unplugging lamps and playing with the dog. He tells us how sorry he was that he had to frighten you, how kind you were once he got to tell you his story . . . and he tells us what happened then, how the two of you made love on the floor." He self-consciously sipped the coffee, set it down, and tapped his fingers on the desktop.

"We didn't make love. . . ." She barely heard her own voice.

"That's none of my business, one way or the other. I'm telling you what's in the diary. For whatever it's worth to you, he wrote about you and your body and the way you handled the situation in a very poetic turn of phrase. Almost like a schoolboy with his first mad crush. Maybe it was his fantasy—you're the only one who knows now. Anyway . . . it's all very sad, really." He caught her eye. "In any case, onward and upward. Sunday he goes on writing about how he's planning to confront Barry with the whole issue, use 'shock tactics' and really scare him back into 'the real world,' 'get him to straighten out and act like a human being tonight.'" He picked up the baseball game again, watching the little lights flashing as if the tiny electrical blips were running amok. "Trying to straighten old Barry out was, I think we can all agree, his big mistake. Barry apparently didn't take kindly to the idea."

He slid open a desk drawer and for a moment she didn't realize what he'd taken out. A book, splotched with what looked like coffee stains, pages stuck together. The diary.

He flipped it open. "Listen to this last entry. 'If Barry thinks life is a movie, I'll play Cagney and read him the riot act! The doctors have already played Pat

O'Brien with him and it sure didn't work.'" He gently closed the bloody book.

"Please believe me, we didn't make love."

He shrugged.

"All right," she flared up, "believe what you want. What happens now?"

"Let me tell you how I see all this. Do you mind?"

"I wish to God you would—"

"Barry has gone all the way over into fantasy now. He's created some movie that's just not listed, it's playing only in his mind. Barry is the star. I think it was reading Bradley's diary that did it to him, I think he read the diary before Bradley ever got to deliver his get-tough speech—I think the diary dictated what Barry did to Bradley. I'd be willing to bet that Barry was sniffing around you, watching you, maybe even bumping into you on the street or something, trying to get up his nerve to tell you that it was okay, the gun incident didn't involve you—just a hunch. He had a real reason to kill Quirk—Quirk had probably threatened him over one thing or another. God knows, it doesn't really matter. Because then Barry read the diary. The problem was, I think he'd been seeing you as his own kind of romantic co-star, a damsel in distress; he was what threatened you and he could also save you—he was creating a relationship between him and you, trying to gird himself up to doing something about it. Like rescuing you by telling you you had nothing to worry about . . . and then he had to read the damn diary.

"And even then, if Bradley hadn't described having sex with you . . . well, he might have gotten out of it

231

alive. But he described it in such lovely, loving detail, that Barry couldn't take it. . . . Hell, Natalie, I know the feeling of jealousy it aroused in me, something I just couldn't help—I mean, this guy writes that he's been intimate with you and I haven't and a man thinks, why him? In this case, Barry thought a good deal more than *why him?* Barry read it, went off the deep end, and wound up turning Bradley's genitals into chow mein. It's the only explanation I can come up with for the intensity of the sexual vengeance in the murder. Make any sense to you?"

She huddled on the chair, clasping her arms around herself. "I don't know. It sounds like we're caught in Barry's movie."

"Precisely. We *are.* We've been locked into his movie ever since he saw you watching him throw the gun away. He's been doing whatever he's wanted to do for some time now—but we know we're in the movie now, which is something. And we've got a pretty good idea of the rest of the plot." He opened a folder on his desk, consulted some notes.

"What happens now?" She felt as if her entire life had passed from her hands. She was helpless. She trembled inside her coat and thought about Bradley, how he'd died.

"We've got to believe he's going to come looking for you. Think of it as one hell of a scary movie. He's living in it, he's going to play it out, he's got to complete the last reel. It's not so hard to figure it out now—now that we're finally in the movie, too. What is he bound inevitably to do? He killed Bradley with a carving knife, we've got

232

him on that, we could pin Quirk to him as well, and we're pretty sure he's slipped over into pure fantasy. Natalie, he has in essence become the carving knife, the light shining on the blade as he raises it—it's *Psycho*, it's a scene we've all watched a thousand times . . . and he's going to come after you. In his mind, you betrayed him on the rug with Bradley. He wants you, Natalie— look at his history—and I'd bet the farm he wants you right where his old roommate had you, on your living- room carpet . . . and then, it's goodbye Natalie. . . ."

"The ladies' room," she whispered. "I'm going to be sick."

He waited outside the door so she wouldn't be in- terrupted.

Chapter Twenty-one

An hour later Natalie, following MacPherson's instructions, was back in her own office, having made no attempt to seek cover. "We've got to assume that he's watching you all the time, even now, when you leave my office," MacPherson had told her. "Go back to your office. We want him to see you go into that building. We want him to feel comfortable, secure, we want him to know that we're all acting out his script. I'll be at your office late this afternoon. Just hang on, Natalie. We're going to get you out of this, no muss, no fuss."

Now she waited in her office, too distracted to work, snapping at Jay because she didn't know how much to tell him. The scenario MacPherson had laid on her had certainly worked: after being sick in the bathroom down the hall from his office, she'd emerged pale, shaky, and haunted by the images she'd heard about in his dreary office. Things hadn't improved as the afternoon lost its light and the city came ablaze. She stood at the window listening to her own shallow breathing, waiting for MacPherson.

He finally arrived at five o'clock. He had Tony Rader with him and he commandeered her office. Danmeier appeared in the doorway wondering what was going on. MacPherson frowned, then told him to come in and close the door. He briefly filled in Danmeier and Tony on the events of the day, stressing the danger he believed was threatening Natalie.

"Now," he said, "here's what's going down, as they say on all my favorite cop shows. Natalie, you're not going home this evening. We now begin waiting for Barry Hughes to come after you. It won't take long—he's a crazy, anxious guy. The bloodlust is up. We had a policewoman go to your home and bring out an over-night bag of your things, toiletries, some underthings, jeans, so on. It's all in an unmarked police car right now, a block from here—we're taking you out through the basement, you're coming out one block north and there's no way in the world he can spot it. In the meantime a policewoman, Officer Grace Farraday, will be arriving here any moment. When she leaves she will be Natalie Rader—she's your size, she'll be wearing your black coat, she'll have a black wig . . . and she'll leave with Mr. Danmeier, just to further declare her identity. She's going to walk home, which will make it easy for Barry to follow her, she'll follow your kind of routine, stop at the cheese place, pick up some pasta, and arrive at your apartment. And then she'll wait. Not alone, however. I'll be waiting with her—I'm going in over the fence into your courtyard and in the back door. So far as the watcher goes, he'll think she's in there alone." He'd been ticking off points on his fingers and looked up at last. "Everybody got that?"

"What about me?" Natalie asked.

"That's where Tony comes in. He says he can't think of a better place than his aunt's house out on Staten Island. He's staying here in town. His aunt is visiting Atlantic City with her girl friends and you'll have the house to yourself."

Tony laughed. "You can take care of the cats, Tiger. Just make yourself at home. How does that sound?"

She nodded numbly. "God, it sounds wonderful—like a vacation." She summoned a smile. "Really, it sounds fine. I like that house."

"All right, then," MacPherson said. "You can just relax and get some rest. I've already alerted the cops on the island. They'll come by and check on you, make sure everything is all right."

"How do I get there?"

"We'll drive you out once we get you to the car."

"Look, could I go on the ferry? I mean, would that be all right? I'd just like to be alone. . . ."

"It's okay with me," MacPherson said. He was looking at his watch. "Once Farraday is here, we'll get her decked out as you, wait for her to get settled at your place, then get you on your way." He was talking mostly to himself. The buzzer sounded on Natalie's desk.

"There's an Officer Farraday here, Natalie."

"Have her come into my office, Lisa."

Farraday did in fact turn out to be a reasonably good duplicate. Natalie wished her luck and the policewoman laughed. "I'm practically an arsenal," she said. "I feel sorry for the guy who messes with me. Now, let me get into my new hairdo and get your coat."

MacPherson followed Farraday into another office and Tony went along with Danmeier for a quick drink. Things were moving quickly but Natalie knew she couldn't just disappear without leaving a trace. She dialed Lew's number and got the answering machine. She started to leave a message but heard the telephone being picked up.

"Natalie? Are you there?"

"Yes. I'm so glad to hear you, Lew."

"What's the matter? You sound funny."

"A lot has happened and I feel funny. MacPherson has got a line on the man with the gun. His name is Barry Hughes and he killed his roommate yesterday, a guy named Brad Nichols—"

"Sure, sure, I heard about it on television—he's the gun thrower, this Barry?"

"Yes. They're setting a trap for him. A policewoman posing as me is going to be at my place tonight—"

"Where are you, Nat?"

"At the office. MacPherson is here. They're taking me out to Tony's aunt's house on Staten Island tonight. I'm going to stay there until it's over—he doesn't think it'll be long. I can't talk more now, but I wanted you to know where I'd be." She gave him the telephone number on Staten Island.

"Look, do you want me to come out with you? Is there anything I can do?"

"No, really, I'll be fine. There's no way he could find

me out there, and the police are turning my place into an armed camp."

"Will you call me once you get settled?"

"Sure I will. And by the way, I saw Dr. Drummond today. I liked him a lot. He wants me to stay in close touch, gave me his private number."

"Good, that's terrific. I told you he was a good guy. Well, you'd better get going. Don't forget—call me when you get there. Promise?"

"Sure."

"Everything's going to be all right, kid."

She dug through her purse until she found the piece of notepaper Drummond had given her. She called his direct number and recognized his voice.

"It's Natalie Rader," she said. She was out of breath.

"Yes, Mrs. Rader. You sound upset. Is everything all right?"

"Well, in a manner of speaking. The police have decided they want me out of the way until they can catch this guy—"

"The killer of the man you told me about this morning?"

"Right. I thought you might try to get hold of me and nobody would tell you where I was. I'm going to my former husband's aunt's house on Staten Island. I'll give you a call when I'm back—"

"I take it they think they're on the killer's trail?"

"Yes. They don't think it will be long until it's all over."

"Well, I'm sure they're right, Mrs. Rader. They know what they're doing. Enjoy your stay on the Island.

It's very peaceful out there. And whatever you do, don't worry. Every nightmare comes to an end. Why don't you give me a number and I'll check on you tomorrow?"

She gave him the number and he told her once again that he was sure the ordeal was just about over. "It's all very exciting, isn't it? In a bizarre way, of course."

"As MacPherson says. It's a movie."

"Well, just relax. I'll give you a call tomorrow."

She hung up the telephone and sighed, sank back in her chair. The two psychiatrists had made her feel immeasurably better.

Now she had only to keep herself tightly under control. She was trying to wait patiently, and it was more of a job than she'd anticipated. When Farraday got to the apartment, the officer had thought she'd been followed. Once inside, she'd called MacPherson at the agency. Time had slowly ticked away while Natalie's street was scanned by a plainclothesman . . . but it had been a false alarm. By then MacPherson was hungry and decided to send out for sandwiches for Tony, Natalie, and himself. But she hardly tasted the food, tuned out of the sparse conversation, spoke briefly with Farraday, who called in hoping to catch them, wondering where the dog food was. Finally it was time to go.

The wind coming off the water was bone chilling. Foghorns groaned and the commuters shuffled anxiously, collars turned up, backs to the cold, waiting to board the ferry. The lights of Manhattan looked warm and cheery behind them and Natalie felt like a little girl, escaping from her cares and worries across the water to the old castle. She felt slightly light-headed, not quite herself. It was the speed of events. And she hadn't eaten anything since breakfast.

MacPherson stomped his feet, banged his hands together. He was quiet and she knew he was thinking past Natalie to what lay ahead. It was Barry Hughes on his mind, not Natalie Rader. She felt as if she had almost faded into the past for him. She remembered the Christmas tree and D'Allessandro, wondered if MacPherson believed her about Saturday night. . . . Her head was beginning to ache. Snow blew like sand across the crusted surface of the water. It was time for the ferry to go. MacPherson grabbed her arm, told her once again that she shouldn't worry, that it was all going to be fine, that she was handling it like a trooper. She nodded, not really listening, not really caring what he was saying. Everybody seemed to be saying the same thing anyway. . . .

She sat alone in the drafty cabin, listening to the chatter of her fellow travelers, hearing the creaking of the ferry and feeling the throb of the engines, half-dozing, letting her body rock to the movement all around her. It had been years since she'd last ridden the ferry but it might have been yesterday. The ride wasn't one of the things that changed.

MacPherson had told her to give a cop named Patterson a call when the ferry docked and he'd run her out to the house, but when she arrived he was waiting for her. MacPherson had called ahead. Patterson carried her bag and she settled into the darkness for the quick ride. She was alone and it felt so wonderful, so incredibly unencumbered and safe. Huddled in the back of the police car, feeling the wheels search out a path in the rutted snow, she experienced one of those moments that came sporadically—one of those moments when she wondered what it would be like to kiss it all goodbye, find a little town upstate or in the Berkshires and open a bookshop and serve tea and coffee and become the town's mysterious spinster. . . . Not exactly an original fantasy, but soothing and better than dreaming of being a disco queen. She was smiling tiredly when the car slushed to a halt at the foot of the long brick walk that led to the dim shape of the old house. She checked her pocket for the key Tony had given her, thanked Patterson, slung her bag over her shoulder, and pushed on up the snowy walk down which Tony had scraped a path barely as wide as the shovel. It was funny, but looking up at the house brooding in the moonlight filtering through the low, heavy cloud layer, she felt as if she were coming home.

The house really was a bit of a Victorian gingerbread monstrosity, more so inside than out. It had been in the Rader family forever, and from the looks of it none of the generations of tenants had ever thrown away anything. It was a world of doilies, antique firescreens before the fireplaces, shawls draped over rickety occasional tables, japanned boxes and bric-a-brac and sheet music from the twenties propped up on the piano, which Auntie Margaret still insisted she played to calm her nerves. Presumably when she wasn't off appreciating John Davidson in Atlantic City. Even the television verged on the prehistoric, an Admiral with rounded corners on the screen. Padded rocking chairs, fringed carpets and lampshades. The firewood in the boot was dry and she laid a fire, built a pile of kindling beneath it, and in no time there was a warm glow radiating from the hearth.

The kitchen was huge. The vast facade of cupboard doors hid endless stacks of dishes, glasses, baking supplies. She found the tea and made a pot, toasted some bread, scrambled a couple of eggs, and finally settled herself in front of the fire. The wind whispered at the windows, and over the second cup of tea she felt the tension draining away from her neck and shoulders, felt her body and psyche letting go.

Her mind turned not to what was going on in New York, at her apartment, where the policewoman and MacPherson waited for the killer, but back, willy-nilly, to her parents, to happy times she had treasured because of their scarcity. She remembered sitting much like this at a lodge one winter, the fire crackling, her parents at ease with each other. Rare, wonderful, an image of what she had wanted her marriage to be. She shook her head, watching the flames lick at the old bricks. A girl's dreams . . .

The telephone rang and for a moment she couldn't quite remember where she was. She groggily found it on a special little table with feet like claws. It was Lew.

"Hey, you didn't call me," he said. "Are you all safe and sound?"

"Safer than you can imagine. It's like being in another century, Lew. I made a fire and some tea and eggs and fell asleep in a rocking chair. It's great."

"Dammit, I wish I'd insisted on coming out with you. Just for the night. I'm going to be thinking about you out there—I could still drive out, Natalie. I'd like to—"

"No, really, Lew. I'm fine. I'm going right to bed and I've got a Robert Benchley I saw in a bookcase picked out for reading myself to sleep—it really is a time machine. I'm fine. Don't worry."

He grudgingly accepted defeat. "But be sure to keep a radio or the TV on, for company. And leave some lights on. I don't want you getting scared out there all by yourself. The house sounds like something out of Mary Roberts Rinehart—"

"It is, it is, and I love it. And there's a huge graveyard next door! Can you believe it?"

"Christ, I wish you hadn't told me." He paused for a moment. "Well, I guess I'll let you go to bed. And, Nat, be safe out there. You're very special."

"Good night, Lewis," she said softly and slowly replaced the receiver.

She was putting the kitchen in order, rinsing off her dishes and putting the milk back into the refrigerator, when a stray thought crossed her mind.

The cats.

Where were the cats?

Tony had specifically said something to her about his aunt's cats. But she hadn't seen a cat since she'd gotten there. Still, there in a corner of the kitchen, on the floor, was a large saucer of milk and beside it a bowl of cat food.

Well, Aunt Margaret must have decided to drop them off with a friend. What else, after all?

She took a long hot bath in a bathroom roughly the size of her own kitchen. She was reading the Benchley when she heard something. At first she thought it was the wind whining outside. But it persisted, the same sound again and again.

Slowly it seemed to clarify itself in her mind.

A cat meowing.

But far away. A faint sound. Coming again and again.

She lay in the steaming water, motionless, listening. Was it a cat? One that had been left behind? But then the wind would whine and obliterate the meowing and when it was still again she couldn't hear the cat. . . .

"Christ," she said aloud, splashing noisily as she stood up and grabbed a towel. "He's on his own tonight," she muttered. Poking through the house in the middle of the night waiting to be scared half to death by a cat jumping from the darkness was way too much like a movie. *Forget it, Natalie*. Bag it, as Julie would have said.

She crawled into the old four-poster, snuggling down under a heavy comforter with the window opened a couple of inches to the night. The inevitable noises an old house made on a windy night kept her half-awake for an hour but she finally drifted off, thinking somewhat defeatedly about Dan MacPherson. . . .

She wasn't sure what time it was when she opened her eyes and lay listening again.

She had heard a door closing, clicking into place.

Her heart was racing.

What was she afraid of?

But surely she had heard among the creaks and groans of the house . . . the closing of a door.

Or had it been a dream?

Chapter Twenty-two

From the kitchen window above the sink Natalie could look out through the scrawny naked branches of the trees in the sloping backyard and see the towers of Manhattan across the water. Low, soft gray clouds scudded across the skyline, and there was fog rising off the water, mist spitting against the window. Manhattan seemed more a mirage than the core of the city: it came and went and the fog seemed almost palpable.

The coffee was finished perking and she poured herself a mug and sipped it carefully, listening to the weather report on the radio, remembering the sound of the cat in the night, the closing of the door. She'd finally drifted off; upon waking the night's fears had receded like misshapen giants straggling back to the black openings of their caves. It was odd how vulnerable one became when the darkness closed in and how carefree even the grayest daylight could make one feel. All she'd heard were some house noises that went on day and night—the kind you only heard in the stillness, the darkness, when your senses were sharpened.

A major winter storm, bigger than the one of the preceding weekend, was on its way, and the weatherman said he expected flurries to begin by noon, turning to full blizzard conditions by mid-afternoon. She was glad to be where she was. The house would be magical with a heavy snowfall outside, like something from a fairy tale.

She poured another cup of coffee and sat on a high stool by the kitchen telephone. She had wakened thinking of MacPherson, wanting to hear his voice, wondering what had happened at her apartment during the night—but for some obscure reasons of self-discipline she had forced herself to wait until she was coffee fortified to call MacPherson's office. It turned out he had come to work directly from her place and he sounded tired, edgy when she was put through. She had almost decided to confront him on the D'Allessandro issue, but no, this wasn't the time.

"No, nothing, he didn't show." She heard him blow his nose. "I tore my pants getting into your backyard, I couldn't sleep at all, and somewhere along the line I've picked up a cold." He sneezed as if to prove his point.

"How's Officer Farraday?"

"Slept like a log. Woman hasn't got a nerve in her body."

"So what happens now?"

"She left the house and went to your office. She'll come home again tonight. We'll wait. I know he's watching, waiting, wondering what to do. Maybe tonight will be the night. How is it out there, Natalie? Snowing yet?"

"Misting. Cozy. I'm fine."

"Well, just relax, sit tight. I can't think of anyone who could use a vacation better than you. This'll be over soon." He was beginning to sound like the needle was stuck, but, she supposed, when you didn't have anything to report, you just didn't. In any case, he didn't sound angry with her, which was something.

She called Julie at her office and told her what was going on. "Well," Julie said, "I won't have you staying out there all by yourself. I'm coming out tonight. Period. End of report."

"Don't be ridiculous," Natalie said, a small hope at the back of her mind. "There's a huge storm coming. It wouldn't be worth the effort. You'd just have to go back in the morning—"

"Not if we're snowed in." Julie cackled triumphantly. "The perfect excuse. I'll be there tonight, one way or another. We can sit around and listen to the house creak and the disappearing cats meow and tell ghost stories—it'll be like Girl Scout camp all over again!"

She wouldn't take no for an answer and Natalie hung up looking forward to her arrival. Somehow, storm or not, Julie would get through.

The first big flakes of snow had begun to blow across the drifts still remaining from the weekend when Natalie got into her sheepskin coat and headed out the door. She was standing on the front porch, feeling the tingling in her cheeks caused by the brisk, wet wind, when she heard the telephone ring behind her. The locks on the outside doors hadn't worked for years, Aunt Margaret was fond of reminding people from Manhattan, and she'd never had a burglary. The result at the moment was that Natalie was able to dash back inside and get to the phone before the caller hung up. She was thrown for a moment: it was an unfamiliar voice. Then it dawned on her that the call was intended for Aunt Margaret.

"Well, where in the world is Margaret?" It was a woman of a certain age. "And who are you? Is this Margaret's house?"

Natalie identified herself. "And Aunt Margaret's gone to Atlantic City with friends." She laughed. "I hope they took along plenty of money—they may get snowed in at the casinos—"

"Oh, no, we didn't go to Atlantic City. We got a much better deal on rooms for the first week in January and what difference did it make to us? Bunch of old biddies out on a tear? December, January, who cares? So we didn't go."

"Well, Margaret isn't here. I came last night and there's not a soul around. Not even the cats. Maybe she decided to go anyway, on her own?"

"Maggie? Oh, I don't think so. She's the life of the party but she does need the party. She's not one to go off by herself. I wonder . . . could she have gone into the city? Well," her voice broke out of the momentary questioning reverie, "she's a big girl, isn't she? She can do what she likes. But the cats, I wonder what she did with the cats."

"I'm sure I don't know," Natalie said. "She's bound to call someone, you or some other friend, or she'll just come home. I'm sure it's perfectly simple." Something about Aunt Margaret's disappearance was making her nervous: it was the state of mind she was in, obviously, and had nothing to do with Aunt Margaret and the cats.

"I suppose you're right," the woman said. "When she gets back, have her call Fanny and explain what she's been up to."

Natalie said she would and jotted down a note on the pad by the telephone. She went back outside and noticed that the flakes of snow were already bigger and blowing harder across the front of the house. She couldn't resist the high iron gates of the cemetery, the way the blowing snow shrouded the monuments as if they were an army crouching against the elements, waiting for nightfall to attack. She leaned into the wind, hands deep in her pockets and chin buried against her chest, barely looking outward, enjoying the simple awareness of where she was. The solitude, the desolate wind, the insistent scraping of the snow on her face like a cat's tongue. She wound around the driveways, seeing the dead, broken flowers in pots, the sheen of ice on the odd monument, the rims of snow growing along the edges of the marble. Someone had scattered breadcrumbs and little dun-colored birds tiptoed daintily along the crust, lunching.

The wind increased as she worked her way up toward the crest of the long slope. To her left she could see Margaret's house, the light she'd left on in the parlor shining through the snow like a safety beacon. Out of breath, she stopped at the top and realized that Manhattan had disappeared in the storm. The towers, the bulk of lower Manhattan, the Brooklyn Bridge—all gone as if by Merlin's wand. Nothing but the increasing gray fury of the storm over the water, where nothing stood in its way.

Damn D'Allessandro and his insinuations! She kicked at the snow, acknowledging her frustration and loneliness. MacPherson had seemed such a nice man, an interesting and interested man, an increasingly rare bird. Hopes . . . she'd obviously felt a flaring hope that Saturday, a hope she hadn't been quite willing to admit.

A man for Natalie . . .

She felt the wind streaking the tears across her face.

She left the cemetery in a thoughtful frame of mind, not upset, but reflective, almost unaware of the weather. She walked for a long time until she found herself in the middle of a shopping area, small drugstores and clothing shops, a market, a couple of restaurants with lights glowing behind windows in fake brick facades. She stopped, looked back the way she'd come and saw a long street blurring in the snow, running straight as a string up a hill and then turning, disappearing. Looking at her watch, she realized she'd been walking for the better part of an hour. The exercise had kept her warm and she was famished.

The restaurant's lunch crowd had thinned to almost nothing and the effort at a nightclub atmosphere struck her as somewhat pathetic, yet oddly endearing in the dim gray light of early afternoon. The hostess gave her a booth with a view of the street through cedar slats and hanging plants, enough hanging plants to remind her of the restaurants in Malibu where what you saw beyond the windows was the Pacific. She ordered a Bushmills on ice and later there was a club sandwich with chips. It was like a little town in Illinois somewhere, like the villages she'd driven through as a college student at Northwestern. New York seemed inconceivably far away. She felt as if the land mass reached hundreds of miles in all directions and there was nothing anywhere to frighten her.

Christmas decorations clung to the ceiling and a tree stood by the cashier's desk. She hadn't seen such old-fashioned bubble lights since she was a child. Her father had come home with boxes of bubble lights shaped like little candles one long-ago Christmas, and they had struck a six- or seven-year-old Natalie as wondrous quite beyond description. Miraculous. Now here they were again and she hadn't seen any since she was a girl. She drank her coffee and realized she'd better go to the bathroom before setting off on her walk home. It was a long walk.

The afternoon turned imperceptibly to twilight and then to darkness as she walked through the curious mixture of fog and snow. Instead of blowing steadily, the snow was now accumulating and the temperature was dropping toward freezing, then below. The footing was increasingly treacherous but still she seemed almost unaware of the process of walking, of her surroundings as she moved past the dark shapes of houses with lights in the windows and the smell of the woodsmoke curling from chimneys. Through the windows she was vaguely cognizant of Christmas-tree lights, the shapes of people moving. Cars sliding carefully into driveways, the slamming of the door muffled by the thickly falling snow. One front lawn featured a team of reindeer pulling Santa's sled, all in plastic, like a store display.

God, she thought, *please let all this be over before Christmas.* It was a child's prayer: *Please grant me my wish, O Lord, and I'll never be a bad girl again.* . . .

Memory doesn't work rationally, doesn't follow nice logical pathways through the maze of the mind and lead inexorably to the truth, the remembered truth. Instead it is constantly making quantum leaps that seem on the surface to make no sense but are instead simply mistakes. Memory, in short, is cleverer and more impatient and a good deal more inspired than those who are merely its keepers.

Which accounts for the fact that it was a snowman that set Natalie to thinking.

He stood somewhat forlornly in a vacant lot next to a small gray house. He wore a plastic bowler hat in an unhappy green shade that surely dated from some Saint Patrick's Day celebration better forgotten. His nose was a candy cane, which struck her as rather a nice touch. His eyes were indeed made of something that looked like coal, and his grin was a curved line of small stones. An ancient plaid scarf had been wrapped around his neck and the fringe fluttered in the wind. Another row of stones stretched down his chest like buttons on a coat.

She stood smiling at him, surprised at the effort that

his creation had required. She had certainly never made such a snowman and doubted that she'd ever seen one like it outside the pages of a book. Or a Christmas card . . .

He seemed almost to deserve a salutation of some kind. Then she saw his shoes! He even had shoes. Two black shoes protruding from the largest of the three boulders of snow, angled slightly as first to remind her of Charlie Chaplin.

But there was something else about the shoes, some snickering blade of memory fighting to emerge, struggling to tell her something, yapping at her even as she walked the last fifteen minutes to the great house where the light she'd left on still burned, making it seem a center of warm family life on a snowy winter night.

She ran a hot tub and sank in gratefully, breathing the steam and feeling the heat soak in, driving the chill from her bones. Those shoes . . . why did they make her think of the anonymous flowers that had come for her? Shoes. Flowers. She closed her eyes, trying to push aside the clouds of memory, all the events that had crowded in on her so distractingly. The shoes. There was something funny, not quite right. . . .

She laughed at the thought of the deliveryman who'd brought the flowers. Same guy both times. Ingratiating, New Yorky kind of character, helpful, proud of having delivered flowers to none other than Mrs. Robert Redford. She remembered standing in the kitchen, dripping wet, a towel around her head, while he got on the stool to reach the vase on top of the cupboard . . . and suddenly memory snapped and crackled.

She saw his black shoes—a stain was it? No, a scratch, a long scratch across the toe of one of his black shoes. Plain black shoes and the scratch had laid back the leather, leaving a pale incision across the toe. . . . The shoes hadn't been polished since the scratch had occurred, otherwise she'd never have seen it—

She sat up in the tub. She felt her stomach turn in on itself. She struggled to her feet and splashed out of the tub, grabbed a towel and began to dry herself furiously. All the signs of terror, the frantic fluttering in her chest, hands shaking . . .

The cop who'd come to her apartment to check on MacPherson. D'Allessandro. She never had seen his shield while he was doing all the shtick about how important seeing the shield was. She'd been amused at what a perfect television cop he was . . . and while she'd listened to the creak of his leather coat and heard his patter she'd cataloged his outfit. Right down to his shoes.

And across the toe of one of his black shoes there had been a pale scar.

The same scar.

But how was that possible?

She struggled into her jeans and sweater and ran down the stairs, out of breath, almost falling on the loose carpet runner.

It was possible only if it was the same pair of shoes.

She had trouble dialing the number, her fingers wouldn't work.

The same pair of shoes . . .

And Barry Hughes wasn't only a murderer.

He was an actor.

Chapter Twenty-three

MacPherson wasn't there and she left an urgent message that he call her as soon as they could locate him.

The view from the kitchen window had disappeared as if a knob had been flicked and the picture gone to black. There was no latticework of bare branches, no slope of hillside, no city across the water. Only the storm now with the constant blowing of the wind rattling the windowpanes, the buckshot of snow and sleet against the glass.

She called Julie at the office and found that she'd left early because of the storm. She called Lew and got the answering machine, debated for an instant, then decided there was no point in dragging him into her neuroses, fears, burgeoning hysteria. She called Dr. Drummond and there was no answer. There was no one home. Everywhere they were sheltering from the storm. On an impulse she called her own apartment, got her answering machine, and hung up.

There was a loud banging riding on the wind from the direction of the stable or barn or whatever the hell it had been and it was driving her crazy. She put on her sheepskin coat and went outside, stood shielding her eyes from the blowing snow, getting her bearings. There were already six new inches atop the old snow and she sank almost to her knees as she fought her way to the outbuilding. A second-story wooden door that had probably once had something to do with a hay mow was swinging wildly on its rusty hinges, smashing itself against the frame. She gave a sigh of *Why me, O Lord?* and went into the ground floor. It was dark and she couldn't see a thing. She fumbled around against the wall until her gloved fingers ran across a switch. The light couldn't have been more than thirty watts and was located just above the doorway. There were worktables, tools, planks, all the odds and ends gathered over the years lurking like the shadows of a vast backstage storage room. It was here that Tony worked on his stained-glass projects and his paraphernalia was everywhere.

A rickety stairway led up one wall to a floor that amounted to half the size of the downstairs. She climbed carefully, hearing mice scuttle in the darkness. The stairs creaked and she smelled barn smells and chemicals from Tony's work and paint and mustiness. When she got to the top she picked her way among the stacks of frames and glass sheets and God only knew what else, heading toward the banging door that whacked away at the building like a metronome. The night through the opening was grayer than the inside of the barn and she felt snow drifting in on her face. It took several tries but she managed to grab the door when it blew to and then fastened it with a brace that had been left to hang idly by. She leaned back against a column of wood, sneezed in the dustiness, and caught her breath. Somewhere far away a horn honked and honked and she imagined a car sliding in the snow and ice. . . .

Natalie poked at the charred remains of the fire from last night, driving the gleaming poker in under the old logs and pushing them toward the back of the grate. She laid two heavy, thickly barked logs on the pile of fresh chips and kindling and got the fire started. After waiting to see that it was drawing, she went back to the kitchen and made coffee. By rummaging around in a pantry she found an extensive liquor supply. She poured a glass of brandy and took it back to the living room with the coffee.

And never once did she stop thinking about the two men who had worn the same pair of black shoes.

And she took her will by the throat and told herself she would not break, she would not go under, she would hold the anxiety at bay. . . .

She was safe. The distance from Manhattan insulated her and the storm further insulated her.

She was safe. She felt hot coffee dribbling down her chin and heard the rattle as she replaced the cup in the saucer.

She turned on the radio. Travel advisories everywhere across not only the tristate area but all through the Northeast. The storm was at its peak. LaGuardia and Kennedy were completely shut down, Logan to the north in Boston was shut. Commuter trains were stuck or not leaving the city at all. Hotel rooms were being snapped up, people were bunking down in their offices. Traffic was barely moving, and even where it might have, vast multiple-car accidents had tied things up.

Poor Julie. Natalie hoped she'd have enough sense to go home and not try the trek to Staten Island.

But she couldn't keep her mind off the black shoes. And she couldn't ignore the fear.

Then she thought she heard the cats again, the faint meowing almost drowned in the wind. She leaped from the chair by the fire, paced back and forth across the room several times, feeling her heartbeat rate going off the top of the scale, and called MacPherson again. He was there and she began babbling, stumbling over everything.

"Hey, hey, give it a rest," he said, trying to tease her. "Now what's going on out there? You sound like you've had a few too many—"

"I'm sorry, but no, I'm just afraid . . . no, no I don't mean that, but I've discovered something, it was a snowman that made me think of it, when I looked down from this green plastic bowler hat and saw two black shoes sticking out of the snow at the bottom and that made me remember. . . ." She knew she sounded crazy but she couldn't quite figure out how to force the facts to make sense.

"What are you trying to tell me, Natalie? Just slow it way, way down and tell me the part that matters." He was good at not getting flustered and transmitted a bit of his calm to her.

She dabbed sweat from her forehead with a sleeve. "All right. Cut to the chase. The deliveryman who brought me the anonymous flowers and the cop who came to investigate you wore the same shoes."

All the joking had seeped from his voice. "Just run that one past me again, please, Natalie."

She explained.

"This cop," he said, "what was his name?"

"D'Allessandro. His shoe had the same scar. Not one like it. The same one."

"And why was he investigating me?"

"He said there had been complaints about your getting too amorous with women in your investigations."

She half-expected a laugh but none came.

"Well," he said at last, "it fits. There's no officer called D'Allessandro investigating me. There's no such unit. I don't make passes at women in my cases . . . well, not enough to get investigated." He laughed mirthlessly. "It sure does fit—"

"Stop saying that! What does it mean? What fits?"

"Listen, in the first place, I think you're right—I think your deliveryman and this D'Allessandro were the same guy. I guess you've probably got an idea who—"

"Well, Barry Hughes was an actor . . . and Bradley said he'd been following me. But, my God, these men were so different—"

"Sure, sure. Different. But differences in style, hair, accents! I talked with Barry Hughes's agent today and he ran down the characters Hughes has played. Including a police detective. What do you want to bet he was doing the same cop in your living room? Christ, what a crazy!

263

He had to get close to you, had to see you for himself, and he did it the best possible way—he walked right in! The bastard." She heard him lighting a cigarette. She heard him exhale. "There's one other thing. . . . You see, Barry Hughes also played a psychiatrist in an off-Broadway production. Agent showed me the reviews, very good they were, said he was very sympathetic, very convincing, the shrink everybody wishes they had—"

"So what? I haven't had any stray psychiatrists dropping in—"

"Now listen, just stay calm."

"Don't be ridiculous—"

"Dr. Goldstein called Dr. Drummond today about something entirely unrelated to you . . . and his nurse said that Drummond flew to Florida over the weekend and hasn't come back yet. His mother had a stroke in Palm Beach—"

"That's impossible. Drummond and I met yesterday morning—"

"No, I'm afraid you didn't, Natalie."

"You're telling me I'm crazy? Great, just great!"

"No, no, I'm not telling you you're crazy—"

"You're telling me I'm dreaming that I talked with him yesterday—"

"Listen to me, Natalie. I am telling you that you didn't see Dr. Drummond, that's what I'm telling you. You saw someone all right—"

It hit her in a rush and she felt herself choking, her throat constricting. "Oh, please, no, don't tell me this—"

"You had a long talk with the wrong man. You spoke

with Barry Hughes. They were all Barry Hughes, all three of them."

"How can you be sure?" Her voice was faint, far away.

"Tell me about him, everything."

She told him everything, from the first sight of him waiting for her in the street. The special telephone number. The painters lousing up his office, the sympathy he'd shown her . . . the whole performance. And by the time she was done she knew MacPherson was right.

"But, and this is important, Natalie," he went on, "it really doesn't make any difference. Unnerving, sure, but it doesn't change anything. He may still be a homicidal maniac, my dear, but he still thinks he knows where you are. And he knows we're closing in on him because you told him—but he doesn't know there's one hell of a surprise waiting for him in your apartment. Natalie, are you crying?"

She bit down hard on her knuckle, forcing it all back into her throat. But she couldn't speak.

"What is it, Natalie?"

"I told him," she said. "I told him where I was going to be."

"Oh, Nat. When? You didn't even know when you saw him, you didn't know anything about this—"

"On the phone, I told him on the phone from my office. I didn't want him to think I'd just disappeared, he wanted me to stay in close touch with him. . . ." She began to sob again but bit down on the knuckle, stopped, wiped her nose. "I told him where I am. I gave him the telephone number, told him it was Tony's aunt's house. . . . He knows, he knows I'm alone—" Her voice was taking off into the upper reaches and she couldn't stop it.

MacPherson's angry shout cut across her consciousness like an icicle falling, shattering.

"Natalie, shut up! Cut it out! Just cut it out! You're forgetting something very important—the storm. He can't get to you. . . ."

"You listen!" she shouted, anger replacing the terror. "He's known since late yesterday afternoon—he's had nearly twenty-four hours to get out here. What makes you think he waited until now? Don't try to kid me—"

"All right. You're right, of course. The only thing I can do this minute is get on to the Staten Island police and have them send a man out to the house. And I'll head out now myself—I don't know how long it'll take me, Natalie. It might be quicker to take a police motor launch. But now, right now, Natalie, I'm going to call the Staten Island cops. Do you understand?"

"I'm scared, MacPherson, not an imbecile." Her mind had switched to practical matters: the doors to the house . . . which made Aunt Margaret so proud. No working locks. "Yes, I understand. Just hurry, for God's sake."

"We will. Now let me get to the cops out there. And remember one thing—if he shows up, if he drops in on you, you're going to have to handle him. Just remember, we're on the way. And remember this—if he should get to you he may come as Dr. Drummond—our people here don't think he's dangerous when he's in character.

It's only Barry-as-Barry who's dangerous. Hang on, Natalie." As an afterthought, he softened his voice: "And remember, nothing D'Allessandro told you is true. If it makes any difference to you . . ."

She sat, almost in a trance, as if she'd covered herself with a protective shroud, in a rocking chair in the parlor before the warm radiance of the fire. In her mind—was it in her mind, after all?—she heard the mournful crying of the cats and the closing of the door in the middle of the night. Had she heard it, the clicking of a door? Or had it come from within herself, born of her dreams and fears?

Was it her imagination? Or was he already there, in the house, waiting for her with a knife . . . the way he'd waited for Bradley Nichols?

She heard the footfalls on the porch and her eyes snapped open. She must have briefly gone catatonic, hiding in the shadows of her psyche. The porch flooring creaked. There was a knock on the door.

She sat rocking, staring into the fire, unable to move. She felt chilled, despite the fire, felt as if she were drawing in upon herself, vacating the premises.

The knocking was increasing in intensity. Pounding.

Julie? Her mind wandered momentarily. Had Julie somehow gotten through? The rocking chair lulled her. She felt drugged by fear.

In her hand she held the poker from the fireplace set. When had she taken it? She couldn't remember. . . .

Someone was calling her. A man's voice piercing the wind.

"Mrs. Rader? Are you in there? Mrs. Rader?"

Of course, the Staten Island cop. MacPherson had gotten his call through. She heard herself sigh. Kept rocking slowly.

She heard the pounding cease, then the front door opening, tentative footsteps in the front hallway.

"Mrs. Rader? Are you there?"

She made herself call out, "Who is it?"

The footsteps came down the hall, closer. She sensed someone in the doorway, couldn't tear her eyes away from the fire.

"My God, Natalie," he said. "Are you all right? Look, it's me." The voice was soothing, calm.

Slowly she looked toward the door.

She felt the breath easing out of her. She felt almost relieved.

"Why, Dr. Drummond, what are you doing here?"

Chapter Twenty-four

"Well, this hits the spot, I must say!"

He sat at the kitchen table, hunched forward in a bankerish gray suit, sipping hot coffee. Then he looked reassuringly at her, shook his head for emphasis, and noisily drank more coffee. His straight gray hair was matted down and his scarf still hung around his neck, though he'd dumped his wet overcoat on a chair in the parlor. He caught her staring at him and offered an avuncular smile. How could it be the same man? The hair, the nose, the bulk of the body . . .

"It's positively hellish out there," he said. "Trees knocked over, telephone wires all tangled up and pulled into the street down in the village, fog, snow—damnedest thing I've ever seen." He looked up at her where she stood by the counter. "Is that a loaf of homemade bread behind you?"

"Yes. I found it in the freezer—"

"If you don't mind, some toast. No, you sit down,

I'll get it myself." He pulled out a chair for her and went to the wooden block that held the knives. She watched him select one, admire the blade. "You want a slice?" She shook her head and he carefully sliced a thick piece, dropped it in the toaster. "At least the electricity isn't out," he said. "If I were you, I'd be ready for anything tonight. I hear there's a god-awful accident on the Verrazano Bridge, completely blocked it off."

She tried to smile. "How did you get here?"

"Came out yesterday, not long after I spoke with you on the phone. Decided to drive out and see a friend, he talked me into staying overnight, and today came the storm." He shrugged, looked into the toaster to see if all was well. "As long as I was here, I figured I'd look you up. The story you told me yesterday worried me. I thought you might welcome a friendly face." He smiled. The toast popped up and he buttered it. "Where's your aunt, by the way? Didn't you say she'd be here?"

"My former husband's aunt, actually. I don't know where she is. Atlantic City, I guess. It's a little confusing." Watching his face, she felt as if she'd entered a fun house—nothing was what it seemed. She was relaxing again, chatting with him. Yet he was Barry . . . God, she had to keep it all straight. He was the friendly deliveryman. He was D'Allessandro. He was Dr. Drummond.

"I've been wondering about your murderer," he said, munching the toast. "Eerie story. Is there any news on that front? Have they found him?" He was staring at her, chewing, reassuring. He had cut Bradley Nichols to pieces.

270

"No, not yet. Still looking."

"They've got a hell of a night for it." He looked out the window over the sink, shook his head, came back and sat down. "I've been going over what you told me yesterday. You really have had a plateful. Lots of stress. Too bad you happened to see the guy with the gun in the first place. Bad luck." He finished the toast and pulled a pipe from his pocket. "Do you mind?"

"Not at all." She had a pain in the middle of her chest and trying to force herself to be calm seemed only to make it worse. She watched him light the pipe, shake out the match, drop it on the plate. He puffed, smiling at her. "Very peaceful here, isn't it? Snug." He frowned. "I suppose I'm being terribly insensitive, given your present anxieties. But it will all be over soon enough." Smoke hung in an aromatic cloud between them.

"We sound like characters in a soap opera," she said. "A dark and stormy night, doctor comes to visit patient, a murderer on the loose—"

"A bit overwrought? Is that what you're saying?"

She nodded. "The stuff of nightmares."

"Yes, I suppose it is. Well, you seem to be holding up very well. More power to you. Think it sounds like a soap opera, do you? Then that makes me a soap-opera psychiatrist." He laughed. "We're all just actors, then." He laughed again.

They went into the parlor. He knelt before the grate and jabbed the fire back to roaring life. He was so bloody convincing! She kept being lulled.

They sat quietly, listening to the crackle of the flames in the dry logs, the wind whipping along the front porch, the snow rattling at the windows, the house protesting.

Suddenly she sat up straight, cocked her head.

"What is it?" he asked.

"Listen . . . do you hear that?"

He listened, puffing. "Sounds like a cat—is that what you mean?"

"I noticed it last night. But I can't find any cats. I'm glad I'm not imagining it."

"Little fellow sounds like he's in trouble somewhere. You're not imagining it. We'd better see if we can find him." He looked at his watch. "Then I'd better be going. God only knows how long it'll take to get back to town."

Natalie stood up and took the poker from the stand beside the fireplace.

"I don't think we need to go armed," Drummond said quietly. He reached for the poker.

She drew back, laughed nervously. "I keep thinking that maybe the cat cornered a rat or something. I'd feel better with this."

"Right. Well, let's go then." He set off into the hallway and up the stairs. "A shrink must be ready for anything." He chuckled.

She watched him go up the stairs ahead of her. A solid, imposing figure, everybody's idea of an authority figure, always ready to help . . . He said he'd be going once they found the cat. She had the poker. She couldn't show him any of her fear, her weakness. She had to hang on. *Hang on, Tiger, be a tiger.* He turned at the landing and held up his hand for her to be quiet. In the stillness they heard the weak meowing.

"Third floor," he said. He felt for a light switch and dim, yellow illumination came on at the top of the narrow stairway. She'd never been to the top floor of the house before. He was halfway up the stairs, looked back. "Well, come on, you've got the weapons."

The sound of the cat grew stronger as they climbed, a pained, wounded sound that made her skin crawl. Drummond looked back. "Scary, isn't it?" he said.

At the top of the stairs she drew even with him, both of them out of breath. She gripped the poker tightly. *Barry-as-Drummond is not dangerous. . . .* She gulped air. *Barry-as-Barry is a homicidal maniac. . . .*

"Why, you're shaking, Natalie," he said. "We're just looking for a cat."

The doors opening off the long, narrow hallway were all closed. The light was so dim she didn't realize at first that there was another door at the far end. Her eyes accustomed themselves to the light and at the same time she heard the cat again.

Then she saw it.

It was crawling toward them, hugging the floor, coming out of the shadows at the far end. It was barely visible, almost a fragment of shadow that had detached itself from the main body of darkness. A tiny, frail creature, moving slowly, moving from side to side as if its gyroscope was out of control. It reminded her of nothing so much as a wind-up animal whose mechanism had just about given up the struggle.

They moved toward it as if it were somehow dangerous. It was making an awful, strangled sound, raw and painful, as it moved, crablike, toward them.

The smell hit her about halfway down the hall.

There was something horribly wrong. . . .

Chapter Twenty-five

Natalie knelt beside the cat just as it stopped moving, gave a tiny mournful whimper, and died.

She watched as the body tipped on its side and she saw the matted fur, touched it, felt the stickiness, then something warm and slippery and wet and realized that her finger had slid through the sliced flesh into the chest cavity.

She screamed, fell backward against Drummond's leg.

"It's been cut," she whispered. A trail of blood lay along the floor, like the mark of a paint brush running out of paint. It led back to the door at the end of the hallway.

"We'd better take a look behind that door, Natalie—"

"No, no," she said, falling backward again, trying to get to her feet, trying to get to the stairway. "No, please, leave the door alone—please. . . ."

She felt the fingers of his right hand close around

her forearm and draw her firmly to her feet. "Now, calm down," he ordered, "be a big girl. You are a big girl, aren't you? Then act like one—come on, face the music, Natalie." His voice had undergone a subtle change, a hardening, a distancing. He sounded as if he was mocking her. He pulled her forward. She turned back, tugging helplessly. Beside the body of the cat lay the poker.

For a moment, before he pushed open the door, the world seemed to stop for her, as if it were imprinting itself on her mind, a kind of terminal sense memory. The wind hammering at the house, the rattling of glass in the ancient frames, the smell of blood, the eyes of the cat staring up at her as she touched its heart . . . The poker gleaming dully, the tightening grip on her arm, the dripping of perspiration down her back, soaking her . . .

He pushed open the door and the smell of blood increased like a stench from the netherworld. It was dark and she saw him feeling against the wall for a light switch. She knew what she would see. All the cats, gutted, dead, rotting . . .

The light came on.

The furry bodies were strewn about the floor of the large closet. Blood matted. Throats cut. Heads twisted at unreal angles.

In the middle of the carnage lay Aunt Margaret.

She'd been slit from her throat to her belly, her dress and flesh laid back by a kind of demented surgeon, legs splayed, blood dried beneath, soaking through her it seemed, soaking into the floor. Her mouth was open. Her eyes stared. In one hand she held a dead cat.

As if from a great distance, Natalie saw herself crack.

She heard the shrieking, heard it echoing and reechoing along the hallway, saw her face twist into a mask she'd never seen before, saw a kind of molten strength born of something close to madness course through her, saw her jerk away from Drummond and slam him back against the wall, heard her making sounds she'd never heard a human make before.

Drummond slipped in the blood, fell heavily against the wall, rolled over struggling to get up: she saw his white hand planted on the side of Aunt Margaret's face, in blood the old woman had smeared there herself, saw him trying to push himself upright.

She turned, staggered down the hallway, stooped to get the poker, fell over the tiny corpse of the cat, hit her head on the floor, got back to her feet. She heard Drummond swearing, panting, turned and saw him standing in the doorway nodding his head, felt the floor shake as he came after her.

She was down the stairway to the second floor, turned the corner, dashed along past her bedroom, negotiated the turn and began rushing down the stairs.

The loose carpet undid her. Her foot caught and she couldn't break the fall. She felt herself landing a million different ways, hurting herself each time. The breath was knocked out of her and she was on her back. Unable to get up. Pain attacking her from every angle.

He was at the top of the stairs; seeing her lying at

the bottom, he stopped. He came down slowly. He was saying her name over and over again.

He knelt over her. Her eyelids were fluttering and she felt herself slipping away, felt the world going. He leaned down. "Natalie?" he said softly.

With the last bit of her consciousness she suddenly clawed at his face, felt her nails dig in, heard him scream in surprise and pain, saw him pulling away . . . saw with mounting, searing horror the bulbous nose come away in her fingernails, felt the gray hair giving way as she tore at his face. . . .

In that last millisecond she saw the face of Dr. Drummond turn into the tortured, maddened face of someone she had never seen before, eyes burning holes in her, teeth flashing like a ferret's, brows furrowing like things with lives of their own.

She was face to face with Barry Hughes.

She woke with a cool, moist cloth bathing her forehead. When she opened her eyes, Barry Hughes leaned back from his ministrations and looked at her curiously, said nothing. He had a plain, nondescript sort of face, thinner than the characters he'd played, light brown hair cut very short and nearly bald on top. His eyes were brown, his expression strangely vacant, like a blank sheet of paper on which his emotions and character were yet to be written. He watched her come fully awake, folded the wet towel, and stood up.

She was stretched out on the couch and her neck was stiff and the fire was still going brightly. He had placed another log on the flames. She blinked, trying to get things clear. He had set her on the couch, gotten the towel for her bruised forehead. Now he was standing at the mantlepiece holding a cup.

"I was afraid you'd really hurt yourself," he said. "You've been out for fifteen minutes anyway. I had time to make some hot chocolate." He nodded at the coffee table and a cup he'd already poured for her. "You want an aspirin or anything?"

She shook her head. "Why haven't you killed me, too?" Her voice seemed unable to rise above a whisper.

"Jesus, give me a break, Mrs. Rader. You think I like killing people? You think I'm crazy or something? I want us to get out of here alive. Both of us . . . Christ, a month ago I was just an actor with a cocaine habit he was having a little trouble supporting—that was me, Barry Hughes, for Christ's sake. Then it all began turning to shit, the pressure kept building up, I didn't know what the hell to do. Now, what a mess . . ."

She nodded. "I'm not exactly a stranger to pressure," she whispered. Her mind was spinning: *He seems to have forgotten his history of mental breakdowns, he's thinking he's just a hard-luck guy and I think he believes it, just a victim of circumstance who's shot a coke dealer, hacked his friend into pieces, and opened a seventy-year-old lady from stem to stern with a butcher knife.* But where was he now? How far from a fourth murder? That was all that mattered and she didn't want to die—

"Well," he said, "what are we going to do?" He was very calm, almost philosophical. He seemed much younger than the florist's deliveryman, D'Allessandro, or Dr. Drummond. "How are we going to get out of this alive? The way I see it, either we both get out alive or neither of us does. But maybe I'm wrong—what do you think, Mrs. Rader? Maybe I've got the plot all wrong . . . the way I see it, I'm the victim of fate, some weird little misfire in the brain that makes me capable of killing people. Like George Segal in *The Terminal Man*, remember? I mean, remember Tony Perkins in *Psycho*? Nice kid, like me—I really am a perfectly nice guy . . . remember Robert Montgomery with the guy's head in the hatbox, carrying it around with him?" He looked at her almost pleadingly and she made herself nod yet again. "So what do you think?"

She sat up on the couch, feeling fingers of pain digging at her head. "Nobody else has to die," she said. "Nothing will happen to you if you give yourself up. You won't die, they won't throw you into prison—" He squinted at her: there was nothing in the face to remind her of Dr. Drummond. Nothing. When in the name of God would the Staten Island cops get here? Where were they? Where was MacPherson and his police launch? How long could she hang on? Stupid questions. She wanted to scream and she had to stay calm.

Barry Hughes was shaking his head. "No, no, please don't insult my intelligence, Mrs. Rader. And I won't insult yours. What I say, you can depend on, it'll be true. But let me give you one word of advice—don't start with the you-need-help crap, okay? You think I'm nuts? Of course I need help—maybe not as bad as you need help, but I need it. Right? But I begin to go crazy when people start insulting my intelligence—Brad Nichols gave me that and I didn't take kindly to it, get it? By the time I was finished with old Brad—well, why bring that up?" He smiled disarmingly. "Not one of my prouder accomplishments. You listening?"

"Yes, I'm listening."

"Are you scared?"

"What are you talking about? Of course I'm scared!"

"That's good, that's the spirit. I may be a class-A psycho or I may not, neither you nor I are really qualified to decide that . . . but I really don't want to wind up in a rubber room somewhere. So you and I had better come up with some alternatives. That is, if you want my opinion."

He poured himself another cup and went back to leaning against the mantelpiece. There were sweat stains spreading from his armpits and his forehead was gleaming. His voice stayed very calm. "While you were unconscious from your fall, I picked up the telephone just to see if it was working—it's not. No pizza for us tonight." He flashed a weird, crooked smile at her. "I turned on the radio and heard an interesting bit of news—a police motor launch just came apart out there when it ran into the Staten Island ferry. Can you believe that? They're picking bodies out of the water now— what's the matter? You look funny—"

"No, nothing funny, just a terrible accident—"

"Yeah. Terrible. My heart goes out to them. Anyway, the bridge is blocked, too. Or did Dr. Drummond tell you that? Seems to me he did." He chuckled at his witticism.

He rattled on, talking to himself. Natalie wondered if MacPherson had wound up in the water. How many motor launches could the cops have out there tonight? But that still left the Staten Island police. . . . My God, where were they? It seemed hours since she'd talked with MacPherson. He was going to call them right away—

"You really didn't know it was me, did you? The deliveryman and D'Allessandro?"

"No, I didn't. Your Dr. Drummond was especially brilliant." *Keep him talking*, she thought, *ask him questions*. "But how did you know about him?"

"Nothing to it," he said smugly. "I was following you, you must have looked right at me a hundred times, but I kept changing who I was. I was fascinated by you, the way a man can be fascinated by a beautiful woman who holds his fate in her hands. I thought maybe you could identify me. Maybe. But I also felt there was something between us, a relationship between you and me, Natalie. I read about you, I followed you, I watched you walk . . . I wanted to know more about you. I wanted to know everything about you. Everything. Body and soul, as they say. You have a really snotty look, arrogant, you know that? You literally have your nose in the air and I thought about you all the time, all kinds of things." He giggled almost shyly. "I wondered what it would be like to kiss your naked belly and pull your panties down and spread you open and look inside, all that stuff . . . but I wanted to talk with you, too, and find out if you were, like afraid. . . ." He grinned at her, a half-smile playing across his small mouth. "Watching you and the cop buying the Christmas tree I wondered how often you fingerfuck yourself, how long it

had been since you'd screwed and if you were going to
fuck the cop. . . . Christ, it made me so hard I couldn't
believe it. But the last thing I wanted to do was hurt
you . . . I don't know what I wanted to do, it was a
game, I wanted to know about you—that's it, I just
wanted to know everything. One day I followed you to
the Algonquin, you were meeting this guy for a drink
and I came in with a copy of *Variety* and sat down near
you, near enough to hear your conversation. That's how I
heard about Drummond, so I called you. If you'd already
talked to Drummond, then I was just a voice at the end
of a telephone and you couldn't find me. . . . And if
you hadn't called him, then I could become Drummond
for you, get closer and closer. I mean, it really was like a
movie, I was right in the middle of a scary movie, it
reminded me of *Flesh and Fantasy*, the Edward G.
Robinson segment where the fortune-teller Podgers,
Thomas Mitchell it was, tells him he's going to kill
somebody and Robinson can't believe it; what I was
doing had that same feel, black and white, lots of
texture, a helluva movie, y'know? I was the innocent guy
driven to shoot that little whore Quirk but I did it, I got
up my courage and rid the world of the rotten bitch, she
wouldn't pay me for doing a fuck movie with her, I
should be a hero, but then—by crazy chance—somebody who's totally uninvolved sees me throw the gun
away . . . and the story gets in the paper . . . and
then the weird fear starts working on me, can she
recognize me? I don't know what I was going to do, I
didn't have a plan, now I never will know—and it's all
that asshole Brad's fault, he had to stick his nose and

more particularly his cock into things—I mean Jesus you were mine and he got you down on the floor and you fucked him and he had to write all that shit down in his diary. I mean I saw 'red, he's coming on all tough and shape-up-Barry to me and I've just read his diary all about what it was like to push it into you, how soft and wet you are, and poor old Brad was a dead man, dead, dead, dead . . . and I knew I had to have you myself. I mean, if you'd do it with him, you were bound to do it with me, made sense, right?" He seemed to become aware of her for the first time in his monologue and shouted at her, "Right? You'd do it with me, too, right?"

"I don't know. Barry. He made it up. I didn't do it with him, truly I didn't—"

"I told you, I warned you, don't insult my intelligence! You fucked him!" Then he calmed down. "Well, we'll get to that in a little while. I'm not sure what movie all this is from—I have a little trouble with movies and real life. Actor, you know. I'm an actor. I get by. Not enough projection, voice, I mean, but I get by, sing a little, dance a little, used to juggle—anyway, fuck all that. Like they say, Actors Equity, where are you when I need you? Does my agent get ten percent of this load of trouble? Ha! I'm finally in the movies and you and I are the only ones who know. So the big question is, how does this end? Is it a night at the movies? Or is it real life? Do I go up the river and say goodbye to Pat O'Brien before I walk the last mile? Or maybe it's *One Flew Over the Cuckoo's Nest* . . . or *Night Must Fall*. . . . Are we Tony Perkins and Janet Leigh or are we Barry Hughes and Natalie Rader?"

He was loving the sound of his own voice and she listened, forcing the images of the gutted woman upstairs, the mangled cats out of her mind, concentrating on Barry, listening, waiting for anything she could use, get hold of.

He was relaxed. *He feels safe*, she thought, *he knows we're alone and going to stay that way.* He kept talking, rattling on about his parents and how he'd always wanted to be an actor, on and on. A character actor, he said, a faceless man. "I can be anyone, Natalie, the invisible man." He went to the coffee table, knelt, and poured himself another steaming cup, poured one for her, held it out to her.

"Here, Natalie, it's really very good—"

With all the strength in her legs she suddenly slammed the coffee table toward him, felt it hit his chest, straightened her legs, pushing with all the force in her hips and thighs, saw the moment disintegrate into its components: the gleaming silver pot tilting toward him, the cup he was holding flying into the air and the steaming liquid hanging in the air, then falling across his face like a whip. She heard him scream, sprawling on his back with the table and the tray of cups and saucers and the pot littering him. He was rubbing at his face and she was on her feet, leaping past him and putting the couch between them, stupidly stopping to look back and see him thrashing about on the floor. While she watched he slowly stopped moving, lay quietly, breathing deeply like a man utterly exhausted. He was staring at the ceiling.

"That was a very predatory act," he said between

gasps. He was wiping his sleeve back and forth across his eyes, wiping away the hot chocolate. There were red streaks across his flesh and on his balding head. A cut above his eye was bleeding. "So, I guess it's going to be a movie, Natalie. So what do you do now in this movie, Natalie? Let's see, let's think it through. I'm going to have to do something just plain god-awful to you when I catch you. . . . So, I'd say you'd better get a move on, Natalie!"

His voice had risen to a shriek on the last few words and suddenly he was horribly alive, like a flashing, thrusting reptile, throwing aside the coffee table and slipping and getting to his feet. . . .

Adrenaline fueled her instincts. She had no sense of what she was doing, she was moving as fast as she could but it seemed like slow motion.

She was in the hallway.

She heard him knock over another piece of furniture.

She was out the front door and across the porch.

She was in the clutches of the storm.

Chapter Twenty-six

For a moment the storm's impact hit her like a hammer and she reeled backward, feet and ankles plunging painfully through the snowcrust, falling to her knees, blinded by the blowing snow. Her mind was clicking, telling her to hide, *don't try to run in this, you'll never make it . . . hide, don't let him get you. . . .*

She struggled back to her feet and plunged off toward the barn, which would be dark and sheltered from the wind. She'd been there before, she knew it better than he did, somehow she could hide there. She needed to get away and she couldn't take time to think . . . she heard him stomping out onto the porch, heard the wind slam the door back on its hinges.

As she lost breath the sound of the night roared in her ears, she felt sweat and panic breaking out, felt her legs weaken each time they sank through the crust.

The barn loomed out of the darkness. Maybe he

wouldn't know where she'd gone, it was too dark and the wind too loud for him actually to see or hear her flailing away. She began to feel faint from lack of oxygen and stopped, desperately sucking at the wind. She looked back, trying to see him, thought she saw his shape thrashing through the snow . . . what she could see was the black, twisting trail she had left behind her, a black scar stretching from him inevitably to her. . . .

Then she heard him scream unintelligibly, heard the cry cut off as if he had fallen in the snow, but it wasn't a human sound. It was the sound of the instrument of her own death and she gulped, struggled on, ripping her ankles on the frozen snow.

She reached the door to the barn, the same door she'd gone in before, only a few hours ago, and she pushed it open, went inside. Suddenly the sound seemed far away, the wind was reduced to the whining and the draft through the chinks in the walls, and it wasn't so cold. She stood quietly, willing her eyes to accustom themselves to the darkness. *Don't turn on that light, Natalie, just find a hiding place, get out of the way . . . feel around for a weapon, a rake, a shovel, anything.*

Instead she tripped over some piece of Tony's apparatus, fell heavily, scraping her hand. She forced herself back to her feet, felt her way slowly toward the narrow stairway she had climbed before, banged into something else in her path, finally reached the bottom step, grabbed on to the handrail, and began climbing past the sacks and boxes and cans stacked on the steps.

The door was ripped open and the night came in again, the wind and the roar like a hungry beast.

"Natalie!" He sounded as if he were speaking in tongues, a different voice, a deep cry from the pit. "Natalie! I'm here! I've come to get you. . . ."

She crouched halfway up the stairs, afraid to move or make a sound. Her mouth was dry and her heartbeat was out of control.

She heard him close the door, sealing them off, heard him stumbling around, muttering. She lay quietly trying to remember what she had seen on the second floor, the balcony where Tony stored his stained glass . . . there were frames of all sizes, long pieces of wood, shreds of soldering material scattered across the floor like droppings, half-finished sheets of stained glass, several huge completed works, boxes and crates and nondescript bags. . . .

The dim light suddenly came on and she saw him standing in the doorway, still wearing his gray suit, which was dusted with snow and hung loosely now that he'd removed the padding from his torso. His face was deathly pale, his eyes flickered around the barn like searchlights tilting and out of control.

She could make herself no smaller and even in the dim light with the shadows and the gloom he saw her. He saw her and he smiled.

"Natalie. There you are. Just wait right there, right where you are, Natalie." He pointed his finger like a schoolteacher warning a difficult student. The burn across his face had bubbled, looked like a parasitic slug clinging to him, eating his flesh.

She was frozen to the spot, trapped.

He began looking around him, making an inventory of materials. He glanced up at her every few seconds, smiling, nodding his head. "Don't be impatient with me, Natalie." He laughed to himself. "Let's take our time with this. . . ."

On a workbench he found what he wanted but she couldn't make it out. He was tinkering with it, looking at it.

Suddenly a dart of flame appeared in the darkness; he held it up, admired it. An acetylene torch. One of Tony's pieces of apparatus, something he used. He admired the flame from all angles, the orange and yellow and blue, adjusted it, stretching the tongue of flame.

"All right, Natalie. Here I come. It's time, Natalie."

Holding the angry, fiery needle before him, he began advancing toward the bottom of the stairway. She felt the tremor as he stood on the first step, grinning up at her. He was only fifteen feet below her and frantically she turned, raced to the top of the stairs. Grinning, he plodded on.

All she could find to save herself were the exquisite pieces of stained glass.

She tipped a large frame over and heaved it down the stairway.

Surprised, he stepped aside, kicked at it, shattered it, sending it exploding into the darkness beneath the stairs.

She hurled down another and he stopped, fended it off, the grin remaining in place. He came on. Another plunged toward him and he kicked it away, laughing.

Huge pieces of stained glass, crimson and green and yellow, broke off and splintered, raining into the barn below.

He came on, the flame darting like a snake's tongue.

Feeling behind her, she found the immense frame, a piece of antique wood, and she tugged it forward, straining, breaking fingernails to slide it across the uneven wooden floorboards. He was halfway up the stairs now, his face like a mask of laughter, laughter at her helplessness, at this lone woman without protection.

With the last reserves of strength she leaned into the frame, pushing with her shoulder, and sent it spinning and toppling off the top stair. So large that for a moment it blocked her view, it teetered, crashed into the wall, and then slowly seemed to split in two, snapping like a giant slab of ice, and she could see him again throwing one arm up to shield himself from its erratic trajectory. But he had brought his free arm up too high and a jagged splinter of dull yellow glass, like a sword, glanced off the wall and drove underneath his arm and entered his chest, between the flaps of the suit jacket, entered through his shirt and drove him back like a fist. . . .

He stood still, leaning back against the wall, the smile slowly fading as he looked down at his chest as if he wasn't quite understanding what had happened. He tried to pull himself together, took a step away from the wall, then another, and then the pain and the weight of the glass that had impaled him began to tear at him. He clutched at his chest as Natalie watched, her hand to her mouth to stop the screaming. . . .

He looked at her again, his eyes rolling back, and grabbed at the great glass pillar implanted in his chest and turned the torch on himself. Instantaneously it burned his chest black and he cried out, stumbled, fell backward, tumbling down the stairs, crashing face down, driving the glass clear through him, the point ripping open the back of his coat. He lay twitching, lying on top of the torch, and as she crouched, rocking on her heels, clutching her arms around her knees, she realized she was smelling the burning of his flesh . . . his body was smoking. . . .

She leaned against the wall and closed her eyes.

Natalie didn't move for a long time.

The wind and the storm seemed far away.

All the fear seemed somehow as if it had never quite happened to her. Pure fantasy. A bad dream. A story to be told late at night.

She tried to remember the night it had begun, the man throwing the gun, the laughter in the hallway outside her door.

She remembered all the men who had played their parts in the story of the last two weeks, all the men in her life who had been passing through and had been concerned, for her, for themselves, all the men who had wanted something from her, had hoped for something from her, who had tried to help her while helping themselves . . . all the decent men and those who weren't so decent. . . .

Tony, who would soon be gone.

Jay, whose past held such awful secrets and who would never change.

Lew Goldstein, who had worried and tried to help.

Rory Linehan, sniveling and weak and drunk and sad. . . .

Bradley Nichols, who had run afoul of fate.

Dr. Drummond, who hadn't been Dr. Drummond at all.

Barry Hughes . . .

And MacPherson. Who had tried to make her Christmas bright.

She wiped her eyes at last and stood up, waited until her legs stopped shaking.

Slowly, like a very careful child, she descended the stairway toward the body of Barry Hughes. There was no way past him. She stopped near the bottom, unable for a moment to step across him. What if he weren't dead yet . . .

In the end—having waited, staring at the still-smoldering body with the stake of glass protruding from its back—she stepped across him and walked out the barn door.

The snow was still blowing and the wind howled.

Through the night she watched as a car pulled off the street and drove slowly up the driveway toward the house.

She stood still in the snow, watching.

The car stopped, lights still on.

A figure was striding toward her, cape swinging, calling to her.

It was Julie. Suddenly Sir was bounding through

the snow, disappearing, reappearing as he struggled happily with the depth of it.

Julie and Sir.

They had gotten through.

Julie stopped, cocked her great head with the long mane.

"What the hell are you doing? You're gonna freeze to death!" She came closer, looked into Natalie's eyes. Then looked back at the car. "MacPherson brought me. . . ." He was coming toward them.

Natalie nodded, saw him, tears running down her cheeks, and as MacPherson reached her Natalie opened her arms wide.

ABOUT THE AUTHOR

DANA CLARINS is a pseudonym for a bestselling novelist who lives and works in New York City.